# "Her Unexpected Delivery"

## Bulbs, Blossoms and Bouquets #7

By Laura Ann

This is a work of fiction. Similarities to real people, places, or events are entirely coincidental.

HER UNEXPECTED DELIVERY

**First edition. August 10, 2021.**

Copyright © 2021 Laura Ann.

Written by Laura Ann.

# DEDICATION

To my running buddy.
You not only keep my feet moving,
But you let me empty my worries and anxieties as well.
You're amazing.
Thank you will never be enough.

# ACKNOWLEDGEMENTS

No author works alone. Thank you, Tami.
You make it Christmas every time
I get a new cover. And thank you to my Beta Team.
Truly, your help with my stories is immeasurable.

# NEWSLETTER

You can get a FREE book by joining my Reading Family!
Every week we share stories, sales and good old fun.
To get in on the action, just click **HER[1]E**

---

1. https://dl.bookfunnel.com/j10fix95s7

# PROLOGUE

**(From the end of "Her Unexpected Star")**

Bennett rolled his eyes when he saw how big the stack of packages was for Brook and Grayson. They'd been married a month now and were still getting mail from every corner of the world. *Half of it's probably hate mail that Brook took Gray off the market.* Benny snorted at his thoughts.

It seemed like a pandemic, these last couple of years, as each of his friends slowly began starting new lives with their significant others. With each wedding, Benny grew more and more restless. And bored. And depressed. But mostly bored.

Rose and Ken were the only other singles in the group now and they only had eyes for each other, even if Rose resisted it. Which left Benny by himself. He couldn't just drop in on his friends unannounced anymore. He actually had to cook all his own meals, leaving his mooching skills severely lacking lately.

And apparently, getting married did something to a person's sense of humor because nobody seemed to want to join in his jokes anymore. Not that they had been incredibly eager before, but they had laughed and given him attention. Now all they did was glare until he stopped.

He didn't want to admit it, but Benny was also lonely. His sister, Melody, was positive that if he would simply find his own significant other, he would feel better, but he had no desire to become the besotted, grumpy man he saw his friends turning into.

He might be a little past thirty, but he still enjoyed his freedom. He didn't want to answer to anyone or anything. He liked to laugh and play, and marriage had a way of draining that from a man, no matter how happy his friends claimed to be. There was no way catering to their wives' every whim was exciting. It just wasn't.

*Maybe I'm too much like my mother.*

The words hit home. His mother was living her best off the grid, carefree boho life down in California, having shirked every responsibility she had once taken on. Or, at least, he thought she was. They hadn't heard from her in so long that Benny actually wasn't sure where she was or what she was doing.

"I'm not nearly as bad as her," he muttered to himself. He held down a good, solid job as the mail carrier of Seaside Bay. He met up with friends and helped when they needed it. He dabbled in art at home as a fun creative outlet, though few knew about it, and he enjoyed surfing on occasion. Life wasn't terrible, just slow.

Whistling a tune to try and cheer himself up, Benny stopped at the next house and made a face. Allison Mayer had graduated school a couple years behind him and yet everybody knew who she was. She'd moved into Seaside Bay in middle school and had shown up looking like the perfect porcelain doll. Even at the young age of thirteen, she wore enough makeup to star in a movie.

Perfect makeup.

Perfect hair.

Perfect clothes.

Perfect grades.

Those were the qualifications of Allison Mayer, and her attitude reflected the fact that nobody else lived up to that ideal. She had been as snobby and jerky as any teenage queen bee had ever been.

Benny had taken great enjoyment in ruffling her feathers any time he got the chance. It had been the ultimate challenge. Nothing ever seemed to break through her stoic face. She showed absolutely no emotion, and only once had he ever seen her lose it. The moment was one for the record books when Allison sent the star quarterback running for his life for daring to ask for a kiss.

Now Allison was the local piano teacher and still lived with her mother, who was the town cougar. Benny doubted if Allison would ever be the type of woman to let a man into her life. Heaven forbid he might burp after dinner. She'd probably kick him out without looking back.

Muttering under his breath, knowing that Allison would either open the door with a glare or her mother would flirt inappropriately, Benny braced himself. He knocked, holding the box in front of him like a shield.

There was some shouting behind the door and Benny held back a groan. The door was still closed and he could already tell this was going to be rough.

"Open the door!" The screeched words became louder as Allison wrenched the door hard enough to nearly pull it off its hinges.

Benny froze. This wasn't an Allison he was familiar with. Not a speck of makeup was on her face. One side of her face was clean and fresh and still beautiful, the other half was covered in a port wine birthmark. He had no idea that it had existed under all that powder she wore.

She must have realized the situation, because as Benny continued to stare, Allison's mouth began to flap like a bass out of water. Her brown eyes were wide and Benny could have sworn a flash of fear went through her gaze before it disappeared behind the icy look he'd seen since they were young.

The door slammed shut just as quickly as it opened and Benny found himself staring at brown painted wood. It kind of reminded him of Allison's eyes, actually.

As he worked to process everything that had just happened, a slow smile spread across his face. His boring, uninspired life had just taken a turn. Benny knew something he hadn't known before.

The door swung back open and Mrs. Mayer stood with her hands on her hips. "Hello," she purred.

Benny held back a shiver. This woman was way too old to speak to him that way. "I need Allison to sign for this," he said, indicating the box.

Mrs. Mayer raised an eyebrow. "I'm her mother. Can't I do it?"

Benny shook his head. "No. It's addressed to her."

Mrs. Mayer started to roll her eyes, then stopped as if realizing she had an audience. "Just a moment," she said breathlessly, then disappeared into the house.

Benny shifted his weight when he heard yelling start again. It was clear only Mrs. Mayer was doing the talking, and Benny found a trickle of sympathy forming toward Allison. He shook himself and shoved it aside. That was the last thing he needed right now. The mystery of her birthmark intrigued him, but he wasn't about to feel sorry for her. She'd been horrible since they were kids, and it wasn't going to change now.

"Allison is...indisposed," Mrs. Mayer said when she returned. "Can I take it in and have her sign it? Then bring it back?"

Benny figured that was as good as he was going to get, so he shrugged and handed her the tablet.

Mrs. Mayer disappeared again, then brought it back with a smirk. "Will that do it for you?"

"Thanks," Benny muttered, handing her all the mail. He tried to glance one more time into the house, but all he saw was the twitch of a curtain. The door closed behind him as he walked away, but the entire situation sat on Benny's mind for the rest of the day.

Allison had a birthmark. Her mother treated her badly. Allison still lived at home and rarely spoke or showed emotion.

It felt like there was a mystery behind the situation, and for a bored, restless bachelor, nothing had ever looked so exciting.

# CHAPTER 1

"Wonderful," Allison said with a smile at her student. "We'll go ahead and pass that one off." Picking up her pencil and the book from the piano stand, Allison signed the name and date. "There," she stated. Flipping back through the book, Allison let out a low whistle. "Look how far you've come!"

Skyla smiled shyly. "I've been working hard."

Allison's grin grew wider. "And that hard work is paying off. You're becoming so good!" Skyla was no more talented than any other student in Allison's care, but Allison always went out of her way to help build her students up. She'd been determined from the start of her teaching career to give them the very thing that had been lacking in her own life.

"What songs are we doing next?" Skyla asked eagerly, bouncing on the bench a little. Her movements caused the legs to creak slightly. The piano wasn't new, but it had held up for all of Allison's life, so she wasn't too worried about it breaking.

Skyla's excited behavior, however, was exactly what Allison hoped to see. Too often music teachers made lessons strict and burdensome, and then young kids petered out before they ever truly gave it a try. As long as the children enjoyed themselves, she knew they were far more likely to continue learning, not to mention it helped them practice and actually progress.

"Looks like page nineteen," Allison said, handing the book back. "This time we're learning about flats." She winked. "Remember how we talked about sharps? How they go up a half-step?"

Skyla nodded and began pressing on black keys on the piano.

"Exactly," Allison agreed, nodding. "A flat is the exact opposite. Instead of going up and to the right, we're going to go down a half-step to the left." The next fifteen minutes were spent helping the eight-year-old understand the concept so she could practice at home during the next week.

After seeing Skyla out the door, Allison found her mood immediately falling. That was her last student of the day, and that meant her mother would emerge from her room. Hurrying to the nearby mirror, Allison double-checked her makeup, making sure not a single bit of her birthmark could be seen. Seeing it was still covered, she closed her eyes and took in a deep breath to prepare herself for the upcoming evening.

"It's about time the brats were gone," Carla Hayer muttered as she entered the room. She patted her hair and glared at Allison. "You're flushed. Why is your makeup not covering that?"

Allison bit back the retort that wanted to escape. She'd had years of practice. "I'm just warm," she said without emotion. "My makeup is fully in place." As if it were her fault that she'd been born with a port wine birthmark. As if she'd asked to have a mother who worried about looks over all else. As if she hadn't spent her entire life, from a young girl, learning how to cover it so no one would ever realize she was damaged.

If funds weren't quite so tight, Allison knew the temptation to leave would be heavy. She had a doctorate in music and was well qualified to teach at the higher levels, but her mother always held her back. Determined for Allison to become a professional performer, rather than a teacher. One-on-one lessons had been a smal compromise because the town they lived in had little to offer someone as educated as Allison.

Her mother huffed. "I'm only trying to help," she complained. "We both know what would happen if your face was ever seen in public." Carla tsked her tongue and shook her head.

Allison knew exactly what lecture was coming. She'd heard it almost every day of her life.

"It isn't my fault that you were born the way you were born." Carla's eyes were drawn to the mirror and she took a moment to admire her own reflection. Allison's mother had been a renowned beauty and budding musician when she was young, and was still a stunning older woman. Her taste in men, however, was not so wonderful.

Allison had barely known her father, who had only stayed married long enough to the dramatic Carla in order to actually create a baby. As soon as the pregnancy hormones had hit, he'd tucked tail and run. Allison had met him a couple of times, but he was just as shallow as her mother and, although extremely handsome and charming, she had put very little effort into trying to keep a relationship with him.

Truly, she didn't care about a relationship with either parent. All Allison wanted was to be free to play the piano and run her own life. Unfortunately, it didn't feel as if she would ever be able to do so. Not unless a Prince Charming who didn't care about looks came to her rescue. Since she'd never met a guy who didn't care about how a woman looked, her chances seemed fairly impossible.

"As long as we keep your face covered, no one ever has to know," her mother continued, speaking over Allison's wandering thoughts. "Someday you'll be able to rise above this podunk town and be seen as the pianist you are, and then we'll both be set for life."

Allison's hands clenched. She couldn't tell her mother, but she didn't want to be a performer. Allison didn't like being in the limelight. She didn't like being watched like a bug under a microscope as every "expert" in the audience waited for her to make a mistake.

Her true love was teaching. Her students brought her more joy than anything else in her life. She adored teaching children the wonders of music. Seeing the delight on their faces when they heard their favorite song from their own fingers was enough to have her floating for days. She just wanted to spend her life introducing children to a new aspect of life and keep her performing for herself and those she was close to. She might be qualified to teach at a university, but it was the young ones who had her heart.

She snorted in her mind. *As if Mother would ever let this be permanent.*

"Just keep yourself looking perfect and someday we'll be out of here."

Allison blinked, bringing herself back to the situation. "Yes, Mother."

Carla sniffed and patted her hair again. "It's time for dinner. What were you planning to make?" Her perfectly manicured finger pointed at Allison. "Remember that it needs to be low in fat. You can't afford to gain another pound or you'll never fit into your concert dress next week."

"I thought we could have chicken caesar salad," Allison said very carefully.

Carla thought about it, then nodded. "That will work. But no dressing on yours." She eyed Allison up and down, pursed her lips when her daughter was obviously found wanting, then marched back out of the room.

Allison wanted to let her back slump now that her mother was gone, but she held herself rigid. Too many times she'd relaxed only to have her mother come back and scold her all over again. It wasn't until she went to bed that Allison could take down the mask she wore. When the real her came out under the cover of darkness, then and only then would she let herself mourn for what might have been. Until then, it was just too hard to hope.

"YEAH, SURE..." BENNY rolled his eyes and shifted until he was sitting back on the couch of his small cabin home. "I totally get it."

*No, I don't.* "You guys enjoy your evening." *I hope your food is burnt.* "Later."

Benny hung up the phone and sighed. He scrunched up his nose, feeling slightly guilty for his mean thoughts during his conversation with Jensen. The guy was his best friend, but ever since he'd married Benny's sister, the distance between them had begun to grow.

Actually, it had grown between him and all his friends. Of all his friends, only himself and two others were still single and it was creating a rift in the group. Benny no longer had free rein of his friends' space or time and attention.

"Stupid marriages," he muttered. Benny found himself torn. On one hand, he was happy that his friends were moving on and fulfilling their dreams. On the other hand, he hated how bored he was. With no one to spend time with, he had too much time to himself and not enough activities to fill it.

Normally he would drop by and mooch dinner off a buddy, but he couldn't do that anymore. Not that anyone would be rude and turn him away, but sitting with all the newlyweds was nauseating. Not to mention, Genni and Cooper had added to their household and had a baby, which, although cute, could scream louder than anyone Benny knew.

No...being bored was much preferable to dealing with googly-eyed couples and loud children.

He sighed again. It was a sound he'd been making far too much lately. Grabbing the remote, he began to flip through the channels. Ten minutes later, absolutely nothing had caught his attention.

"Maybe I need a hobby," he grumbled. As the mail carrier for Seaside Bay, Benny's schedule was fairly fixed and he always had holidays and evenings off. If the last few months were any indication of things to come, he definitely needed to come up with something else to pass the time. "Especially since you're not getting married any time soon," he reminded himself, finally letting the TV rest on a crime show. Maybe if he left it on long enough, he would forget about the fact that he was sitting by himself...on a Friday night...and all his friends had plans.

As he forced himself to relax in front of the television, his mind wandered back to a couple weeks ago when he delivered a package and found a surprise. "Oh yeah..." He grinned as he thought of seeing Allison Mayer without makeup on. It had been the find of the century.

And yet, instead of shouting his find to the world, Benny found himself strangely intrigued with the mystery. Usually he dreaded delivering packages to the Mayer household. Mrs. Mayor always seemed to hit on him and Allison was as close to an ice queen as anyone had ever met in real life.

But after their little moment at the door, Benny was beginning to wonder if there was more to her than her bratty personality. During the five minutes he'd been on her doorstep, he'd heard Mrs. Mayer shout horrible words, had seen Allison not looking like the perfect porcelain doll, and most of all, had seen Allison's stoic face break into something emotional.

Benny frowned, letting the scene run through his mind again. There was something in Allison's eyes when she'd realized Benny was seeing her without makeup that called to him.

Fear.

Benny stiffened and sat upright. She'd been afraid. He began twiddling his thumbs. "But who was she afraid of? Her mother...or me?" The second idea actually caused him physical pain. Who the heck would be afraid of him? Of all his friends, Benny was known for being the most laid back and goofy. He got along with everybody. "As long as they have a sense of humor," he muttered.

That had been part of the problem when he and Allison had been in school together. She was a couple years behind him, but her beauty had caught the attention of the entire high school. When the whole high school was less than three hundred people, anything different stood out like a sore thumb. Which made Allison's personality as noticeable as her looks.

Despite being watched by the entire male population at Seaside Bay High, no one had ever made any progress in regards to Allison. She turned down every date or dance offer. She walked the halls without a single wrinkle ever marring her perfect skin, which meant not a single emotion ever graced her face either. She'd been intriguing, but frustrating, and it hadn't taken long for the teenage boys to move onto more willing pastures.

The more he thought about it, the more Benny began to put together a few pieces of the Allison Mayer puzzle. He couldn't remember ever seeing her with a friend. Not even one. She walked the halls like a queen, but rarely spoke to anyone. Any words that came from her mouth were usually cutting and meant to put the peasant in their place.

He did recall that she was very into music. It seemed like she was always coming and going from the music room, but Benny had no idea what she played or if she sang. It had only taken one barb from her perfectly plump lips for Benny to back off and keep his distance, though no one could ignore her completely.

"But she's not quite as perfect as she puts on," he mused. The TV show was completely forgotten at this point. In fact, she had a really big flaw, if one wanted to call it that. The port wine birthmark took up almost half her face and made Benny curious.

He grinned and settled back on his couch again. There was definitely something mysterious about her situation, and as bored as he was...Benny began to think maybe he should be the one to figure it out.

Being the first person to break that icy facade would be a fun feather to put in his cap and would definitely give him something to look forward to since he had too much time on his hands.

He slapped his hands together and rubbed them eagerly. "It's settled," he said to his empty room. "Operation 'Figure Out Allison Mayer' will commence right now." He glanced at his cell phone. "Or first thing in the morning."

He wasn't really sure what he was going to do, but the first step was probably to see if he could get her to talk to him. Once he'd opened a line of communication, the rest should be easy peasy.

He pushed a hand through his longish hair. No one could resist his playfulness for long, especially if he put his mind to it. Allison might put off a tough vibe, but even she wouldn't be able to hold out for long. But in the meantime, he would enjoy every minute of his challenge.

# CHAPTER 2

Allison took a deep breath. A small smile tried to break free, but she kept it from showing. The salty sea air was strong in the grocery store parking lot and she was beyond grateful for the break from her mother's constant criticism and bemoaning.

Despite being free for a few minutes, Allison was still in public, and that meant she had to maintain the facade she'd perfected over the years. She spoke to no one, showed no emotion, and would eventually walk out with her guilt feeling heavier than ever. If she broke from that routine, however, she would hear about it at home. It had just become easier to follow through with her mother's wishes, rather than beat her head against a brick wall.

Allison walked across the parking lot, grabbed a cart, took a fortifying breath, and prepared herself for the performance ahead. She held her head high and marched inside. Air conditioning slapped her in the face as she went in and blew her hair all over. With one hand, Allison smoothed it back down so it looked just the way her mother had taught her and continued inside.

Quiet music was playing and luckily the store wasn't very busy, which made Allison's task much easier. She headed to the fresh produce and began sifting through the bananas in order to find some that didn't look brown. She hated when bananas got mushy. The texture made her want to throw up.

"Do you like bananas?"

Allison jolted slightly, not expecting anyone to speak to her, but instead of turning around, she continued what she was doing.

"Me too. Although, I think banana bread is the way to go." The male voice chuckled. "My mom always said I didn't need any more sugar considering how hyper I tended to be, but you know...she's a little on the crazy side, so..."

Allison knew that voice. But from where? She kept her back to the intruder, focusing only on the produce. It didn't really matter who it was. She couldn't talk to them, so hopefully they would get the hint soon.

"And now she's living her best life down in Cali eating only whole foods and missing out completely on the best parts of life. So yeah...I don't think we can really trust anything she says. No one who avoids doughnuts or cookies can be trusted in any aspect of life...amiright?"

There was that deep chuckle again. It sent a pleasurable shiver up Allison's spine and she immediately stiffened. She wasn't supposed to feel anything. Finishing bagging her bananas, she turned to put the bag in the cart and nearly dropped it. Luckily, she had plenty of practice keeping herself in check and only the most astute watcher would have noticed her slip.

*Anyone but him.*

Bennett Frasier was the *worst* person she could have run into. He was a fun-loving dork who loved everyone, and everyone loved him. When they'd been in high school together, he'd been one of the most popular upperclassmen in the entire school. He'd been a prankster, but not a bully, and that had always intrigued her, not that Allison could show it. They'd only interacted once and she had played true to form with a sharp comeback, and Bennett had never spoken to her again.

She couldn't figure out why in the world he was speaking to her now, but it wasn't good. A couple of weeks ago, she'd had a *very* rare slip and had answered the door without her makeup on. Other than her mother, Bennett was the only person in the entire town who had seen her birthmark. She was surprised he wasn't announcing his coup to the entire world, but then again...she'd never seen him hurt someone on purpose. And she'd been watching, at least she had when she was younger.

His bright white smile, blond-streaked hair, and pleasantly tanned skin was hard for anyone to ignore, but to a teenage girl who lived under a perpetual rain cloud, he had seemed like a ray of sunshine.

Forcing her eyes to look straight ahead, Allison began to walk. Apparently, Bennett didn't get the hint, because he stepped up and walked with her.

"Did you know that Melody and Jensen have been married for over a year now?"

*She did.*

"Jensen plays the guitar."

*She knew.*

Bennett grinned. "He once played on television, but the crowds were more than he could handle."

*Allison had watched.*

"Okay, maybe that isn't the right way to put it, but he didn't like all the drama of it and ended up coming home to marry Mel."

Allison stopped in front of the lettuce display and plucked up a package of romaine.

"I heard that you're also musical. What do you play?"

She began pushing her cart again, but her heart was beginning to beat an unnatural rhythm. Why couldn't he just leave? If her mother found out about this, she was going to be so mad.

"Or maybe you sing? I'll bet you've got a great voice."

Strawberries were next. Allison took her time looking them over until she found a package that had no bruising.

"Do you use your music for work? Wait..." Bennett held out his hand and tilted his head like a curious puppy. "You don't teach music at the high school, with Jensen, do you?"

Allison pressed on, but it was getting difficult. She was ready to scream. No one had ever stuck around so long and she wasn't sure how to handle it.

"I dropped off the mail in your mailbox today." Bennett grabbed a bag of tortillas as they passed an endcap and dumped them inside his basket. "You know...like I do every day." He smiled at her and Allison's stomach gave a little flip.

This was so dangerous. *Peanut butter!* She turned and hunted for the brand her mother preferred. It was always so difficult to find since her mother's tastes ran against the norm. *There it is.* She put a couple in the cart and pushed on again. *Please get the hint. Please get the hint.*

"No nut allergies, huh?" Bennett continued his one-sided conversation as if he didn't have a care in the world. "None in my family either." He sighed. "In fact, I don't know anyone who has a nut allergy, but you sure see them all over the news, don't you? They use them in the movies enough that you'd think half the population had them."

Allison picked up a couple loaves of bread.

"I wonder what percentage of the population actually has a nut allergy," he mumbled as if speaking to himself.

Allison continued onward, almost sighing audibly in relief when he fell behind. His sudden reemergence had her biting her tongue to keep from squeaking in surprise.

"Only one-point-one-percent." Bennett stuffed his phone back in his pocket. "Huh. With all the talk about it, I would have expected it to be more." He shrugged. "Of course, I always thought quicksand would be more of a problem when I became an adult as well, so...what do I know?"

*What in the world is he talking about?* Allison was so lost. She was torn between wanting to laugh at the bizarreness of it all or cry that he wouldn't leave her alone, and she was afraid her mother would find out.

"Have you ever seen quicksand?" he continued. "It was always in the shows growing up. You know, Batman? Princess Bride? Wonder Woman? Every hero had to struggle through quicksand in order to win, and yet not once have I ever run into actual quicksand." He snorted. "The more I talk about it, the more I'm starting to feel jipped."

Allison's hand twitched as she passed the Oreos. She loved the sandwich cookie, but there was no way her mother would ever be okay with them coming into the house. They'd just be thrown away and Allison would waste her money.

As if he'd read her thoughts, Bennett grabbed a package of the double-stuffed and put them in his basket.

Allison dared to glance at his bounty and she bit her tongue to keep from laughing. It was a hodgepodge of random food items, none of which actually went together. *What in the world is he planning to make for dinner with all that stuff?*

BENNETT HAD CAUGHT her glance and it only spurred him on. Seeing her walk ahead of him into the grocery store had been a crazy coincidence, but he wasn't about to let it go to waste. Allison presented a mystery and a challenge, but judging from how good she was at ignoring him, breaking down her barriers was going to be more difficult than he'd imagined.

*Perfect.*

He was desperate for something to keep him busy, but he'd assumed this little obsession would only take a week or two at most. She was quickly showing him that wouldn't be the case.

"I suppose that one of these days Mel and Jensen'll have a kid," Benny drawled, grabbing a pack of bagels to put in his basket. He had no idea what all he'd been dumping in there, but there were bound to be some things he could eat. It wasn't like he did a lot of cooking anyway. Mostly he snacked around until he felt full, or he ordered out. If Mel knew, she'd have a conniption.

He kept his face forward, but watched Allison out of his peripheral vision. She didn't so much as flinch at his conversation. She was so good at it that Benny wasn't sure whether to laugh or be offended. Maybe it wasn't that life was boring, but that he was.

He scratched his chin. "Someone will have to take on the role of the 'fun uncle.'" He used the fingers on his free hand to create quotation marks. "I doubt anyone else will be up to the job, so I'll just plan on taking one for the team."

Truth was, he would be the baby's only uncle, but Allison didn't need to know that. Benny already had plenty of ideas of how he would spoil his eventual niece or nephew rotten, then send them home for his or her parents to take care of the aftermath. It was going to be epic.

"Funny...my mom always worried I'd never amount to anything. Yet here I am, a full-time job and already named the world's greatest uncle." He blew on his nails, then buffed them on his shirt. "It's a rough life, but someone has to do it."

Allison studied the ingredients in some chips and Benny frowned. What was she looking for? Maybe she was part of that one percent he'd talked about earlier. Did she have some allergies? Is that why she was so slim?

She wasn't an unattractive slim, though it was close. She was taller than the average woman, coming in probably close to five-foot-nine, and her willowy frame was attractive, but if she lost any weight she'd probably look like she was ill. She'd been that way for as long as Benny had known her. When the other girls had all rounded out, Allison had barely budged. Curves had formed, but they were just enough to not mistake her for a child, rather than an adult.

His phone buzzed. He grabbed it and grinned. "Well, Allison, dear. It's been a pleasure, but it looks like I have to run. Duty calls." He winked at her, even knowing she probably didn't see it. "Catch you soon."

Spinning on his heel, he walked swiftly to the front of the store and paid for his groceries. It only took a few minutes for him to be outside and headed to his car. Now that he was out of the store, he let himself laugh about the situation. She had been so stoic, so emotionless.

He supposed it had been the result of years of practice, since she'd been that way since middle school. What he was curious about was, what made her that way? People weren't blocks of ice by nature, it was a learned behavior. Was it her terrible mother? Was it the birthmark? Was it something else he didn't know about?

The questions swirled through his head as he headed home to drop off his groceries. Afterward, he would go to Caro and Jack's, but first he needed to put things away.

"But why would a birthmark make her withdrawn?" Benny mused as he unloaded his car. "Nobody even knows about it. Maybe someone made fun of her as a kid?"

Benny snorted and shook his head. Everybody got made fun of as a kid. That wasn't a life-altering experience. And surely it couldn't be the mother. Benny had the world's nuttiest mom ever and he was the exact opposite of Allison. Besides...she was an adult. Why would she still listen to her mother at all?

"But she still lives with her." He made a face as he hopped back in the car and drove back to town. It wasn't far, just a few minutes, but today it seemed longer with all the thoughts and questions churning.

Throwing the car into park, Benny hopped out of his vehicle and sauntered inside. "You begged? I came!" He threw his arms wide, startling the small party of patrons inside.

Several sets of eyes were staring at him, wide as saucers, but instead of being embarrassed, Benny just smiled his best smile and put his hands on his hips. "Afternoon, folks. Finding anything good?"

"Benny. Would you hush before you scare off my customers?" Caro's Southern drawl came from the side and Benny looked over to see her standing in the doorway between the kitchen and the sales counter.

"Caro, my love! I knew this day would come!"

She rolled her eyes and shook her head. "Jack is right behind me. If you pick a fight, my money's on him."

Benny's grin grew wider. He began walking toward the back, winking at the still staring group. A teenage girl blushed and ducked her head and Benny had to hold back a chuckle. After Allison's refusal to acknowledge him, he had had a few moments of concern that he was losing his touch. Good to know that wasn't the case.

"You're such a dork," Caro grumbled as he walked past her.

"If by dork, you mean the most awesome mailman that ever was in existence, then yes, I suppose I am a dork."

"Heaven help me," she said with a shake of her head.

"Hey, Benny!" Jack called from deeper in the kitchen. "Thanks for coming."

Benny shrugged. "Dare I admit that I didn't have anything else going on?"

"What? Your list of people to mooch from growing small?" Caro said with a sickly sweet smile. She was back at a stainless steel counter, her hands covered in chocolate as she hand-dipped some of her famous truffles.

Benny put a hand over his heart. "My life stopped the day you got married."

She rolled her eyes, while Jack laughed.

"If I had to lose you, at least it was to someone who brought something good to the table," Benny continued.

"Speaking of which," Jack interrupted. "You gonna come try this new recipe or not?"

"On it!" Benny walked over to Jack's side of the kitchen. He loved it when he was the guinea pig for new recipes. Most of them turned out amazing, though a few had been hard to swallow.

"White chocolate, strawberries, and dark chocolate," Jack said, eyeing his creation critically. "I'm worried there are too many flavors, but I like these flavors, so it's hard to know for sure."

"Allow me to be your humble tester," Benny said, picking up a warm cookie.

"Humble my foot," Caro shot back.

Benny chuckled. This. He missed this. It happened far less often than it used to and he hated it, though it made him feel guilty. He really wasn't begrudging anyone finding their spouse. He just wished he still had a social life. Good thing he had a new project to keep him busy. Though he doubted Allison would say the same.

# CHAPTER 3

Allison could barely concentrate on the badly performed version of "Fur Elise" being played on her piano. Truly, it was an insult to the composer, but she barely noticed. Her mind was a few miles away at the grocery store.

It had been two days since Bennett Frasier had all but stalked her through the aisles. She should be frustrated. She should be furious. She should vow to never see him again.

But she just couldn't sum up the enthusiasm.

Her mother would have a fit if she knew, but Allison had very carefully left out any mention of the handsome beachbum during her errands. It was a new sensation for her. Having a delicious secret that was for her and her alone. It made the experience seem more intimate, though it had been anything but. Bennett hadn't paid attention to any other person at the store though, so she soothed herself by soaking in the fact that she and she alone had kept his attention.

"Ms. Mayer?"

Allison blinked herself back to the present. An automatic smile came to her face. "Sorry about that," she said to Jordan. She glanced purposefully at the sheet music. "How much time did you get to practice this week?"

Jordan dropped his gaze to his lap. "None," he admitted.

"Ah..." Allison nodded slowly. "I see. Well, it sounds to me like we need a little more time to nail this one down, huh?"

Jordan gave her a sheepish grin. "Yeah, probably."

"Okay, good." Allison spent the next few minutes talking him through some of the more difficult passages before his lesson was over. "All right," she said, slapping her thighs. "Looks like we're done for today. Remember, when you practice for at least three days, you can choose from the candy bowl, okay?" She knew that probably wasn't as attractive to a twelve-year-old as it would be to someone younger, but she was hoping that the insatiable appetite of a boy would help motivate him to earn the treat.

Jordan rolled his eyes. "Got it." He pulled the strap of his backpack over his shoulder and stood up from the bench. "See ya later."

"I'll walk you out." Allison stood and led him to the door, pulling it open. "Thanks for coming. I'll see you next week." She smiled down at him, then looked out the door and froze.

"Hey, Allison!"

*What is he doing here?*

Bennett looked down at Jordan. "Hey, bud. What have you been up to?"

Jordan grinned at Bennett. "My mom's making me take piano lessons." He rolled his eyes. "She says it'll help me in school."

Bennett ruffled the boy's hair. "She's right. Always listen to your mother." He put a hand to the side of his mouth. "Unless she's wrong. Then, don't listen to her at all."

Allison's jaw dropped and a squeak came out of her without permission. When Bennett looked her way, she snapped it shut and put on the face she showed the world.

"How do I know when she's wrong?" Jordan scratched his head.

Bennett gave the boy his attention again and shrugged. "I don't know. It doesn't happen very often. Moms are pretty amazing." He winked. "Probably better just listen to her."

Jordan groaned. "Dang it."

Chuckling, Bennett stepped to the side and let Jordan run home. Once he was down the street, Bennett turned back to Allison. "You teach piano lessons?"

Allison didn't answer. She debated whether she should just shut the door, but something had to have brought Bennett to her doorstep. She just needed to find out what, then get him to leave.

"Guess that answers my question at the store the other day." His friendly grin never wavered and Allison wondered how he did it. Nothing seemed to bother him, at all.

Allison pinched her lips together, then immediately tried to relax them. They would be a dead giveaway if Bennett looked too close. She should ask him what he wanted, but he was far too dangerous to her mental health to deal with like a normal person. She began to back into the house, intent on closing the door.

"I've got something for you."

Allison couldn't explain why her heart leapt at those words. It made no sense and it wasn't worth investigating, but leap it did, and she paused as a result.

Bennett's smile was a little too smug for her liking as he waved her mail in the air. "There's a certified letter in here that needs to be signed for."

Allison held out her hand, keeping her nose in the air. *Show no weakness. Don't let him see how he's affecting you.*

Bennett didn't move. Instead, he dropped the stack of mail back into his other palm. "Were you expecting something special? I don't deliver a lot of letters like this."

*Ugh! Are you kidding me?* She held her ground, but it was difficult. This guy annoyed and amused her all at the same time. But laughter would probably just encourage him and anger would only let him know he'd gotten under her skin. She had been taught to be above all that and no one, not even a fun-loving, handsome mailman, was going to break her.

"Don't want to share?" His grin grew mischievous, like a little boy about to do something naughty.

Allison would never admit how attractive she found that look.

"Maybe I'll just guess." He tapped the envelopes against his lips. "I've got it!" His eyebrows rose high. "You won the lottery!"

Allison forced herself to stay still. This wasn't funny. Not at all.

"No? Don't play the lottery?" Bennett frowned. "Hmmm...that makes it harder." He looked at the ground for a few moments before raising his eyes again. "A trip to Disneyland?"

*Really?* It took great effort not to show her response on her face.

"Okay...you seem like the type who gets motion sickness, so that can't be it." He chuckled. "Or if it is, it's a bummer of a giveaway."

She bit her tongue. The pain helped her keep her face solemn. Knowing she couldn't hold out much longer, Allison made a point of holding out her hand again.

"Tell you what," Bennett said conspiratorially. He put the letters behind his back and leaned forward, dropping his voice as he did. "You take a walk with me and I'll give you the mail."

If her eyebrows rose, it wasn't Allison's fault. Considering how she wanted to react, the small movement slipped through the cracks.

The widening of Bennett's smile, however, said the small movement hadn't gone unnoticed. "You won't even have to talk," he said enticingly. "If you haven't noticed, I'm *really* good at carrying a conversation."

BENNY WAS USING ALL his self-control, what little of it there was, to keep from laughing out loud. He'd finally managed to shock Allison, but of all the things he'd said, it was the offer for a walk that had sent her over the edge.

The reaction had been small—he had to give her credit—but it had still been there, and it was more than he'd received thus far. The hand she was holding out for the mail began to shake slightly and Benny had a fleeting thought that he'd pushed her too far.

*Just what is it that is making her so scared?*

He couldn't get the question out of his head. He'd never seen anyone so reserved. How did people manage to go through life without ever feeling? It made no sense.

Her eyes flared ever so slightly before a shrill voice came through the doorway.

"What are you doing?" Mrs. Mayer snapped, coming up to Allison's side.

Allison dropped her hand that had been asking for the mail and stood stiff as a board.

Another tally in the "it's the mother" column marked itself in Benny's head. "Hello, Mrs. Mayer," Benny said conversationally. "How are you today?"

The older woman raised an eyebrow at him in an alluring manner. Or at least it would have been if she wasn't old enough to be his parent. "I'm well, thank you, Bennett. What brings you by today?"

He held out the mail. "I have a certified letter that needs to be signed for," he said quickly. "Allison was just about to help me out."

Mrs. Mayer looked at her daughter, then back to Benny. "I'm sure she was," the woman muttered under her breath. "But Allison is a busy woman and I'm sure she has something else to do." She waved her hand dismissively. "I'll sign for it."

Benny hoped his panic didn't show in his face. He didn't want Allison to leave for multiple reasons. But at this point, it was mostly because he didn't want to be left alone with her mother. Mrs. Mayer was way too flirtatious, even for him. "Actually, it's Allison's signature I need." Benny was grateful the law was on his side for this one. "It's her name on the letter."

Mrs. Mayer huffed. "Didn't you tell me that story only a couple of weeks ago?"

Benny shrugged. "The law's the law," he said. "I don't make the rules."

Mrs. Mayer rolled her eyes. "Get on with it, then." Apparently, she had no intention of leaving, because she stayed right next to Allison's side as he pulled out the tablet to let her sign for the delivery.

Allison's handwriting was slightly shaky and Benny knew then and there that if he was ever going to get her to talk to him, he would have to get her away from the house. Her mother was going to have to go.

"Looks good," Benny said with his normal grin. "Thank you." He winked at Allison. "I'll see you around."

Mrs. Mayer shot him a dirty look, then yanked Allison back and slammed the door in his face.

Benny kept his smile on his face, whistling as he walked down the sidewalk until he knew he was out of sight of the Mayer house. Then he let a dramatic shiver run through his body and scrubbed his face with his hands, as if he could wash away the weirdness of that woman. "She's not right in the head," he muttered to himself.

An inkling of pity tried to surface once more for Allison, but Benny pushed it down. He didn't like pity and he doubted someone like Allison would like it either. No, if he was going to break down this mystery, it was because he wanted to help Allison see past the end of her nose, not because he felt bad for her. She was an adult. She had every capability to do what she wanted, especially in regards to her mother.

As he continued down his route, he began to whistle again, his normally upbeat personality coming back the more he worked. The attitude made work go faster and almost sooner than Benny would have liked, he was clocking out and heading home. But what to do with the rest of his day? He'd already poked Allison enough, he needed to let that one sit for a while. He'd eaten himself sick on Jack's new cookie recipe the other day, so that wasn't an option.

"I wonder what Ken's doing," Benny muttered. He pulled up his texting app.

**Hey, Mr. Popo. How many tickets have you given out today?**

Stuffing his phone in his back pocket, Benny headed to the kitchen to find a snack. He smirked when he saw the bag of groceries from two days ago. He'd put the cold stuff away, but hadn't bothered with the pantry stuff. Now was as good a time as any to figure out what he actually bought that day.

"Not bad," he muttered as he unloaded cookies and some fruit. "Balance in all things." With a grin, he broke open the packet of cookies just as his phone chirped.

**Not enough. Want to drive by?**

Benny chuckled.

**Don't you wish. I still haven't paid my last ticket.**

**I've never arrested a friend before. This ought to be interesting.**

**I dare you.**

Just as Benny pressed send, his doorbell rang. "Who the heck is that?"

Loud knocking came next. "Open up! It's the police!"

Benny rushed over, but didn't open the door. "How do I know you're telling the truth?" he asked through the closed door.

"I know about the time you switched the sugar for salt in Mel's kitchen," Ken said wryly. "If that was illegal, you'd have spent the night in the slammer."

Benny pulled open the door. "Keeeen!" he drawled. "So good to see you."

Ken gave him a sarcastic smile. "That's what everyone says...until they find out why I'm here."

For the first time since their conversation started, Benny dropped his smile. "Are you really here on business? I thought it was a joke."

Ken held his face a moment longer before he broke down laughing.

Benny groaned and let his head fall back. "How did I fall for that?" He shook his head at his friend. "You're good, man. Too good. Someone give this guy an Oscar."

Ken slapped Benny's shoulder as he came inside. Benny had to step back in order for there to be room. Ken's over six-foot, football-sized frame made Benny feel small in comparison, though Benny wasn't exactly a scrawny teen. He was a respectable six-foot, and he had visible muscles. He just wasn't built like a linebacker.

"You off duty?" Benny asked as he closed the door. Ken was in uniform, but that didn't always mean he was working.

"Just clocked out," Ken said, plopping himself on the sofa and putting his hands behind his head.

"Sweet," Benny crowed. "No arrest in sight."

"Do you really have an outstanding ticket?"

Benny waggled his eyebrows. "Wouldn't you like to know?"

Ken rolled his eyes. "Guess I know what I'm doing tomorrow morning."

"So...what brought you by?" Benny asked, relaxing in a recliner. "Besides my sparkling personality, that is."

Ken shook his head. "Cable. I was hoping you wouldn't mind if I watched the Ducks play tonight since I don't get ESPN."

"Ken." Benny gasped, putting a hand on his chest. "Are you asking me on a date?"

"You're kidding...right?" Ken raised a single eyebrow. It was the same move as Mrs. Mayer, but this time it didn't give Benny the willies. "If I wanted a date, she'd sure be a lot better-looking than you."

"I'm wounded."

"Not enough, but I've still got my gun within reach."

Benny chuckled. "I haven't eaten yet. You?"

Ken shook his head.

"Pizza or sandwiches from the cafe?" Benny asked.

"You get sandwiches and I'll buy dessert."

Ken stood up to grab his phone from the kitchen. "This is sounding more and more like a date, Kenny Boy."

"Tell anyone and I really will lock you up."

Benny cracked up. "Promises, promises," he shot back. Looked like tonight wouldn't be so bad after all.

# CHAPTER 4

That man was going to be the death of her. Allison's mother had spent the entire rest of the day grilling her about having a relationship with "a no-good, podunk, mailman with no ambition beyond living in this tiny town".

Truthfully speaking, Allison didn't think that sounded too bad. She liked living in a small town. Or at least, she thought she would if she had any friends. Or if life had given her a circumstance where she *could* have friends. She'd learned the hard way, however, that her face was enough to drive off any kindness and her mother made sure she never forgot it.

"How many students do you have today?" Carla demanded as she sauntered into the kitchen for breakfast.

"Five," Allison said automatically. "It's Friday. I always have one less on Fridays."

Carla huffed, but didn't comment. "As long as we don't get any packages, it'll be fine," she muttered.

The thought of Bennett never knocking on her door again created a physical pain in Allison's chest. Not that she would ever admit it out loud, but she kind of enjoyed his persistent presence. She had no idea what he was trying to accomplish, but the fact that someone, *anyone*, was trying to talk to her was a novel experience. It made her feel less alone, even though she couldn't bring herself to break down her walls and answer back.

She'd done it before and all it had led to was pain. Lesson learned.

"What was in that letter yesterday?" Allison asked before she could think better of it. Her mother had taken it and opened it while

Allison took care of another student, and she'd forgotten to ask last night. Carla had a habit of taking Allison's mail anyway, so it wasn't an unusual occurrence for things to slip by. But this was a certified letter, which meant it probably had something important inside.

"Nothing you need to worry about," her mother said with a sly smile. She couldn't quite hide the smugness in her look and an immediate frisson of worry went up Allison's spine.

"But what was it?"

Her mother slammed her fork down on the table and Allison immediately ducked her head. Carla had never hit her before, but her words could be sharper than any sword. "All I want is to help my daughter," Carla began in a low tone. "I work and slave, trying to pull us out of obscurity, and this is what I get in return?" She shook her head slowly. "I never thought you would be so ungrateful for all the sacrifices I've done on your behalf. The piano lessons in Portland. The hours spent helping you practice even when you were too young to want to. Not every mother would give up her entire life in order to push for the success of her daughter."

Allison kept her eyes on the floor. "I know," she whispered.

"I don't think you do," Carl continued, her voice growing stronger. "I've raised you by myself. Work myself to the bone to put food and clothing in our house. I gave up my own career so that I could take care of you." Her bottom lip trembled. "I could have been big. Famous, my teacher said. I had everything it took. Talent, dedication, and looks." She turned her head to look out the window. "But instead, your father seduced me, making me believe life would be better with him." A vicious snort escaped. "He was wrong. Nothing about that marriage made life better."

Hot shame bubbled up in Allison. She was a result of that marriage. Her mother always made it very clear how much she regretted having a child, claiming her life had been ruined once her figure was gone. She couldn't very well perform in front of millions if she didn't look perfect, so in essence, Allison had taken that from her.

"Having a child ruined it all."

Allison tried not to wince that her mother's words reflected her very thoughts.

"I left behind the glamour, adoration, and wealth...all for diapers and bottles." Carla sighed longingly. "And I did it all on my own. With a deformed baby."

A fierce anger began to bubble in Allison's gut. How she hated the way her mother spoke about her birthmark. She hated being looked down on for something that was out of her control. But she also had nowhere else to go. She'd actually been hospitalized as a twelve-year-old for a suicide watch because the bullying at school had gotten so bad, so Allison knew first-hand how cruel the world could be. Others couldn't accept her looks, they couldn't stand to have her around. Her mother didn't like it, but at least she didn't kick her out.

"A baby with such talent," Carla said breathlessly. "One that I developed and pushed and have shaped into the perfect prodigy." Her cold eyes finally turned to Allison. "All except for your face." The last words were practically spat in derision. "If I wasn't so good with makeup, you'd have never made it as far as you have. You have to be perfect to make it on stage." Her lips pulled into a cruel smile. "You aren't perfect, but with my help, we'll fool them all that you're worth investing in."

Allison didn't say a word as her mother flounced dramatically from the room. But inside, she was a boiling volcano. She wanted to scream at the injustice of it all. She wanted to shout that a mother should love her child for who she was. She wanted to demand to never have to play another concert again. She wanted to put her foot down, declaring her desire to teach children and possibly pursue a job teaching at the elementary school.

She let out a breath of air and deflated a little. There were so many things she wanted, yet none of them were within reach. She had no prospects, no friends, and no hope.

What would Allison do if she left? Become the town recluse? At least her mother spoke to her.

*Bennett speaks to you.*

"Yes, but why?" The words slipped out before Allison thought them out. Bennett had seen her birthmark, or at least, part of it. Why was he so dead set on getting her to talk to him? There had to be an ulterior motive. Was it possible he was trying to set her up so he could announce her deformity to the world?

Allison shook her head. "That can't be it." She'd never seen Bennett, of all people, be intentionally cruel. He was a people person and his goal had always seemed to make people smile.

*So what does he want with me?*

There was no true answer to her question. At least not that she could answer right now. She could give in. She could answer his questions. She could open herself up to people again...but all it took was a few memories of lying in that hospital, doctors and nurses treating her like some kind of science experiment, for her to throw that idea away.

People, whether friends or not, meant pain.

Smart people avoided pain.

Unfortunately, Allison was starting to think she just wasn't that smart.

"FOOD!" BENNY CROWED as the women set up the table.

Felix snickered. "Been starving lately, Ben?"

Benny glared at his friend. Or...ex-friend. "It's not my fault you all stopped feeding me."

Jensen was laughing as he slapped Benny on the shoulder. "You know you're always welcome to come eat with us. We're family after all."

Benny groaned and threw his head back. "I'm more than happy to come eat with you if you two can stop staring at each other with wide eyes long enough for me to get down the main course."

"No promises," Jensen said with a smug grin. "I mean, my wife is hot. How am I—"

"Stop!" Benny put his hands over his ears. "That's my sister!"

Jensen's grin never faltered. "Trust me. I know."

The other men were all laughing at this point. "You're cruel," Felix pointed out.

Jensen shrugged. "I just called my wife hot. I don't think I'm in the doghouse."

"Nope." Mel walked up behind him and leaned over to kiss his cheek. "What woman doesn't want to hear that?"

Benny leaned over, holding his stomach and gagging. He stopped when someone smacked the back of his head. Sitting up, he glared and rubbed the spot. "You guys are going to give me a concussion if you don't stop it. Then who'll deliver your mail? Huh? I won't be able to read straight and then everyone else will get your letters and packages, and who knows if you'll ever get them back."

"If you haven't gotten one yet, somehow I doubt it'll happen now," Charli drawled as she plunked down in the chair next to her husband Bronson. Their hands automatically joined and came to rest on Bronson's thigh.

Benny held back another groan. He was so surrounded by PDA that it was literally everywhere he turned. Slapping his knees, he stood. "I'm hungry. Who's hungry?"

"Apparently us single men," Ken said as he walked up to the circle. The glowing fire lit up his grin as he approached, dumping his camping chair in the sand.

"Well, you're in luck, my friend," Benny stated. "If you hurry, we'll be first in line." He pointed at Ken. "Jack's cookies are mine."

"I brought too many even for you to eat," Jack said from the corner he and Caro were snuggled in.

"That's what you think!" Benny grinned as chuckles rang through the group. He had the best group of friends, even if life was messed up with them all married. For the most part, he still enjoyed their company. He just didn't like all the romance tainting the air.

"Sorry I'm late," Rose said breathlessly as she sped-walked to the group.

"ROSE!" Caro jumped to her feet and rushed over for a hug. "You haven't come in forever!"

Rose sighed when Caro let go and opened her chair to sit down. "I know, and I almost didn't make it tonight. Lily was on a total high from her piano lesson today and I had a hard time getting her to calm down enough for bed."

Benny had just begun to lament the fact that he'd lost Ken, who was totally in love with Rose, but at the mention of piano lessons, his ears perked back up. "Piano lessons?"

Rose nodded, slumping back and closing her eyes. "Yep. She started a few months ago. She loves it, but she's moving a little slow because she has a hard time differentiating the note sounds."

"Who does she take from?" he asked casually.

When Ken turned away from Rose and raised an eyebrow, Benny knew he hadn't been as nonchalant as he'd hoped.

"Allison Mayer," Rose responded, not seeming the least bit upset at the question. "Word was, she's the best teacher in town." Rose opened her eyes and frowned. "I think we only have three in town as it is." She shrugged. "Anyway, she's who I was recommended to and it's been great."

"Allison?" Mel made a face. "I recall her being difficult to get along with." She quickly put up a hand. "Not that she can't be a good teacher, it's just...she was so cold in school, I'm surprised any child would warm up to her."

Rose shook her head. "I don't know what to tell you. Lilly loves her. She always comes home determined to be the world's best pianist. Ms. Mayer seems to do a really good job of making Lilly feel like her handicap is not an issue at all."

Benny had lost his interest in the food as an idea began to churn in his head. He'd already figured out that Allison taught, but he had to admit that he hadn't believed she was any good. Jordan wasn't crying when he left, but he hadn't looked too enthused either. Lilly, on the other hand, was deaf and a little girl. She would be far more sensitive to an uncaring teacher than a teenage boy. "Have you sat through any of her lessons?"

Rose straightened, obviously catching onto the fact that Benny was asking more questions than he should have. "Yes..." She gave him a look. "Why do you ask?"

Benny shrugged and turned back to the table. "No reason. I was just curious."

"Give it up, Benny," Charli called out. "You're after something."

"What does this Allison look like?" Bronson asked.

"Long dark hair, and a picture-perfect face," Charli said, answering her husband's question without ever taking her eyes off Benny. "You can't miss her. She's the most beautiful woman in town. Problem is, she knows it."

"No, she doesn't." *Crap. Crappity crap.* Benny knew he should have kept his mouth shut. Every eye in the group immediately turned his way.

"I think you better explain," Mel said softly. "I thought you didn't like Allison. She was pretty rude to you back in high school."

Benny shrugged. "I'm just...curious."

Jensen snorted. "You mean bored."

"Same thing," Benny shot back.

"Benny..." Mel started. "Don't do something mean. Revenge is beneath you, not to mention high school was over a decade ago."

Benny scowled. "This has absolutely nothing to do with revenge."

"Then what is it about?" Felix asked.

Benny grinned and bit into a carrot. "I believe I have a sudden hankering to learn the piano."

# CHAPTER 5

Allison's knees were nearly knocking together as she stood in the wings of the stage. It was almost time for her entrance and that always meant the same thing. Nausea, trembling limbs, blurry vision, and a determination to overcome it all.

Just like the rest of her life, this was all an act. Allison knew well how to put a smile on her face, walk across the stage as if she wasn't about to fall on her face, and force her fingers to play the songs they'd practiced thousands of times. If she didn't practice as much as she did, Allison was positive she wouldn't be able to do this at all. For that, she had to give her mother credit. The songs were second nature to her at this point and it required very little effort to actually play them. It was controlling the shaking that gave her fits.

"Allison Mayer!"

Applause erupted, sending Allison's heart into her throat. She swallowed hard, but it wasn't until her mother gave her a push from behind that she actually moved her feet. The lights hit her face, blinding her to the size of the audience, and a gracious smile crossed her face immediately. It was basically a Pavlovian response to the lights at this point.

As she nodded to the conductor and sat down at the piano, Allison could feel the back of her dress starting to grow damp with sweat. She sent a prayer heavenward to any God that might actually listen to someone like her, to help her makeup survive the heat. If her caked on foundation dripped at all, her mother would go on for days. Allison had to be perfect...in everything.

Her fingers poised above the keys, she did her best to tune out the audience and listen to the orchestra. Her entrance was in four...three...two... Using every bit of self control she owned, she brought her hands down and let them take over. At first they were stiff, and she felt slightly clumsy for the first few bars, but the more she played, the more Allison was able to focus on only the music.

She might not enjoy playing in front of audiences like this, but she did enjoy music. Her mother often complained about having to force her to practice, but anyone viewing the situation from the outside would have recognized that Allison put up very little fight. Not only did she enjoy playing, but what else was she going to do?

Music and her mother were the only constants in her life, so Allison had had very little other activities to spend her time on.

Her fingers slowed as the song came to a close and Allison snatched in a breath when the audience broke into applause, ripping her from her concentration. She blinked then turned her ready made, if not completely sincere, smile to the director. At his invitation, she stood and nodded to him, then bowed to the audience.

Her dress was plastered to her back and the heat of the overhead lights was starting to wreak havoc on her hair. After sitting back down, she surreptitiously patted her hairline, wincing when it felt damp. *Please, please, please.*

The next song started and once again, after a forced beginning, Allison was able to get her fingers into the rhythm. The rest of the concert went quickly and soon she was headed out from behind the curtains for her final bow.

The conductor stepped down from his stand, walked over, and took her hand, giving it a crowd-pleasing kiss, then turned them both to the clapping audience. Once it was over, Allison walked stiffly backstage, her emotionless mask slowly coming back into place. There would be no celebrating the concert or reveling in the enjoyment of the audience. She couldn't let anyone get too close or she risked letting them in on her secret.

She walked calmly, only taking the time to nod to the congratulations she received backstage, quickly arriving at her dressing room. Inside, the noise dropped dramatically, but the scolding had only just begun.

"It's about time you got back here," Carla snapped. She pursed her lips and shook her head. Leaning forward, she clasped her hands and rested her elbows on her knees. "You slipped tonight." Hanging her head, she made a show of disappointment. "We've been over that run a thousand times, Allison. Does our practice do nothing for you?"

Allison took a calming breath in through her nose. She could do this. She'd been through her mother's lectures a million times. What was one more?

"In order to stay on stage, you must be perfect." Carla tsked her tongue. "Especially with your other notable failures. Your playing, of all things, can't fail." When Allison didn't move, her eyes stuck on the back wall in a way of buffering herself against the harsh words. Carla's face softened. She stood and walked over, holding out her hands.

It looked for a moment like she would cup Allison's face, but Allison knew better. Her mother never touched her face. Ever.

Instead, her hands went to Allison's shoulders. "You know I'm only trying to help you," Carla said in a soothing tone. "I'm doing this for *you*. You deserve to be famous...and rich. You deserve to be in the spotlight with your talent, but in order to do that, we have to fix the things that are wrong." She shook her head slowly, her eyes tearing up. "It's so hard to say those things. As your mother, I want to lie and tell you how wonderful it all was, but I would be doing you an injustice. You can't get better unless you know what was wrong, and as hard as it is...it's my job to point them out." She moved her head around until she forced Allison to look at her. "You know that, don't you?"

"Yes, Mother." It was Allison's rote response. It was the only way to get Carla off her back. More times than she could count, Allison had tried arguing. Had tried pointing out how much the audience loved her and how kind the other musicians were, but her mother was an expert at helping Allison remember what life was like when she'd tried to listen to outsiders before.

It was no wonder she still had nightmares about her time in the mental wing of the hospital. Her mother utilized the nightmare like a weapon.

There was a knock on the dressing room door. Allison waited just a tick before turning. Her mother huffed and rolled her eyes, but didn't complain, so Allison opened the door.

The conductor stood in the doorway with a wide smile. "Allison," he said in his deep baritone. "You were magnificent." His hands also came out, but unlike her mother, the man cupped her face and left a kiss on each cheek.

Allison tried to keep from being too stiff, but she was sure he noticed, since he let go of her quite quickly. "Thank you," she said politely.

The man glanced over her shoulder and Allison could have sworn his eyes narrowed when he spotted her mother. When they came back to meet her own eyes, they were softer, filled with something similar to compassion. "You are a treasure," he continued, his eyes darting one more time over her shoulder. "And don't let *anyone* tell you otherwise."

Before Allison could respond, the man was gone, but he left a funny feeling in his wake. That was the second time in a week that someone had made a comment about not listening to her mother. It seemed odd that the topic should creep up so many times, but it spoke to a small part of her that was growing more and more rebellious at her confined life.

"We have work to do," Carla snapped. She came to Allison's side and slammed the door. "We need to get you out of that dress before you ruin it." Walking away, Carla continued to mutter. "We're lucky nobody saw your face with the way you sweat."

Allison put her self-control back in place and turned to do her mother's bidding. It didn't matter what ideas were ruminating in her head. Right now she needed to focus on getting through tonight. She could worry about tomorrow when it came.

"SHOOT," BENNY MUTTERED, waving his burning hand through the air. That boiling water was stinkin' hot! He blew on the red fingertips and then ran them under some cool water while he waited for the pain to subside.

Just as the sensation was starting to calm down, someone knocked on his door. Benny looked over his shoulder and groaned. "Perfect timing." Grabbing a towel to wipe his fingers on, he rushed over and pulled it open. "Mel! Jensen!" Benny smiled. "What are you two doing here?"

Jensen was shifting his weight back and forth, looking pretty uncomfortable for someone who had known Benny since they were little kids. They'd been best friends for years until Jensen married Mel. Much to Benny's dismay, apparently Mel had taken his spot as top dog and Benny was relegated to number two. Just another reason marriage stunk.

"Can we come in?" Mel asked.

Benny backed up. "You're my sister. I don't think you have to ask." He gave a chin tilt to Jensen as he followed behind his wife. "Wassup?"

Jensen nodded back. "Did we interrupt your dinner?"

Benny shrugged. "It's just some ramen. It's not a big deal."

Jensen chuckled. "Sorry I stole your cook."

"Yeah..." Benny sighed as he flopped into his recliner. "I might never forgive you for that."

Mel sat on the edge of the couch, stiff with anxiety.

Benny wanted to roll his eyes. Surely things couldn't be that bad. Why were girls dramatic all the time?

Jensen sat next to his wife, leaned back and slightly more relaxed, but only a little. He reached out and massaged the back of her neck.

"Are you two hungry?" Benny asked with a smirk.

Mel made a face. "No thanks," she responded.

Ramen had never been her thing. Mel made a living making fresh fruit smoothies, while her own brother ate every piece of saturated fat he could find. "Are you going to spit it out, or is my dinner going to get cold?"

Mel sighed. "I'm sorry. I'm a little nervous, I guess." She looked back and Jensen sat up enough to grab her hand. "First of all, we wanted to share some really good news with you." Her cheeks were flushed and in a rush of genius, Benny knew exactly what she was going to say. "We're expecting."

A slow grin spread across Benny's face. "Really? For sure?"

Mel nodded, her smile more genuine than it had been at the door, and her free hand resting on her abdomen. "We just found out, but we felt like since you're family, you should know before we eventually tell everybody else."

Benny laughed and stood up, walking over to the couch with his arms outstretched. Mel stood up and met him. He gave his sister a gentle squeeze. "I'm excited for you guys." After he let go of Mel, he pulled Jensen off the couch and gave him a back-slapping hug as well. "Look at you!" he teased, stepping back. "You're gonna be a dad!"

Jensen paled slightly. "Yep." He tugged on his collar.

Benny snickered. "What? You're not nervous, are you?"

Jensen's eyes darted to Mel, then came back to glare at Benny. "No. I work with kids all day. I know exactly what I'm doing."

Benny's laughing grew. "Good luck with that."

"That wasn't the only reason we came over," Mel said.

*Of course it wasn't.* Benny went back to his recliner. Leaning back, he put one ankle over the other knee. "Shoot."

Mel and Jensen sat back down. Mel's hands were fidgeting, giving away how nervous she was.

"Come on, Mel. Just say it."

Mel took a deep breath, pinching her lips together. "I think we need to talk about your plan to take piano lessons."

*Oh. That.* Benny did his best to continue to look carefree. "What about it?"

"I'm worried you're going to do something to hurt Allison," Mel said too fast. "I know she's not very nice, but if you just stay out of her way, she doesn't bother people."

Benny smirked. "Do you really think I'm in this for revenge? I've only spoken to her like five times my entire life." *Three of which were in the last couple of weeks.*

Mel gave him a look. "Seriously, Benny. Why are you so interested in Allison?"

Benny spread his hands. "What's not to be interested in? You can't deny she's a beautiful woman." *One with a secret...or two.*

"You've never shown any interest in her before."

"Maybe I've never had the time to be interested."

Mel deflated a little. "Benny...what's going on?"

He shook his head. "Nothing. I just want to learn a musical instrument." He waved at Jensen. "Your husband plays guitar. Why can't I learn something?" He winked. "Maybe it'll help me catch the attention of a woman." He knew that would get his sister's hopes up that he was interested in settling down, but her interest in his current plans couldn't continue. Allison was going to be hard enough to crack without Mel's interference.

"Benny..." She groaned. "You forget. I'm your sister. I know when you're up to something."

Benny kept grinning, but didn't answer.

Mel's face grew more serious. "Do you promise you aren't going to hurt her?"

Benny put his hands up in surrender. "I promise I'm not trying to hurt her."

"But you *are* trying to....what?"

"Learn the piano."

Mel shook her head and rolled her eyes. "I know I can't stop you, but please...don't make an enemy, okay?"

"You've never been the type to play with people," Jensen said, studying Benny. "Why start now?"

Mel's eyes opened. "Oh my goodness! You're lonely!"

It took a great deal of self-discipline to keep from wincing at her statement. While it was partly true, Benny really was curious about what was going on with Allison. Things just didn't add up with her and he wanted to figure out what was going on. "Mel." He groaned. "Just because you're happy being joined at the hip with someone, doesn't mean we all want to be."

She pointed a finger at him. "No. You're lonely and that's why you're doing this." She gave him a pitying look. "I'm sorry we've been neglecting you. Do you want to make a standing dinner date with us each week? Can you come over every Sunday?"

Benny jumped to his feet. "Okay. I'm starving, so I think it's probably time for you to head on home, so I can stuff my face in peace." *Please just go. This is ridiculous. Go while I still have my pride.*

Mel and Jensen both stood. "Okay, but think about what I said, okay? I know things are different—"

"Goodnight, Mel!"

Mel rolled her eyes and walked to the door. "Fine," she snapped. "We'll leave you to your scheming."

"The only scheming I'm doing is figuring out how to completely spoil that kid when they finally make their appearance." Benny tapped his chin. "Sugar'll do it, I think. Lots and lots of sugar."

"Do that and you'll never be invited over again!" Jensen shot over his shoulder.

"If I'm going to get lectured, that might be worth it!" Benny grinned and shut the door. Shoot, his sister knew him too well. He'd have to be a little more low key in his pursuit of answers. If Mel got involved, it would ruin everything and his chance of breaking down Allison's walls would die an untimely death.

Sighing, he headed to the kitchen. He always thought better on a full stomach. Time to eat. Then he'd worry about the other stuff, including his sister, later.

# CHAPTER 6

"We'll see you next week!" Allison said as she opened the door for Eve. "Keep practicing and I'm sure you'll pass that song off next time."

Eve gave a cute wave, then skipped down the front steps and headed out to the sidewalk. The seven-year-old only lived two houses down, but Allison always liked to watch until she was sure Eve was home safe.

She was so caught up in watching the child that she didn't notice someone coming up her walk until the shadows passed over her. Frowning, she turned, then immediately stiffened. How was it this man was constantly catching her off-guard?

"Hello, Allison," Bennett said, his usual grin in place.

Allison swallowed hard, realizing her reaction too late. She straightened her shoulders, put her chin in the air, and began to turn back to the house.

"Don't you even want to know why I'm here?"

She couldn't help it. She faltered. *Isn't he here for the mail?* The answer made her turn back around. It was nearly evening. The mail had been delivered several hours before and Allison just now realized that Bennett wasn't in his uniform.

His grin widened, letting her know he knew he'd won a point. "I have a question."

Inside, she sighed. She wanted to roll her eyes and go back inside. A question? That was it? There was no way this was important enough for her to stand around on the doorstep waiting.

"Do you have any openings in your schedule?"

She stared harder. What was that supposed to mean?

"You know," Bennett said. "Your piano schedule. Do you have room for another student?"

Her eyes widened. "Another student?"

Bennett's eyebrows rose high and his jaw dropped in an open mouth smile. "YES!" he shouted, pumping a fist in the air.

"What's going on here?"

Allison snapped her mouth shut and stepped back as her mother shoved her way to stand between her and Benny.

Benny's exuberant smile fell some until he looked more normal. "Hello, Mrs. Mayer. I was just inquiring of Allison whether or not she had room for another student in her piano-teaching schedule."

Carla narrowed her gaze, then slowly turned to look over her shoulder at Allison suspiciously. Allison nodded subtly, but she knew her mom would catch it. She was the queen of details.

She turned back to Bennett. "You know someone who wants lessons?"

Bennett nodded slowly. "I do."

Allison relaxed just a hair when her mother smiled. It wasn't necessarily a kind smile, but Allison had two open spots on her schedule and another student just meant more money each month, something her mother struggled to turn down.

"She has room on Friday evenings. From five to five-thirty."

Bennett nodded. "Perfect. We'll take it."

Carla nodded back graciously. "If you'll just give us the child's name, we'll fill out the paperwork."

Bennett beamed and Allison grew immediately suspicious. "Bennett Frasier."

*No...*

"Excuse me?" Carla asked sharply.

"Me. I'm the student."

Allison's jaw dropped again. This day was definitely not turning out how she expected.

"You can't be a student," Carla all but growled.

"Ah, ah, ah," Bennett said with a finger in the air. "Would you really deny someone who had a desire to learn music the chance to learn from the best?"

Allison's eyes darted to her mother, watching her back stiffen.

"I've heard your daughter is the best in town." Bennett winked. "I've got no experience at all, so I figured the best teacher would be the best chance I had for success. Don't you think your daughter is capable of teaching someone like me?"

*Oh, he's good...* Allison had to give him credit. Somehow he knew just how to pull on her mother's strings. Pride and flattery. They were good choices.

"Of course, she can teach you!" Carla said in defense.

"Great! I look forward to starting on Friday." Bennett completely bulldozed over any more objections and turned to Allison. "Do you have paperwork for me to fill out?"

Allison's mouth went up and down a few times before she found her voice. "Yes," she croaked. She glanced to see her mother fuming, but she wouldn't go back on what she'd said. She'd been roped into agreeing and Carla Mayer never broke a promise. She wouldn't be able to handle how people would view her if she did. "Come on in." Allison backed up, still keeping a wary eye on her mother.

Bennett sucked in a breath and puffed out his cheeks as he slid past Carla. The dramatic look on his face almost made Allison laugh. Her guard was down at the moment, so it would have been easy for a giggle to escape if she wasn't so shocked by everything that had just happened. Her head felt fuzzy and she wasn't quite sure she was aware enough to know what was going on.

*I'm going to teach Bennett Frasier piano? Why? Is that why he's been trying to talk to me so much? He just wanted lessons?*

Her heart sank a little at the thought. Deep inside she had hoped he had a better reason for singling her out, but wanting piano lessons made more sense. It wasn't like she gave him any encouragement to want to spend time with her because of her sparkling personality.

*Wait!*

She skidded to a stop. Bennett hadn't even known she taught piano when he'd first started bugging her in the grocery store. It was something he'd only learned later. A smile crept across her face before she could stop it. *So he was talking to me because he wanted to talk to ME!*

Bennett stepped into her space, nearly nose to nose.

Allison's smile immediately fell and she blinked rapidly, shocked at his sudden appearance.

"That's what I like to see," he said softly.

"What?" Allison asked.

One half of Bennett's mouth lifted into an adorable smile. He pulled off the innocent, boyish charm so well. "You smiled. You should do it more often." He looked away and ticked his head back and forth. "And speak. Having you speak has been pretty awesome as well."

All humor and excitement fled. Her emotionless mask slid back into place and Allison could actually feel the wall forming between them. For just a moment, she'd had a glimpse of something fun and bright, but with one sentence he reminded her of who she was supposed to be. Her mother would be here any second and if she thought for a second that Allison was encouraging a relationship with Bennett, Carla would make life horrible. Her grand goals were for them to eventually escape Seaside Bay. A boyfriend would only hold them back.

Bennett sighed and narrowed his eyes playfully. "Don't worry," he whispered. "I've seen it once. Now that I know it exists, it's only a matter of time before I glory in that look again."

BENNY COULDN'T HELP grinning at the shocked look in her pretty dark eyes. She had done such a good job of keeping her emotions behind that prison wall that any break in them was something to celebrate.

He'd managed to shock her enough to not only make her speak, but he saw surprise, fear, and a smile. Today was a pretty darn good day.

He also had to give himself props for how he'd handled Mrs. Mayer. That woman was wily and manipulative. He was going to have to be careful whenever he was over here. He had a feeling Mrs. Mayer would be watching him very carefully.

"Paperwork?" he asked Allison when she didn't move from her spot.

She blinked, breaking whatever spell she was currently under. "Hold on just a moment, please." She disappeared further into the house, leaving Benny in the front room with the piano.

He wandered over and sat down on the bench. He stared at the black and white keys. His mother had been a little too loose in her parenting to have put any responsibilities on him such as taking lessons. Her lax style might have contributed to his carefree personality, but it had gone the opposite way with Mel. She thrived on order and organization. Though her health nut side was more than likely a trait she got genetically.

He sat down and chuckled as he thought about how opposite they were. Yet he wouldn't trade his sister for anything, despite her determination to poke her head into his business once in a while. "She'll probably leave me alone if I ever get married," he muttered under his breath.

"Mr. Frasier?"

Benny spun on the bench, hoping she hadn't heard his muttered words. That particular sentence wouldn't help him on his quest, he was sure. "Got that paper?"

Allison's stoic face nodded.

Man, he wanted to break it down again. She was so much more attractive when she let go. Her looks were almost exotic in their depth. Her eyes were slightly tilted at the corners and her rich-colored hair and eyes were a perfect contrast to the porcelain skin that looked as if it had never seen the sun. No wrinkle would ever dare mar such beauty, although Benny figured it had more to do with the fact that she never smiled than her Spanish ancestry.

If she would ever get over whatever was holding her back, she would probably have men lining up around the block to date her.

Benny held out his hand for the paper. "Do you have a pen or pencil? I'm afraid I didn't come prepared."

A huff of disgust carried around the room and Benny looked over to see Mrs. Mayer leaving the room.

He found himself relieved that she wasn't sticking around. It would give him a chance to speak to Allison a little.

"Let me get you one," Allison said softly. She walked to the other side of the bench he was sitting on and reached into a small glass full of glass beads. Several pens were poked into the beads, standing straight up.

*I probably should have seen those.* He gave Allison a sheepish grin. "Sorry. Didn't see those there."

Allison nodded, her face still emotionless even with her mother gone. "That's all right. If you'd like to use the bench to fill that out, I'll put it in my records."

*Now to draw this out...*

"How long have you been playing?" he asked, keeping his face down as he wrote down his name. When she didn't answer right away, Benny looked up from under his lashes. "Don't tell me you don't know," he teased.

Her lip twitched, but stayed neutral. "Since I was three."

Benny's eyes widened and he sat up straight, whistling low under his breath. "Three? Are you serious?"

She gave a single nod.

"Wow." He rubbed the back of his head. "I was still eating mud at that point, you know...like a normal kid." Her lips twitched again and Benny grew a little bolder. He glanced at the hallway where her mother disappeared, then leaned in. "It's okay to laugh," he whispered. "She's not watching."

Allison's eyes flared.

"You're really beautiful when you smile," he continued. That apparently was the wrong way to take the conversation. The shutters that came over her eyes were almost visible. *Looks...bad topic. So noted.*

At this point, he figured it didn't matter if he kept going since she was already upset with him. "Why do you let her run your life?"

"Are you finished with your paperwork?"

Benny sighed internally, but he made sure his frustration didn't show on his face. "Did you know that the first post office was in a bar?"

"What?" Allison jerked back slightly.

"I'm serious. The very first post office was in a bar."

"That...can't be true," Allison responded, but her tone said she was unsure.

Benny shrugged. "You're trying to convince me that you played piano when you were three years old. Why can't the post office be in a bar?"

"How is that even remotely the same?"

The look of surprise on her face let Benny know she hadn't meant to respond to him at all. *Surprising facts work. So noted.* His mental list of how to handle Allison was starting to get some information on it and that spurred him onward.

"They're not," Benny admitted easily. "Except that they're both hard to believe."

She relaxed just a little, her shoulders dropping from their stiff stance. She tilted her head, studying him as if he were a science experiment. "Somehow I get the feeling that you have a lot of hard to believe facts in your head."

He buffed his nails on his shirt. "I might or might not be excellent at useless information." He waggled his eyebrows. "Want to hear another one?" He continued before she could turn him down. "The Postmaster General earns more than the Vice President."

"No," she breathed.

"Absolutely true." Noises came from down the hall and Benny knew his stalling was up. He quickly scribbled down the rest of the information. "Why don't you send me a quick text to confirm my number."

Allison slowly picked up her phone from the side of the piano and did just that.

"Great." Benny sent back a smiley face emoji. "Now we've exchanged numbers." He winked. "Just like a real date!" A squeak managed to escape as he shot out the door, but he was down the sidewalk well before any true repercussions could hit him upside the head.

Pleased with his sneaky mission, Benny put his phone in his back pocket, his hands in his front ones, and slowed his walk to a saunter. A few more steps and he began to whistle a cheerful tune. He'd made quite a bit of progress today and he had a feeling it would only get better. Now Allison was forced to see him at least once a week and he would absolutely make sure he got his money's worth.

# CHAPTER 7

Allison's nerves had been jumping all day. Bennett was coming tonight for his first lesson and Allison wasn't sure whether to be elated or scared to death. She'd never taught an adult before, but that wasn't exactly the issue.

Bennett was different.

He pushed when others stayed back.

He prodded when most ignored.

He drove her completely crazy and refused to back down when others looked away from her death glare like she was a monster.

"Ms. Mayer?"

Allison jolted slightly, then forced a smile onto her face. "Sorry," she said automatically. "I'm afraid I got caught in my thoughts."

Jordan rolled his eyes. "Yeah. I don't think piano's very interesting either."

Allison pinched her lips together to keep from laughing. This poor boy. No matter what incentive she tried, she just couldn't seem to capture his attention. He wasn't rude, just...not interested. "Well, I find piano fascinating," Allison said in an upbeat manner. "I love playing songs I hear on the radio or making up new ones." She shrugged. "I think making music is great."

"It's not when you want to play the electric guitar instead," Jordan grumbled, slumping in his seat.

"Did you know that playing piano can help you when you eventually learn guitar?"

He gave her a look. "Really?"

Allison nodded. "Yep. By knowing all your theory and being able to read music, you'll be way ahead of the other students when you start taking guitar lessons."

Jordan sighed as if the weight of the world was on his shoulders. Grumbling slightly, he put his fingers back on the keys and stiltingly pounded out the song they were working on.

"Great!" Allison gushed. "You're already making progress." She wrote down his practice assignments for the week and then the lesson was over. Standing up, Allison walked the young man to the door, and her heart gave a flip when Bennett was waiting for them on the doorstep. She'd managed to forget her anxiety for the last couple minutes of Jordan's lesson, but now the nerves seemed to come back double what they were before.

"Hey, man," Bennett said to Jordan, giving him knuckles. "How'd your lesson go?"

Jordan shrugged. "Fine, I guess." He squinted up at Bennett. "What're you doing here? You're not wearing your uniform."

Bennett grinned and his blue eyes flashed up to Allison. "I'm here for piano lessons."

Jordan's jaw fell, but his eyebrows rose. "What? You're taking lessons?"

Bennett nodded. "Yep. I thought it would be a good idea to learn something new."

Jordan shook his head, obviously unsure what to think of the situation. "Good luck, I guess." Shrugging, the tween walked past them both and escaped to the sidewalk.

Allison watched him go with trepidation. With Jordan gone, it was just her and Bennett. Her mother was actually in Portland and wouldn't be home until late, which was a rare occurrence. "Please, come in," she said softly, stepping aside so Bennett could enter the house. She held her breath when his shoulder brushed against her arm. Her body didn't seem to be able to control itself when Bennett

Frasier was around and once again, she found herself stuck between frustration and intrigue. He seemed to have a knack for knocking her off her guard.

Bennett stopped at the bench and looked down, then up at her. "I can scoot this back, right?"

A smile pulled at her lips, but Allison did her best to stay strong. "Of course. Move the bench to a comfortable position for you." Leaving him to make the adjustments, Allison sat down in her chair, then jumped when a body landed next to her. "What are you doing?" she squeaked, leaning back from his overwhelming presence.

Bennett winked. "You said to put it where I was comfortable. Sitting next to you is comfortable."

Allison barely resisted the urge to roll her eyes like Jordan had done only moments previous. "Move it so you're comfortable at the piano, please," she said firmly. She could *not* let this man continue to push her buttons. Allison knew she would just have to stand up for herself. If he knew she meant business from the beginning, then hopefully they could get through these lessons without too much awkwardness.

"Bummer," Bennett mumbled before moving back to the keyboard.

"Please remember this lesson is for me to teach you piano," Allison said loftily. "Not a flirting session."

"Another bummer," Bennett said with his usual grin.

Allison could just imagine this man getting away with anything he wanted when he was a boy. His blue eyes sparkled with mischief, his slightly too long hair hung adoringly over his forehead, his skin was tan and smooth-looking, and his personality was positively addicting...when he wasn't making her want to throttle him, that is. "Have you ever played an instrument before?" she asked, forcing her eyes to move back to her notes.

"Nope," he said easily. "In fact, maybe you should sit on the bench here with me. Learning so late in life might mean I'll need...extra help."

"Mr. Frasier," Allison began.

"Benny."

She paused. "I can't call you that."

"Why not?"

"It wouldn't be professional."

Benny shrugged. "We're in your home and I'm older than you. I think it'd be fine to bend the rules a bit."

"I'm afraid not," Allison replied, putting her face back down. She just had to stop staring at him. Then she'd be able to concentrate on her job. When warm fingers landed on her chin, however, her plan was thwarted.

"Don't you ever break the rules?" he asked, searching her face as if it would hold the answers he sought.

"Never," she whispered, more breathlessly than she would have liked. He didn't need to know the effect he had on her. It would only spur on his outrageous behavior.

His pointed finger traced along her cheek. "Tell me about your birthmark."

Allison jerked back. "I don't know what you're talking about," she said crisply. "Please pick up the book on the right-hand side of the piano."

She ignored Bennett...Benny's...beleaguered sigh as he plopped the book on the piano. "What now, O Wondrous Piano Teacher?"

"If you'll notice, on page one, it talks about the different mechanics of a piano," Allison began, knowing the information from memory. "In the body of the piano, you'll find the soundboard. This is where the music comes from." She continued droning on, no emotion in her tone. This was a safe place. She knew how to behave like this, no feelings, no emotions, no stimuli. She could just do her job and once the half-hour was over, she'd let herself break down in her room, lamenting the one day where she'd ruined a lifetime's worth of work.

HE'D PUSHED TOO FAR, too fast. It was time to back off a little before trying again. He didn't see Mrs. Mayer anywhere, so it seemed like a good time to see what he could find out about her background, but Allison hadn't been prepared for his probing. Even without her mother, she apparently was going to be a tough nut to crack.

"Like this?" he asked, splaying his fingers across the keys.

Her eyes barely came up to view his fingers. "No. Try curling your fingers as if they were going around a ball. Your palm should be up, and your wrist not resting against the front board."

Benny squished his lips to the side. "Maybe you can show me?" He scooted over and made room for her on the bench.

Allison glared at him.

Benny raised an eyebrow. "Do you always treat your students like this?"

"Do you always pretend not to be able to do things you're perfectly capable of?"

"Yes," he said without preamble. "I do that all the time. I'm excellent at pretending I don't know how to do dishes, or cook, or be responsible in general." He beamed at her, a smile others had told him was dangerous to the female population. *Dangerous to everyone except Allison, apparently.* She didn't budge.

"I don't think this is going to work out," Allison said, jumping to her feet. "I'll walk you to the door."

"What?" Benny raced after her, grabbing her arm. "You can't just kick me out. I'm a paying customer."

"I'm not a retail store," Allison said sharply, pulling her arm out of his hold. She rubbed the spot unconsciously with her other hand and Benny frowned a moment.

"Did I hurt you?"

Dark eyebrows pulled together. "What?"

He nodded toward her arm. "Your arm. Did I hurt you? You're rubbing it like I did."

She looked down and surprise spread across her face. Immediately, Allison dropped her hand. "No. You didn't hurt me." She began to turn toward the door again, but Benny stopped her yet again.

"Let me look." He paused slightly, waiting to see if she would push him away, but instead she just stared, like she couldn't quite figure him out. Slowly, as if dealing with a skittish colt, he gently took her arm and ran his fingers over the spot he had been holding. Goosebumps skittered over her skin and he heard a ragged breath escape. He wanted to grin at the small win. She wasn't completely unaffected by him. This would go a long way into helping him in his mission to figure out her story. He could use this. He had to admit though, he wasn't completely unaffected himself. His neck felt warm and he was very much enjoying the feel of her soft skin under his fingers. "No bruises?" he asked, his voice slightly husky. *Oops.* He cleared his throat. The fact that she found him attractive would be useful, but just like asking about her birthmark, he knew full well it was too soon.

"No," she croaked. Blinking rapidly, as if coming back to herself, Allison stepped back, once again pulling out of his hold. "What do you want from me?" Her voice was stronger now.

Benny gave her an easy smile. "I want to learn piano."

"Then why did you ask about..." She was breathing heavily, as if even speaking of the topic forced her to exert herself. "My life?"

Benny stuffed his hands in his pockets. "I'm a curious guy." He tilted his head to the side and pulled out his best innocent expression. "No one has any idea that you have a port wine mark."

She flinched and ducked into herself.

"But you know what?" Benny immediately backed up, his hands in the air. "It really doesn't matter. I'm here to learn piano. Nothing more."

She narrowed her gaze. "I find that hard to believe."

He smiled and walked back to the bench. "That's what I paid for and I totally want to get my money's worth."

Slowly, Allison came back to her own chair, still looking wary, but seemingly willing to follow his lead. "Okay, then, let's put your hands back on the piano."

For the next twenty minutes, they went through exercises and the beginnings of notes. Benny had to admit, it was kinda interesting. He hadn't expected to actually like his lesson, it was mainly a tactic to get close to Allison. If he actually found a new hobby in the process, then he had to admit that was just a bonus.

Allison finished writing down his assignment for the week. "I'm assuming you have a piano to practice on?"

Benny snapped his mouth shut. He hadn't thought that far ahead in this matter.

Allison looked up from under her perfectly styled eyelashes. "Bennett?"

"Benny." Maybe he could distract her and then this week he would solve the issue.

Allison put down her pen. "Does everyone call you Benny?"

"Yep."

"You never go by your full name?"

Benny shook his head. "Nope." He raised his eyebrows. "Do you ever go by a nickname?"

"No." Her answer was quick and succinct, with no room for error.

Benny tapped his lips. He swiveled on the bench so he was straddling it so he could face her. "Never?"

"Never."

Benny shook his head. "That won't work. We need to find you a nickname."

Allison made a face before it was quickly smoothed away. "I don't think we should do that."

A slow grin grew across his face. "Oh, we totally should."

"Why? Why would we want to find me a nickname?" She looked honestly perplexed.

Benny threw his hands up in the air. "They're fun."

Allison just blinked at him.

"Why do I get the feeling that you never have any fun?" Benny put his chin in his hand and studied his teacher.

"I have fun." Her jaw snapped shut after that lie and Benny felt that familiar swirling of pity again.

Allison needed help and once again, he was positive that he was the one to give it to her. "Come on," he said, standing up and grabbing her hand.

"What are you doing?" Allison screeched as he dragged her to the door.

"We're going for a walk."

"A walk? Why would we do that?"

Benny stopped at the door. "You don't have any more students, right?"

"Well, no."

"And we need to find you a nickname, right?"

She started to shake her head, but Benny opened the door, interrupting any response.

"We also need to teach you what having fun means, because I think your view is skewed." She wasn't exactly walking eagerly, but she wasn't objecting, and Benny gave himself a mental high five. One more little victory to put on his side of the chart.

# CHAPTER 8

Allison had no idea what she was doing. The idea of taking a walk and figuring out a nickname was so ludicrous, and yet here she was...tripping in Benn...y's wake like a clumsy puppy. If her mother could see her now, she'd lock Allison up until kingdom come.

"Relax," Benny said with a chuckle. "You can't enjoy this if you're walking around like a stiff board."

*I don't know how to relax like that.* Allison bit her tongue to make sure those words didn't slip through her lips. They were almost as embarrassing as her birthmark. She was twenty-six years old, and she didn't know how to relax or have fun. *What kind of life have I lived?*

Old feelings began to resurface, ones she had buried as a child. Feelings of missing out, of watching the world from the outside. When other children were playing on swing sets, she was at the piano bench. When the teenagers were going to movies, Allison was getting makeup lessons or competing in concerts. When college kids were partying all night, Allison was pretending to be the perfect little protege her mother wanted.

She tried to bury them once more, but they refused to go back to the dark hole she'd kept them in. The more the warmth from Benny's hand penetrated her fingers, the more he laughed and pointed out fun things in nature, the more he refused to back away from her, the more she didn't want to go back to where she'd come from.

But thinking about changing made her feel lost. If she wasn't her mother's perfect pianist...who was she? Who was Allison Mayer?

*A permanently scarred woman with no personality and no friends. That's who.*

The words swept through her brain, the voice of her mother loud and clear.

"Whoa, whoa, whoa," Benny said, coming to a stop right in front of her. He put his hands on her shoulders. "None of that."

Allison shook her head a little, dispelling the words. "What?"

"I was losing you," he said. "That's not what we're doing right now."

"I..." Allison let her mouth hang open, but no more words came. She felt like a scared little girl, not the strong, confident woman she usually pretended to be. He had been right.

"Look around," Benny said gently.

Allison frowned.

He clicked his tongue. "Come on, it's not that hard."

Still feeling wary, Allison forced her head to turn around. She noticed they'd gotten fairly close to town. Other people were walking down the boardwalk, very few paying any attention to her and Benny. Children laughed and danced around their parents. In the distance, she could hear the waves of the ocean and the squeals of yet more children. Her heart slowly softened at the noise. No one would ever know it, but Allison loved children. They were the only people who treated her like someone normal.

"Ally."

Her head jerked back to Benny. It was only then that she realized just how close they were standing and that his hands were still resting on her shoulders. That pleasant warmth continued to penetrate her body and she had to lock her knees to keep from shivering at his nearness. *Great. That's all I need is him knowing I'm attracted to him. Benny could have any woman he wanted. He's not going to pick the ice cold, town jerk with a ruined face.*

"Your nickname," he clarified. "I've decided it's going to be Ally."

She started to shake her head, but stopped. "Ally," she whispered, as if tasting the name on her tongue. It sounded...fun. It sounded like someone who knew how to smile and laugh, who didn't miss out on life because of fear or other frailties. "I think I like it," she said.

Benny winked, sending her heart fluttering again. "I knew you would." He tweaked her nose. "It suits you."

*No, it doesn't,* she argued mentally. *But I want it to.*

"Come on." Benny took her hand again, but he slowed his walk down to an amble. Their hands swung between them and Allison had to wonder if he treated every woman like this.

*Probably.*

"Do you know what kind of birds those are?" Benny pointed to a large bird on a fence post.

Allison chewed her lip. "No. I don't think I do. It looks like some kind of pelican. The beak is kind of big."

Benny's smile was enough to have her feel overheated, though the day was mild in temperature. "Right. It's a brown pelican. Did you know that they're the only bird who drop into water from like...thirty feet in the air to dive bomb their prey?"

"Really?" Allison looked at the bird again. It seemed so docile, not at all like something that would drop from the sky like an atomic bomb.

"Really." Benny started walking with her again. "However, despite how high they dive from, they actually don't go very deep. They have a pouch which causes them to be buoyant, so they never sink very far."

Allison slowly shook her head, an unbidden smile pulling on her lips.

"It's the smallest of the pelican family and can fly at speeds up to thirty miles an hour."

"How in the world do you know all that?" Allison asked, completely amazed. He seemed like such a dork most of the time. She would never have guessed he'd be so knowledgeable.

Benny grinned at her. "I've got a thing for random, useless knowledge."

She pursed her lips in thought. "I don't know...it seems like that's the kind of information that always wins on *Jeopardy!*, you know?"

"Ah..." Benny put a hand over his chest. "We only started talking a few weeks ago and yet you already know my highest aspirations."

Allison had no idea if he was being serious or not. How in the world was she supposed to figure this guy out? Everything he said was dramatic. "Uh...do you really want to be on a game show?"

"Wouldn't you?" he asked back.

"Absolutely not." The words were out before she could stop them, though they were completely true. She'd never told anyone how much she hated the limelight.

He stopped and turned to her. "Why not?"

She ducked her head and tucked a loose piece of hair behind her ear. "I just wouldn't."

Once again, Benny refused to let her off the hook. He reached and lifted up her chin until they were looking at each other again. "Why not?" he asked more deliberately.

Several ragged breaths went by before Allison answered. "Because I hate being the center of attention," she whispered.

Benny kept looking at her, but didn't ask more. Finally, he nodded and they continued down the sidewalk. "Ever been zapped by a jellyfish?"

BENNY COULD TELL HE was confusing her, but he figured she needed a little shake up. Not so much she would retreat into her icy shell, but enough to make her question the status quo. He was starting to believe more firmly that she wasn't the jerk everyone thought she was.

He'd seen her with her piano students, at least for a few unguarded seconds in the doorway. He'd seen her smile and compliment, appearing happy and content...all until a grownup or her mother came. He'd seen her without makeup, and knew she hid secrets, one she didn't even want to acknowledge existed.

And now he knew she didn't like being the center of attention. That particular piece of information seemed completely at odds with her life. She commanded attention everywhere she went, whether she wanted to or not. Between her picture-perfect looks and her wicked witch facade, no one didn't notice Allison Mayer.

"Uh, no I don't think I have," Allison said softly, her eyes drifting toward the water.

"I wouldn't recommend it," Benny said conversationally. "It stings like the dickens."

She smiled softly. "I've heard that."

He hated to ruin the moment by asking, but he needed to know. "Where's your mom today?"

Allison's smile disappeared so quickly, he wondered if it had been real. "She's in Portland."

*Perfect.* He was hoping she would be gone long enough for Allison not to get into trouble.

"Why do you ask?"

Benny glanced sideways at her and smiled. "Because I wanted to know how long I can keep you out without getting you in trouble."

Her mouth opened slightly, then snapped shut. He could practically see the wheels turning in her mind.

"Do you like ice cream?" He tugged her a little faster toward a cart selling cones and other sweet treats. There was almost no line since summer was winding down. Soon the cart would be put away for the winter, but the owner always held out as long as possible to catch the last of the tourists. Allison tugged on his hand.

"I can't..."

Benny stopped and turned toward her. "You can't? Are you lactose intolerant?"

She gave a short shake of her head. "No."

He waited for her to explain, but the situation just grew more awkward. *Okay, now I really gotta know.* "If you don't like ice cream, I can always take you to Sassy Sweets. Caro and Jack have the best desserts ever." He put a hand to the side of his mouth. "But don't tell Caro I said that. She's feisty enough as it is."

Again, Allison shook her head.

Benny frowned. "I don't understand. You can't...meaning you can't eat...what? Sugar? Milk? Dessert?" He said the last one jokingly, but when Allison didn't even begin to smile, Benny's humor slowly faded. "That's it, isn't it? You're not allowed to eat desserts."

The icy walls were painstakingly put back into place. Benny watched brick by brick as Allison began to protect herself and her mother. "I have a duty to those I perform for to look a certain way," she started, the words sounding stiff and rehearsed.

Once again, pity filled Benny's gut. He didn't like feeling sorry for her, but geez, this was just wrong. His childhood hadn't been ideal either, but just what did Mrs. Mayer do to Allison to make her so...robotic?

His eyes fluttered over her figure, thin to the point of almost looking ill. Nope. He wasn't about to stand by and let her pull that card. "That's the biggest load of bull I've ever heard," Benny muttered, marching toward the stand again. "Ice cream is the heart of our country. Ninety-six percent of Americans eat ice cream." He pulled to a stop in front of the cart and grabbed his wallet from his back pocket. It was a bit awkward since the hand he needed was still holding Allison's, but he wasn't about to let her bolt.

"You made that up," she accused.

Benny shook his head. "Nope. It's true." He gave her a half-grin. "Want to know the most popular flavors?" He faced the vendor. "Two, please. One scoop chocolate, one vanilla, on each."

Allison gasped behind him, but Benny ignored her. If nothing else ever came from this situation, he was bound and determined to undermine Mrs. Carla Mayer and corrupt Allison's view of the world. In a good way.

"Thank you," Benny said, leaving the vendor a generous tip. The man was a retired vet and Benny always liked to support where he could. Turning, he handed one of the large cones to Allison. "Chocolate is the number one flavor, followed by vanilla, and third, butter pecan."

"I can't eat this," she said breathlessly.

"You might be surprised," Benny said brightly. He took her to sit on one of the benches located just off the boardwalk. "See, ice cream is one of those special treats we always have time for. It melts and fills in all the cracks even when we're full."

A soft snort escaped Allison and Benny put another tally mark on his victory chart. "That I *know* you made up."

"Wrong again!" Benny sang out. "There might not have been a study on it, but I can guarantee I spent years and years studying the matter."

Her laughter grew and Benny couldn't help but smile at the sound. It was a side of her she rarely shared, and he felt a strange bout of gratefulness that he was one of the privileged few.

Still smiling, Allison took a lick of her cone. "Mmm…" she hummed, closing her eyes as if savoring every drop.

"How long has it been since you had dessert?" he asked, too fascinated with watching her reactions to eat his own cone.

"Too long," she said, giving him a sarcastic smile. Her eyes widened. "You're dripping."

"Crud." Benny licked his knuckle, then got busy taking care of the melting cream. "So...do you follow the masses, or are your tastes unique?"

Her brows pulled together and the edges of her mouth drooped. "What do you mean?"

"The ice cream." Benny nodded toward her hand. "Is chocolate your favorite? Or do you like something else?"

Allison studied the treat in her hand. "I...don't know. I just like ice cream."

"That is an excellent answer," Benny said. "I eat *almost* any flavor."

"What flavors do you not like?" she asked right before licking the cone again.

"Pickled Mango."

Allison straightened. "That's not a real flavor."

"It was," Benny assured her. "So was Foie Gras, Pear and Blue Cheese, and Ghost Pepper."

Her perfectly small nose scrunched up in an adorable way, taking years off her face. "That's disgusting."

"Yep. They were."

"You tried them all!" Allison gaped at him.

"One thing you should know about me," Benny said in all seriousness. "I eat everything."

Her eyebrows shot up. "Everything?"

"Yep. Everything."

# CHAPTER 9

The next two days were spent in a weird haze. Allison was still floating on cloud nine from her evening with Benny, but the non-hormonal crazed part of her brain spent every moment terrified that her mother would somehow read her mind and figure out what she'd been up to.

Carla had come home from Portland with a gleam in her eye that had worried Allison, but had kept Carla too occupied to dig into her daughter's life. It usually meant she had managed to get Allison involved in some kind of concert, but Carla had yet to announce whatever had her so giddy. Which was just another piece of stress to add to Allison's shoulders.

She was feeling the weight of it all quite heavily one night when cooking dinner and Carla slapped a manilla folder down on the kitchen counter.

"This is it," she crowed.

Allison glanced over her shoulder. "What is it?"

Carla settled onto a bar stool, her face smug. "Our future."

Fear skittered down Allison's spine. She didn't like the sound of this. "Oh?" She hoped her voice sounded steady, because it felt anything but.

"You've been offered a job."

Allison turned fully from the stove, wiping her hands on a kitchen towel. "I have a job."

Carla waved her hand dismissively through the air. "I don't mean teaching those brats for a few pennies a day. I mean a *real* job." Putting her palms flat on the counter, Carla leaned in. "You've been offered a contract to teach at Eastern up in Washington. You'll be teaching theory, on top of private piano lessons. The contract offers a full-time salary, along with time for you to continue pursuing your professional career. In time, you could even be department head!" Carla's smile was so wide, it looked like it could split her face in half.

Dread pooled in Allison's stomach. "I..." She didn't want to do it. She didn't want to keep pursuing a professional career. She didn't want to have to teach college students or anyone older than the age of twelve. *With the exception of Benny.*

After having the slightest taste of freedom the other day, Allison had more words to add to her internal rant. She wanted more walks on the boardwalk. She wanted to keep teaching little children, even those who were only there because their parents forced them to be. She wanted to play in church or compose at her leisure. She wanted to have the freedom to enjoy her life and not constantly be at the beck and call of the professional world or a thousand piano students, or a board of academic musicians who had forgotten what it was like to enjoy music.

"Allison!"

She snapped out of her thoughts and forced her attention to her mother. "Yes?"

"What is the problem?" Carla huffed. "I thought you'd be excited about this."

Allison pinched her lips together. "I'd...I'd rather stay here." There she'd said it. Let the chips fall where they may. She was an adult, she had a say in her life...right?

Carla's face slowly morphed into a look that Allison did her best to avoid. "You want to stay here?" she demanded. "After all I've done for you? All I've sacrificed. All the times I pushed you to be more than just a deformed face."

Allison couldn't stop the flinch. Her mother spoke of her face often, but no matter what Allison did, it never stopped hurting.

"The doctors told me you wouldn't accomplish anything," Carla sneered, standing up from her seat. "They even hinted someone like you might have brain damage, but I didn't listen. Even when I became a single mother, I didn't listen. I pushed. Pushed you to be your best and to develop a talent at the cost of my own." She put a hand to her heart and her eyes filled with tears.

It didn't matter that Allison knew the emotions were completely manufactured. She still felt a tug inside to soothe and rectify the situation. She absolutely hated hurting her mother, and she hated she had been such a burden her whole life.

"I scrimped and saved and all I ask in return is for you to use the education you've been given to help support us. I've spent everything I had to get you to this point." Carla choked on a sob. "And yet you can't even take the time to think about it? This job would be the security we need. You've been given the best musical education a person could ask for, and while we both know you're far from perfect, we're barely getting by."

Carla turned away, her bottom lip trembling. "But if that's what you want. To stay in this town, working for peanuts and spending the rest of our lives in poverty, then who am I to stop us?" She dabbed at her eyes. "I suppose when it comes time for me to go into a home, we'll just have to take out a loan. There are plenty of others who have to do the same."

An instant headache slammed into Allison's forehead. She hated her mother's manipulations. And that's exactly what this was. She *knew* it was. Allison might have very little control over their money, but she had a fair idea of what they made. She wasn't wealthy and famous, but she had plenty to live on, especially in a town like Seaside Bay. But her mother's words hurt, and they absolutely did their job in making Allison feel guilty for putting her mother through such turmoil, feigned or not.

Carla sniffled, keeping her back to Allison.

"I'll think about it." Allison closed her eyes and dropped her head. She hadn't wanted to say it. For once, she wanted to be strong enough to just say no and let her mother explode as she would, but years of habit took over and the words slipped easily between her lips.

Carla immediately stiffened, then she relaxed and turned with a teary smile. "Thank you," she gushed. "That's all I ask." She came closer to Allison. "I know that with time, you'll see what an opportunity this is." A calculating glint came into her eye. "It's probably a good thing to make them wait a bit anyway. There were a couple parts of the contract that weren't my favorite. Perhaps if we stand our ground, I'll be able to figure out some leverage to change it to our advantage."

Allison didn't say anything more. She didn't need to. Her mother was leaving the room, mumbling under her breath about how they could get more out of the contract. Sighing, Allison turned back to the stove. She wasn't really hungry anymore, but she also didn't want to waste a perfectly good meal.

Draining the pasta and mixing it with the marinara took almost no time at all. Despite her worries, Allison dished herself up a plate, then in a fit of defiance, got herself some parmesan out of the fridge and dumped a bunch of it over her meal. Since her mother had not shown up again to eat, Allison took the plate to her room and locked herself in. Her stomach protested, but she forced down every bite, until she couldn't eat any more.

She set the plate on the ground, not even bothering to take it to the kitchen, then laid flat on her bed, sleepy from her first real food coma. Something about it was as comforting as it was painful. Twice now she'd gotten away with breaking her mother's rules and so far, she had survived.

"What else can you change about your life?" she murmured to the darkened room.

Thoughts of the job floated back in and Allison put a hand to her stomach, suddenly nauseous. But perhaps that was the answer. Perhaps that was where she needed to put her foot down. She wanted to repay her mother for all her years of help and sacrifice, but she had no desire to teach at that college. Eastern was known for its music program, and Allison knew she'd be so inundated with students she'd barely be able to breathe. Especially with her face. It was difficult enough to keep her birthmark hidden from a handful of kids, let alone hundreds of adults.

Allison set her jaw as she made up her mind. She had no idea how she was going to do it, but someway, somehow, she was going to stay here. She knew she'd be miserable in Washington, but here...well, it looked like there just might be some light at the end of a very long tunnel.

"COME ON," BENNY WHINED. "You know you miss me." He sighed and listened to Mel explain why they weren't available for dinner. "Meeeeellllll," he wheedled. "I'm your brother. Can't you celebrate your anniversary another time?" Benny grumbled under his breath. "Yeah, yeah, I'm just joking. Uh-huh. Have a good time. I mean, I don't know why it takes an entire week to celebrate, but whatever." Though his sister wasn't in the room, Benny put his hands in the air in defense. "Sorry! I said I'm sorry! Go! Enjoy Cali! Just be careful of the baby, huh?" He smiled. It had worked. Any time Mel got frustrated with him, all he had to do was bring up his future niece or nephew and she immediately melted. "Yeah. Have a good time. And happy anniversary."

Shaking his head, Benny turned off the phone. "Too bad that baby doesn't help me get a decent meal," he said to the empty room. Setting the phone on the counter, Benny leaned his back on it and folded his arms over his chest. He hated this. His house was way too quiet. It felt like a tomb and the walls were closing in.

Grabbing his phone again and then his keys and wallet, Benny marched out the front door. He couldn't stay in that place one moment longer. Something shriveled inside of him every time he spent an evening alone.

Grabbing the nearest fast food, he parked himself at the police station. "This is what I've come to," Benny grumbled, looking at the lights inside. He shook his head. "Spending the night at the jail and I didn't even do anything wrong. Should've had some fun at least before this."

Grabbing the food, he burst inside. "Hey, Steve!"

The man at the front desk raised his head. "Hi, Benny. What brings you by tonight?"

Benny dangled the bag. "I happened to be free for a date."

Steve snorted. "He'll demote me if I tell him that."

Benny grinned wickedly and began to saunter past the desk. "Don't worry. I'll do it for you." Benny's smile didn't falter as he listened to the laughter behind him. He approached Ken's office and slowed, putting his ear to the door. He didn't mind busting in, but he didn't want to interrupt a phone conversation or something.

When he didn't hear anything, Benny threw the door open and swung his arms wide. "Never fear! I'm here!"

After recovering from his shock, Ken rolled his eyes to the ceiling, shaking his head and mumbling under his breath. "And I thought today was going to be a quiet one."

Benny laughed. "Aren't you lucky it didn't turn out that way?"

"I happen to like quiet, thank you very much," Ken drawled, leaning back in his seat, bending it back just a little.

"Quiet is overrated," Benny retorted.

"Only for the extroverts."

Benny shrugged. "Which I am, so why are we arguing about this?" He grinned. "You know, if you ever manage to get Rose to agree to a date, you might have to change your stance on quiet. I've heard Lilly squeal."

A small smile played on Ken's mouth. "I think I could handle that in my life," he admitted.

Benny groaned. "No. I've had enough of lovebirds."

"I wish," Ken huffed.

For once, Benny eased up on his teasing. He was beginning to get a small sense of what Ken went through on a regular basis. Allison's constant rejections would be easy to get discouraged over, especially if Benny's behavior was because he was lovestruck like Ken was.

Benny usually just barreled over Allison's objections, but in Ken's case, that wasn't an option. He could only imagine how hard that must be. Ken had held a torch for Rose for several years now and everyone was pretty sure Rose felt the same. The reasons behind her rejections were anybody's guess.

"Hungry?" Benny began digging through the bag and handed his friend a wrapped meal.

"I'm gonna end up fat if I keep eating this stuff," Ken grumbled, though he took the hamburger and fries.

Benny's eyebrows rose high. "Are you kidding? You have muscle on muscle. I'm not exactly embarrassed by my physique, but you make me look like a scrawny teenager."

"I feel like you should be more afraid of me if that was the case."

Benny grinned. "Have I also mentioned how intelligent I am?"

"No need," Ken said before taking a big bite. "I've seen it in action."

The room was quiet for a few moments while they both ate.

"Tell me about Ms. Mayer," Ken said between bites.

Benny paused momentarily. "What about her?"

"I was there the other night when you mentioned piano lessons and despite any insinuations, I'm not a dummy."

"I think I implied that about myself," Benny corrected. "Not you."

"You haven't answered the question," Ken pointed out. "Avoidance won't work."

"I brought you dinner," Benny complained. "Aren't you supposed to be nicer to me?"

Ken gave him an unimpressed look.

"Fine." Benny threw a fry down on the desk. "What exactly are you wanting to know?" For some reason, a protective side had risen up in defense of Ally. Normally Benny had no trouble talking about whatever, or whoever, he pleased, but the more time he spent with the secretive beauty, the more he wanted to protect her. Mostly from her mother, but also from anyone else who would hurt her. He had a feeling she had been hurt enough to last a lifetime.

"Just what's going on between the two of you," Ken said. "She's not exactly the type I would have pegged you with."

"We're not together," Benny quickly corrected. He stopped himself from grimacing. He'd spoken too quickly, which automatically sounded defensive, even if he was telling the truth.

"You're not, huh?"

Benny shook his head.

"Yet Brook told Caro, who told me, that she saw you two walking down the boardwalk the other day."

Benny hung his head back and groaned toward the ceiling. "Small towns are the worst."

Ken chuckled, stuffing more ketchup-covered fries in his mouth. "You could always move."

"And go where? All my friends are here."

"Ah...so maybe small towns aren't as bad as you think."

Benny gave him a wry look. "Whatever."

"You going to finish telling me about the two of you?" Ken pulled the conversation back in line.

"There's really not anything to tell," Benny said, swirling his fry through his sauce. "I'm bored. She's teaching me piano. I bought her an ice cream to say thank you."

"That's it?" It was clear Ken didn't believe him, but he didn't call Benny an outright liar.

Benny took a large bite, hoping Ken wouldn't see past the small fib. "That's it," he said around a mouthful of meat. He grinned when Ken made a face. Looked like bad manners were all he needed to protect Ally. He'd take it.

# CHAPTER 10

Allison didn't bring up the topic of her new job prospect and neither did her mother. It appeared that it would be the elephant in the room. At least, it felt that way to Allison. It hung heavy on her shoulders, weighing down every decision she made, and everything she said.

She might have decided she didn't want to leave, but she had yet to tell anyone. Carla was happy as a clam at the moment, which only made Allison believe she was up to something. *More than likely trying to get more out of that contract.*

It felt like a small truce and Allison was loath to upset it. As long as her mother was busy and didn't push, Allison was left to her own devices in order to figure out how to circumvent her mother's scheming.

She glanced at her watch. Her first student would be here in ten minutes. The afternoons always seemed to fly by once the children started coming. Shifting on the piano bench, Allison glanced at the blank staff paper in front of her. Normally she enjoyed composing, but today nothing came to her.

Her mind was too consumed with jobs, mothers...and handsome mail carriers.

Scowling, Allison shook her head. She couldn't let herself continue to have any hope in that direction. Benny was being very nice to her. She wasn't quite sure why, but she wasn't angry about it anymore either. The most she could possibly hope for was a weird sort of friendship. Her lips twitched. She imagined that any type of friendship with Benny was slightly odd.

A knock on her door snapped her out of her thoughts. Scrambling, Allison put away her nonproductive work and hurried to let in her first student. It was time to get her head out of the clouds and back on the keys.

Several hours later, she sighed and rested her forehead against the closed door. There must have been something in the water this last week because not a single student was prepared today. Each and every lesson was a painful experience as she helped them all through their songs so they could try again next week.

Her forehead bounced a little when another knock came. Straightening, Allison pushed her face into submission. She didn't have any more students, so this had to be someone else. She slowly pulled the door open...

"Benny," she breathed, then snapped her mouth shut.

"Ally!" he cried. He jabbed a thumb over his shoulder. "I just saw a kid carrying piano books, and he informed me he was your last student." Benny tapped his lips playfully. "I think his name was Devin?"

Allison nodded numbly. "Yes."

Benny nodded enthusiastically and rubbed his hands together. He leaned in. "Where's your mom?"

Allison was still in a bit of shock, so she pointed over her shoulder. "She's in the back."

"And you don't have any more students today?"

She shook her head.

"Perfect." Benny grabbed her hand and tugged her outside with him.

Out of habit, Allison pulled the door shut behind her, but it closed her off from her escape route and she began to panic. "What are you doing?" she snapped, defaulting to her normal irritated tone.

"Taking you on a date," he said casually.

"What?"

Benny grinned over his shoulder from where she trailed behind slightly. "You heard me. I'm taking you on a date."

Digging in her heels, Allison pulled them to a stop. "I don't understand."

Benny chuckled. "It's not that hard. I'm a man. You're a woman. I'm taking you out to dinner. It's called a date."

Her mouth opened, then snapped shut, only to do that a few more times. Allison was at a total loss for words. A date. Bennett Frasier was taking her on a date. It made no sense. They weren't a couple. They weren't really even friends, although he seemed determined to change that. What in the world made him think they should go on a date?

"No need to thank me," he said with a wink, then began walking again, pulling her feet back into motion.

"Thank you for what?" she asked, completely lost. The world had obviously gone topsy turvy.

"For taking you on a date," Benny clarified. He laughed. "Come on, Ally. You've got more education than I do. Keep up!"

"How can I keep up when you keep doing things without asking me?" she muttered in exasperation. "I don't know that this is the best idea..." Right now things were good with her mom. No, they didn't agree on the future, but there wasn't a bunch of yelling or demanding going on either. Carla would *not* be happy if she found out Allison was out with Benny. Allison's mother detested relationships in general, and anything that would tie Allison to Seaside Bay especially would be seen as a declaration of war.

"It's a great idea," Benny said. "Why wouldn't it be?"

Allison continued to stumble beside him, still feeling like her world had been turned upside down. She wasn't sure how to stop the avalanche that was Bennett Frasier. "I don't know if my mom—"

Benny came to a screeching stop and turned to look at her. "What do you want?"

Allison blinked rapidly. "Excuse me?"

"What do you want?" he asked more slowly. "Not your mom, not your audience, not even your students." He gave her a significant look. "You. Ally Mayer. What. Do. *You*. Want?"

*I want to be free to live my life. I want to stop being afraid of people. I want to stay in Seaside Bay and keep doing my little job of teaching music to children. And most of all...I want a relationship that will never come.*

The problem was, she couldn't say any of those things to him. He wouldn't understand. Benny had never been anything but free. Even when he'd still lived with his mother, he'd had more freedom than most. His mom was a bit of a hippy, and apparently had gone completely off the grid once her kids were old enough. Everyone knew her parenting style was a bit on the loose side. It was sheer luck that Melody was such a good person and had done a decent job of keeping Benny in line.

"Let's start with something simple," Benny said in a soothing tone. He let go of her hand and rubbed his palms against her upper arms. "Do you want to spend the evening at home or in town?"

She immediately opened her mouth, but Benny put a finger to her lips.

"What do you *want*? Not what *should* you do?"

Allison drooped a little. He was right. She hadn't even had to think about it. It was complete to answer in favor of her mother's wishes.

"Well?"

Allison took a deep breath and for the second time ever, pulled on her courage. Just like the other night, alone in her bedroom, she let the rebellious side of her have a say. He wanted to know what she wanted? Then she would give it to him. "I want to spend the evening in town."

IT TOOK GREATER EFFORT than it should have for Benny to keep from puffing up like a stupid rooster. Those words had been a fight. He'd watched the entire thing through the emotions in her eyes and been mentally rooting for her the entire time.

The more time he spent with her, the more he came to understand the emotions she was hiding. Ally was extremely good at wiping her face of emotions, but her eyes were a different story. Her gold brown eyes were truly the windows to her soul.

"Excellent," Benny praised. He grinned at the flush creeping up her neck. Man...she really was a beautiful woman.

He mentally slapped himself. That wasn't why he was here.

"Question number two. Would you rather be alone or spend time with me?"

She gave him a small smile. "I don't get the option of another person?"

Benny snorted. "Uh, no. Me or nothing. Take it or leave it."

She laughed softly.

Something weird fluttered in Benny's chest at the sound. He rubbed the spot. Usually he liked her laugh, so he wasn't sure why it felt like it was giving him heartburn now. Maybe it was something he ate?

"I think your company would be preferable to being alone," she said.

"Niiice," Benny drawled. He turned, took her hand, and began walking toward town again. "Way to keep a guy's ego in check."

"Someone has to," she said with a shrug.

A loud bark of laughter escaped him. Little by little, he was uncovering some very interesting things in Ally. Who'd have thought she had a sarcastic side? He'd barely been able to get her to speak not too long ago.

"I probably shouldn't have said that," Ally said, her face toward the ocean.

"Never censor yourself around me," Benny said adamantly. "I like hearing what you have to say."

She turned his way as they walked and Benny made sure to keep looking forward. He could practically feel her trying to dig into his brain to see if he was sincere.

"I'm not your mother." He glanced in her direction.

Ally snapped to the front. "I didn't say you were."

"No, but you were wondering if I really want you to speak your mind, and that's why I reminded you." He gave her a cheeky grin. "If you haven't noticed, I don't get offended very easily. You might as well take advantage of it."

She peeked at him sideways. "I can't quite figure you out."

Benny shrugged. "Eh. What's life without a little mystery?"

She laughed again and that same fluttering feeling tickled his chest.

*What the heck is that?*

"Sandwiches or fish?"

Ally frowned. "Should I be the one making all the choices here? It doesn't really seem fair."

Benny squeezed her hand. "I think it's your turn." He meant that in a general life sense, though he didn't clarify that. She didn't need to hear his worry about her. But best as he could tell, she'd been denied a choice her entire life. What were a few chances now? It's not like where they went to dinner was a life-altering decision.

"Sandwich?"

"Is that a question or a choice?" Benny teased.

"A choice...I think," she said.

Benny snickered. "All that college and you don't know?"

Ally rolled her eyes. "How do you know how much college education I've had?"

"Are you kidding?" Benny's eyes bugged out. "Everyone knows. Your mother announced your doctorate degree to everyone."

A soft sigh escaped her beautiful, full lips and he could actually see her fold into herself.

*Crap. Didn't mean to do that.*

He tugged her a little closer to his side, ignoring how good it felt to have her close. He was starved for company at the moment, that's the only reason he liked having her near. It had nothing to do with who she was, just the fact that she was a person.

"Don't be embarrassed about it," he whispered. "Some of us wish our mother bragged about our accomplishments."

She gave him a soft smile. "I'll bet your mother is very proud of you."

Benny shook his head. "Nope. She's convinced I'm helping the government spy on everyone by delivering their mail. Heaven forbid I actually bring letters and packages that people want. It's all about Big Brother recording our every move."

They arrived at the cafe just as he finished speaking.

"Hey, Benny," Sarah, the hostess, said with a smile. Her eyes flitted to Ally, her smile faltering just slightly.

Benny squeezed Ally's hand. "Table for two, please."

Sarah's eyes flared, but she nodded. "Sure. Give me just a moment." She moved a few things around on her tablet, then waved over a waitress. "Table four." She handed the young woman two menus.

She smiled and tilted her head. "Welcome. Let's get you two taken care of."

Benny kept Ally close as they walked. Several locals were inside and he saw most of them glance their way. His protective instincts rose to the surface, but he didn't want Ally to freak out. Instead, Benny did what he did best.

He put on a smile and nodded and greeted everyone they passed. He knew full well they were curious why he was with Ally, but really, it wasn't their business. Who he chose to hang out with was a personal choice.

"Is this table okay?" The young woman waved toward a small window table.

"Looks great," Benny said, then stopped. He turned to Ally. "Would you like to sit at this table or another one?"

Her smile of gratitude was one he would never forget. "This one is fine, thanks."

Benny turned back to the hostess. "Looks like we're good. Thanks."

After seeing them seated, the young woman left so they could have time to look over the menu.

"Anything look good?" Benny asked, breaking the awkward silence. He hated that feeling.

Allison shrugged, her eyes telling him she was uncertain. "I've eaten here a couple of times, so I'll probably order the chicken salad."

Benny shook his head. "Nope. Order something else."

She slowly set down the menu. "Why?"

Benny leaned in closer so that their conversation remained between them. He wanted to push her, not make a spectacle of her. "Because that's what your mother would tell you to order. I want you to order what Ally wants, not Carla."

She stared. Again. She seemed to be doing that a lot.

Benny smirked. "You're right," he teased. "I don't have any boundaries."

That laugh escaped, warming his chest all over again. "No, you don't."

"And yet, I still have friends." Benny pumped his eyebrows up and down. "People might say otherwise, but they all want a friend like me, if only for comedic entertainment."

"I can only imagine," she murmured.

"Why only imagine?" Benny said, smiling and frowning at the same time. "I'm *your* friend. You have first-hand experience."

# CHAPTER 11

Once again, Allison was at a loss for words. This man had quite the knack for throwing her world off balance. She could barely believe she was eating dinner with him, and now he was declaring they were friends. Yes, he had been friendly, but she knew better than to assume he actually thought they were anything more than acquaintances.

"We're...friends?" she choked out.

Benny gave her a look like she should have known that. "We're sitting down, talking civilly, and eating dinner together. What else would you call it?"

*A date?*

She absolutely could not say that. "I guess we are," she said slowly. "Friends." The word felt foreign on her tongue. Did she actually have anyone that she counted as a friend? Her mother had never let her get close enough to anyone to say they were more than an acquaintance, unless she counted her students.

And when she was younger, Allison had learned the hard way that friends weren't all they were cracked up to be. Sometimes they become a person's worst nightmare.

"Are you two ready to order?"

Their server was back and Allison hadn't looked beyond the usual salad menu.

"Normally I would say let the lovely lady order first, but I think she needs just a couple more minutes," Benny said, drawing the attention his way.

Allison sent him a grateful look and quickly began to scan the rest of the dishes. She was proud of herself for only hesitating twice as she mentally calculated all the fat and calories that would be in the other dishes. Her mother's voice tried to infiltrate her thoughts more than once, but Allison pushed them away.

She'd held back her own voice for years, and now she simply swapped it for her mother's criticism. Logically, she knew this...whatever it was...with Benny couldn't last, but she couldn't say she wasn't beginning to enjoy it. Weirdly enough, Benny was breaking down her reticence, but if she was being honest, Allison kept waiting for the other shoe to drop.

Although it had been awhile, she had been through something similar before. She'd had friends when she was little. Even before she started to wear makeup, her birthmark on display for the whole world to see. Then she'd entered middle school and life had almost ended. Literally.

"Miss?"

Allison snapped out of her old memories and panicked. She still hadn't figured out what to order. "Uh..." Glancing down, she ordered the first thing she saw. "Can I get the California BLTA, please?" Even as the words came out of her mouth, Allison wanted to take them back.

"Perfect. Do you want fries or a salad with that?" Their server waited patiently.

"She'll have the fries," Benny interrupted.

Allison started to glare at him before she stopped herself. There would be time to berate him in a moment after the server was gone. She smiled and waited until they were alone before leaning over the table. "Why did you do that?" she hissed.

Benny, to his credit, looked completely unconcerned with her ire. "Because you were about to order the side salad," he explained, shrugging. "I couldn't let you do that."

"But why?" she asked, still upset. "Why does this mean anything to you? Why did you even bring me here?" She shook her head.

"It makes no sense. You claim we're friends, but again, I have to ask...why? You've never spoken to me before. What's causing this behavior now? Some kind of challenge? A bet?"

The words slipped out in anger, but as they settled in her brain, Allison knew she had to be right. She'd wondered if there was an ulterior motive to his behavior and here it was. Benny had seen her secret and was setting her up for some kind of prank.

When he didn't answer right away, Allison pushed her chair back. She didn't have to stick around for this.

"Wait!" Benny reached across the table and grabbed her hand. "Where are you going?"

"Home," she snapped, pulling away as best she could without making a scene. "I don't know what you've got up your sleeve, but I don't have to stick around for it." Her heart felt like it was going to break. She had been skeptical at first, but for a few short days, she had hoped Benny had been sincere. He'd fed her ice cream, pushed her out of her comfort zone, and made her laugh. Things she hadn't experienced in a really long time.

Feeling like an idiot, Allison walked straight out. She didn't need to hear his explanation. She didn't need anything or anyone. For the first time in her life, Allison was grateful for her terrible childhood. If she hadn't already been through a set-up similar to this one, she wouldn't have recognized the signs.

She stuck her chin in the air as she walked, her face back to the one she had practiced for so many years. She couldn't quite blame herself for hoping. Benny...Bennett...was handsome and completely charismatic. He was like a whirlwind and had a tendency to pick up anything in his path.

Well, she was no longer in his path.

Her feet were firmly planted on the ground and she could focus on the red flags she had ignored earlier. Nobody befriended people like her out of the blue. She had never encouraged friendship or even acquaintanceship with anyone in the town. The only people who saw anything other than her cold side were the children.

And that's what she would continue doing. She still didn't want to take the job teaching at the college, but she did enjoy teaching her students. One-on-one lessons with children were the only part of her life that brought her joy.

Her chin shot up another notch.

She could be strong. She had just walked away from Bennett and she could put her foot down with her mother. This was *her* life. *Her* job. *Her* future. While she was grateful to her mother for protecting her and sacrificing for her all this time, Allison knew it couldn't continue.

She didn't want to keep dancing around issues at home and at town. She'd just shut down the socializing problem. Now she would do the same for the one at home.

An odd sense of empowerment went through Allison as she walked. Too much of her life had been ruled by fear. She was afraid of people seeing her birthmark. She was afraid of risking her heart to make friends. She was afraid of upsetting her mother. She was afraid of disappointing her audiences. She was afraid of adults, the public, calories, fat, sugar... She was afraid of everything!

"No more," she murmured to herself. "No. More." She refused to continue this horrible existence. She was an adult. It was time to act like it. "No matter what Mother thinks."

The sidewalk leading to her house came into view and Carla was standing in the doorway with her arms folded over her chest.

For just a split second, Allison faltered. She knew the next hour or so would be very unpleasant, maybe even horrific, but it needed to be done. *Maybe something good did come out of Bennett's weird challenge.*

She wasn't afraid to give credit where credit was due. She sent mental thanks his way, even as she marched up to her mother. If he tried to deceive her, she might never have gained the courage necessary to take her life into her own hands. In an odd way, Bennett had truly helped her, even if her heart was still in shatters.

"Good evening, Mother," Allison said crisply. "We have some things to talk about." Without waiting for a response, she walked inside. The neighbors definitely didn't need to be a part of this conversation.

BENNY SAT STUNNED FOR only about thirty seconds before he jumped into action. He had no idea what had set Ally off, but he had worked too hard to get her to speak to him. He wasn't going to let all that go to waste.

Benny cornered their server and ordered their meals to go. He had a feeling he might need the food in order to get his foot back in the door at Ally's house. Waiting, however, was torturous. The longer he waited for the food, the longer he knew Ally was stewing in her anger. *What made her so mad?*

The question gnawed at him. He couldn't figure it out. He'd been teasing, though he would be the first to admit he was pushing her buttons. Not that it was a hard thing to do. Ally was extremely sensitive, though he figured there was good reason for it.

But what exactly had set her off today? Benny had thought he was getting pretty good at reading her moods, but apparently he still had a ways to go.

"Here you go," Sarah said with a smile. She was holding a bag as she walked from the back.

"Thanks." Benny gave her a stiff smile, took the bag, and rushed out the door. He blinked against the bright sunlight, but even not being able to see, he plowed onward. His eyes transitioned quickly and he barely dodged running into a tourist. "Sorry," he muttered as he shifted around her shocked expression.

It took far too long to get to Ally's house, yet when he arrived, Benny came to a screeching halt. Raised voices were coming from inside, or at least, one raised voice could be heard from out on the sidewalk. He scowled, those new protective feelings rising up in his chest once again.

*Don't get involved.*

The voice was loud and clear in his head, causing Benny to hesitate. Should he step in? He was trying to do a good deed by introducing Ally to her own life, and it helped him with his boredom, but was it fair of him to step in between a mother and daughter? The question was a good one. So far, he hadn't been paying attention to it. He'd been plowing ahead without a second thought, but now, listening to Mrs. Mayer chew Ally out, Benny wondered if he'd gone too far.

"You *know* what happens when you go out in public!" Mrs. Mayer screamed. "Do you want a repeat of when you were twelve?"

Benny's eyebrows went up. His curiosity was piqued again. "What happened when she was twelve?" he mused. A breeze brushed the bag of food against his leg, pushing Benny into action. He wanted to know what had happened when she was a little girl. But if he was being honest, Benny also was a little angry. It was an emotion he didn't deal with very often.

*What mother uses an experience from over a decade ago to keep their child in line?*

Mrs. Mayer's manipulations were really starting to irk him. If Ally shut him down and shut herself in by her own free will and choice, that was one thing. But if it was mostly because of her mother's machinations, which was what Benny suspected, then he wanted to help her break free. The idea of her being shut away by force made him want to punch something.

If his knuckles were clenched a little tighter than normal, nobody could blame Benny as he knocked on the front door.

The quiet that ensued from his actions was almost comical. He almost called out, "I know you're in there!" But he held himself back. Jokes were probably not going to help his cause at the moment. Pity.

"What do you want?" Mrs. Mayer sneered.

Benny gave her a polite, but definitely not warm, smile. "I brought Ally her dinner. She left it behind." He held the bag up, emphasizing his point.

"She's not hungry." Mrs. Mayer began to push the door closed.

Without conscious thought, Benny reached out and held the door open. "Why don't you let her decide that?"

Mrs. Mayer rolled her eyes and stepped away from the door. "*Allison...*" She emphasized the full name. "Tell Mr. Frasier you're not interested in what he's selling."

Ally walked up to the door and Benny changed his smile to be much more welcoming. "Hello, Ally," he said softly. "You forgot your dinner."

Her brows furrowed together and she glanced from him to the food and back several times. Stepping close to the door, she spoke in a whisper. "Why did you come?"

Benny leaned in just a little. He wanted their conversation to be private, but didn't want her mother to come rushing back by making things intimate. "I told you I was buying you dinner tonight. I don't go back on my promises."

"But..." Her mouth gaped. "Why would you go this far for a prank? Or a bet?"

Benny scowled. "I don't know where you got that idea, but my taking you to dinner had nothing to do with a bet or a prank." He shook his head. "Why would you even think that?"

"Why else would you take me out?" She folded her arms around herself. Her normally straight shoulders were rounded forward as if she wanted to disappear into the background. "Why else would you even speak to me?" she continued. "You've never spoken to me before, not even when we were kids. Then, all a sudden, you pop into my life and act like we're besties." Her dark eyes met his and they looked torn.

The pain tugged on Benny's heart, to his surprise. He wasn't normally pulled in by sob stories, but there was something about Ally he just couldn't let go of…yet. He shrugged. "To be honest, I kind of do that with everyone. Everybody's a friend, until they say otherwise."

She looked taken aback. "I don't understand that mentality."

"Allison!" her mother snapped from behind her. "Tell him goodbye. We have other things to do tonight."

"Ally," Benny said tenderly. "Come eat dinner with me on the beach. We'll have a chat." He winked. "I'll bet it's more fun than the one with your mother."

A teary laugh broke through and she wiped at the corner of her eye. "Anything is preferable to that."

"Allison!" Mrs. Mayer was sounding more desperate.

"Ally is going to come eat her dinner before it gets cold," Benny said loudly, though he kept his eyes on Ally. He raised his eyebrows in question. Yes, he was pushing, but he wanted her to know she had a way out if she wanted. He didn't want to ever be compared to her mother.

"I think you've done enough, Mr. Frasier." Mrs. Mayer stormed to the door, grabbing it out of Ally's hands. "Leave. This is private property."

Benny waited, still watching Ally. He mentally begged her to accept his invitation. Not only did he want her to eat the meal she chose, but he also wanted a chance to defend himself. Maybe he wasn't taking her out because he had romantic feelings for her, but he did enjoy her company, when she let down her guard. And there was something so interesting about watching her discover new things and come into her own. "Ally?" he asked. "What do *you* want?"

"This isn't about what she—"

"I'm going to eat dinner," Ally interrupted her mom. Her eyes were on Benny, so she probably didn't notice the shock and anger on Mrs. Mayer's face. "I'll be back in a while."

Benny grinned, feeling like he'd won a battle, and held out his hand. He probably didn't need to hold her hand—it wasn't like she was going to run away—but he enjoyed the feel of her small fingers in his. It warmed him in a way a sunny afternoon never quite managed.

With a shy smile, Ally put her hand in his and Benny strutted down the sidewalk as he led her down to a bench on the boardwalk just a few minutes walk toward town.

# CHAPTER 12

Allison wasn't quite sure why she'd followed Benny, but she couldn't quite bring herself to regret it. Her mother's tirade had been worse than she'd expected and her courage had begun to wane by the time Benny had shown up at the door.

She was still unsure about whether or not she could trust him, but she couldn't deny that she wanted to. She was so shocked he had followed her, she hadn't been sure what to say when he'd come to the door. But the fact that he had come said a lot to her. If this was just a joke to him, why would he continue or want to prove her wrong, especially after she stormed off like a child? Why bother?

"How about right here?" Benny asked, walking to an unoccupied bench.

"This is fine." They couldn't see the water from here, but that's part of why the bench was empty. Closer to the beach, the city benches were almost always full. This one held a view of wild grasses and wasn't quite as popular. A fact Allison was grateful for at the moment. She didn't really want to be around a bunch of other people.

"I believe this one is yours," Benny said, handing her the Styrofoam container.

"Thank you." Allison set it in her lap and opened the steamy lid. Her hot sandwich was probably soggy by now, but she didn't care. Anything was better than dealing with her mother. Even squishy toast. She took a bite and nearly sighed in contentment. It had been a long time since she'd had bacon. The salty, smokiness was perfect.

"Good?"

She turned toward Benny and swallowed. "Yeah."

He grinned, that teasing glint back in his eye. It had been missing while they were at her house. In fact, when dealing with her mother, Allison could have sworn he'd looked protective, which was ridiculous.

"If you'd forget your mother's weird rules, you could eat like this all the time."

Allison slowly set her sandwich down. "I know." She sighed. And she did. But she also struggled to blame her mother for trying to help her look appropriate. Allison knew her face was enough to frighten others, so it made sense that trying to make the rest of her look good was a way to make up for her deficiencies.

"I was intrigued."

Allison blinked a few times. "What?"

Benny tore a large bite of his own meal and chewed before answering. "You asked why I was suddenly your friend." He wiped his mouth. "I was intrigued."

"By what?" Once again, her sandwich was forgotten.

He gave her a sheepish look. "By what I saw that day when I delivered your package."

"Oh." Allison dropped her gaze to her lap. "So this is a pity party."

"What?" Benny scowled. "How do you go from A to Z so quickly?"

"It's a gift." She gave him a sarcastic smile.

Benny rolled his eyes. "There are a lot of letters between and they're all better answers than this being a pity party."

"Okay." Allison set down her food and folded her arms over her chest. "Explain it to me. You saw my birthmark and you wanted to...what? Befriend the freak? Find out my sad backstory? Make a public example of me?"

"Bzz!" Benny made an annoying buzzer sound. "Wrong on all counts, Ms. Mayer. Care to try again?"

This time it was Allison's turn to roll her eyes. "Why don't you just explain it to me."

"Okay..." Benny nodded, then leaned forward a bit to make sure he had her attention. "All my friends are married." He made a face. "Well, almost all of them, but I can only hang out with him for so long before I'll end up behind bars."

Allison couldn't help the snort that escaped her lips. She put her fingers on her mouth to stop the laughter, but it slipped through anyway.

"You can see my problem," Benny said seriously. "So..." He shrugged. "I decided I needed to make a few more friends." He gave her a considering look. "You seemed like a good candidate and I'm not as intimidated by your aloofness as I was when I was a kid."

Allison leaned back. "You were intimidated by me?" She was utterly shocked. Benny Frasier wasn't intimidated by anyone. Or at least it had appeared that way. He was friends with everyone from the football quarterback to the nerdy kid on the science team. Well...everyone except her. But that wasn't remarkable. Nobody was friends with her. She had made sure of that.

Benny nodded as he chewed another bite. "Everyone was. You were so confident and so apart from the rest of us." He grinned, that childlike mischief coming through. "And the time you socked Ethan for trying to sneak a kiss was the clincher in me ever being brave enough to approach you."

Allison pinched her lips together. "I shouldn't have done that."

Benny snorted. "Uh, yeah, you should have. Any girl should have. He just grabbed you and kissed you. Even I'm not that bold. A girl...or woman..." He gave her a significant look. "Should always have a choice. He didn't give you one."

Benny had no way of knowing that he had hit a tender spot with her. Ever since her hospital stay as a twelve-year-old, her mother had taken away so many choices, stating that Allison couldn't be trusted to think for herself.

At first it had been welcome, since Allison hadn't trusted herself either, but now, nearly sixteen years later, Allison wanted freedom. Nightmares of her hospital stay and the entire situation, however, still held her back. That and her mother refusing to see her as the grown woman she was. It was just easier to give in, rather than fight, but Allison knew she wasn't going to be able to handle it for much longer.

The side of her that wanted to break out was rising to the surface more and more. It had completely taken over just thirty minutes ago. She'd stormed home feeling self-righteous from her argument with Benny and ready to take on even her formidable mother. But it wasn't quite strong enough to survive on its own, as seen by the fact that she'd been deflating by the time Benny had followed her to the house.

"Thank you for that," she finally said, grimacing at the taste of her cold fry.

Benny preened. "I'll come to your rescue anytime," he flirted with a wink.

She shuffled a quiet laugh. "Like you did tonight?"

"I suppose..." Benny pushed his lips to one side. "I might have been desperate for a non-attached friend, but I'll admit that I'm curious."

"About?"

"About you and your mom." Benny stuffed an entire fry in his mouth. "I mean, I know what it's like to have an off-the-wall mom, but yours, well, she's a new level of wacko."

Allison sighed, stirring her ketchup with another fry. "She's dealt with a lot over the years," she finally said.

"What do you mean? Raising a kid on her own?"

Allison shook her head. "No, I mean dealing with me."

He scowled. "She's your mom. It's her job to deal with you."

"No, not like that." Allison paused. She wasn't sure she wanted to share all this. Could she really trust Benny? Did he really just want a friend? Part of that hurt. Despite knowing it couldn't go anywhere, Allison was really attracted to Benny. *Maybe it's just because he lives the kind of life I wish I could.*

That was probably it. She wasn't attracted to *him*, per se, she was just attracted to his lifestyle. Yeah...that felt better to say.

"Then how was it?" he pressed.

The words swirled in her head. What to say? How much to say? She didn't really want to spill her deepest secrets. He just wouldn't understand.

ALLY HAD NAILED IT when she asked if he was just curious, but it wasn't in the way she was implying. He didn't see a freak when he looked at the beautiful Allison Mayer. He saw something tragic, but definitely not a freak. "Ally?"

She sighed, long and loud, and he almost backed off. The problem was, he wasn't sure why she was so afraid to say anything. Was her past that horrible? Or did she just not trust him? The reason behind her hesitation would make a big difference in how he would go about trying to convince her to tell him. "You still don't trust me." He didn't mean it to sound like an accusation, but by the time the words spilled out of his mouth, that's what happened.

Her cheeks flushed pink and she glanced at him in her peripheral vision. "I...don't know," she admitted.

"Tell me why," he asked.

A small smile tugged at her lips and she shook her head. "That is a perfect example."

"Uh..."

"You're a living contradiction, Benny," she told him. "You tell me I should always have a choice. Yet you push me more than anyone. You didn't ask me if I would tell you, you demanded it."

Her words kind of hurt, but when Benny opened his mouth to defend himself, he found that he couldn't. She was right. He did believe in choice, but he also had a tendency to steamroll when he felt strongly about something. He rubbed the back of his hot neck. "That might be a little too true."

She laughed softly. "I'm not upset about it," she continued. "Your pushing has actually helped open my eyes to how much of a shut-in I've become, but you telling me one thing and showing another makes it hard to believe you're sincere."

He rubbed his chin. "Fair enough." He nodded thoughtfully. "I wouldn't trust someone like that either."

She gave him a sad look. "I don't know that I think you were really trying to be deceptive. But I've had...issues...in the past with people, and it makes me wary."

Benny reached out and took her hand, rubbing his thumb over her knuckles. He wasn't usually quite so touchy, but his protective side just enjoyed having Ally close. "Will you tell me about it?" he asked, then batted his eyelashes. "Please?"

She grinned. "It's not really a happy story."

"I figured as much. It couldn't be a good one if it led to you distrusting everyone." He watched the fight in her eyes. She was still worried about telling him. Holding still, except for his thumb, he tried to let her know he was trustworthy. Yes, he was a joker, but he cared for his friends and would do anything to help them. And he wanted Ally to be one of those friends. She needed that and he wanted that. He had a feeling that if she let herself, they could get along really well.

"I didn't always wear six inches worth of makeup," she said with a derisive huff.

Benny held his tongue, though it was hard.

"When I was in elementary school, I walked around with my birthmark on full display, despite what my mother said would happen." She gave him a sad smile. "She warned me that there would be people who would be bothered by it, but like most little kids, I was happy and wasn't worried about it." Another long sigh and she set her food aside. It was only half-gone, but apparently talking about her childhood was enough to put her off her appetite.

"After my father left, we moved and I quickly became friends with a girl, who I thought accepted me exactly as I was." Her lips pinched with tension. "We were friends for the last few years of elementary school and then went into middle school together. I thought of her more like a sister than anything." Her fingers tucked a piece of hair behind her ear, and they were shaking.

Benny entwined their fingers, trying to give her the courage she needed to keep going. He had a feeling he knew where this was going and it was exactly the type of story he had hoped not to hear.

"My mom told me middle school would be different. That the kids would be meaner, but I didn't believe her." She laughed. "Emily and I were such good friends that I wasn't worried about what anyone else thought." Her head shook back and forth, almost unconsciously. "It turned out my mother was right." She took in a shuddering breath. "The bullying started almost immediately, but grew progressively worse as the year went on. The biggest problem was...I was losing Emily."

She paused and Benny almost expired as he held his breath in anticipation. When she didn't continue, he gave her fingers a squeeze. "You can do it," he whispered.

She gave him a quick smile. "It shouldn't be that big of a deal," she whispered. "It was so long ago."

He squeezed her fingers again, but stayed quiet. He knew things like this haunted people and there was no way her story was going to be a happy one.

"One night, I went to the football game, expecting to meet Emily. She had started to hang out with some of the popular kids, but still spent enough time with me to make me feel like we were still friends." Ally made a face. "I ended up sitting by myself, and then went to walk home after the game, but the popular kids cornered me under the bleachers." Ally rolled her eyes. "How cliche is that? Being cornered under the bleachers. It seems like that's always where the bad things happen."

"I don't know," Benny admitted. "I had a couple of decent kisses under the bleachers..." She laughed like he intended and he smiled back, grateful to have broken the tension at least a little bit. Humor *almost* always made things better.

"Well, I'm glad your experience was different from mine. I ended up with soda and popcorn in my hair, the official title of freak-face, and the pleasure of watching my best friend side with my bullies."

"Ah, Ally," Benny said. He dropped her hand to move all the food off the bench, then scooted closer so he could wrap his arms around her. He'd only ever treated Mel like this, but something inside of Benny urged him to comfort her.

She was shaking slightly, though she was mostly composed, but when he held her, he felt her slowly relax into his shoulder and the pride that gave him was different than anything he'd ever felt before. It wasn't quite the same as when he watched Mel succeed at something, though it was close.

"Thank you for telling me," he said into her hair. "I'm sorry it was so hard for you, and I'm sorry some kids are total punks. No one deserves to be treated like that."

"Thanks," she said softly, her tension draining more and more as she allowed her weight to lean into Benny's chest.

"Want me to go beat them up?"

She laughed and straightened.

A strange sense of loss accompanied her movement, but Benny ignored it.

"Thanks, but I have no idea where they are anymore." She grinned at him, though it wasn't entirely sincere. "I'm afraid I lost track of them when we moved to Seaside Bay."

"Is that why you moved here?"

Allison pursed her lips and shrugged. "Mostly. Mom thought we would do better financially in a smaller town. She signed me up for classes on makeup and we made the transition here." She tucked that hair back again. "And I have to admit that I started school with a huge chip on my shoulder. I wasn't going to be caught off guard again."

"No one can blame you for how you felt," Benny soothed. "But thank you for explaining it to me." He scratched his chin. "You did a good job of hiding it all. No one had any idea about your birthmark or your background."

"That was the idea."

"Well..." Benny took her hand again. "Now you're among friends, and you don't need to hide anymore."

# CHAPTER 13

**T**here's a carnival up in Florence. Want to go?

Allison grinned. Apparently, he was taking her criticism to heart and was giving her a choice. "But is it really a choice?" she murmured, her thumbs poised over the phone. She had a feeling that if she turned him down, he would still do his best to get her to go.

**A carniva—**

She hesitated as she thought about her mother. Allison had gotten home last week expecting a massive blow-up, which is exactly what she had left behind, but instead, her mother had gone into silent mode. On one hand, that gave Allison some peace, but on the other hand, it meant she would eventually explode and it would be worse than before.

Shaking her head, Allison forced herself to move on. She wanted what Benny was offering, even if it wasn't romantic. Truth be told, she wanted that as well, but it was clear that Benny did not. Problem was, the more he pushed, pulled, and spent time with her, the more she wanted from him.

She missed him on days they didn't talk. She wanted more of his teasing, his laughter, and his bright outlook on life. Ever so slowly, she was finding herself responding to him, but inside, it was still slightly painful. Stepping out more was fun, an unrequited crush...was not.

**A carnival sounds fun.**

**There's one catch.**

She frowned. He'd never put rules on the few times they'd spent time together.

**What's that?**

**No makeup.**

Allison's eyes nearly bugged out of her head. There was no way on God's green Earth that she was going to go anywhere without makeup on. Benny had *seen* her without makeup and she still wouldn't show him her face. He'd gone too far. Frustration and hurt began to simmer in her stomach. He didn't have the right to ask that of her. He was well-liked by everyone, even if he did have an unusual mother. He would have no way of knowing what it was like to be whispered about, to be bullied, to be called a freak.

She dropped her phone like it was a live coal and turned away from it. She had told him most of the story about how she was bullied as a young girl, and now he wanted her to risk doing it again?

Not happening.

Allison rushed to the piano, not bothering to answer his request. Her fingers flew over the keys as she pounded out her frustration, her anger, her hurt, and eventually her longing.

*How does he know?*

What she wouldn't give for the opportunity to be free of the confines of her makeup routine. She hated having to hide who she was, but she had experienced for herself what people thought when they saw the real her. It had almost cost her her life.

She hated starving herself in order to stay attractively thin. She hated having to adjust her budget in order to afford the best makeup lines. She hated pretending to be something she wasn't.

How did Benny know that dangling something like that in front of her would be so enticing yet terrifying?

Yet, no matter how enticing, she knew she couldn't do it. That's what hurt so much. Her hope was to stay in Seaside Bay, not be driven out of town on a rail.

What young student would come sit at her side and actually learn anything about the piano and joys of music if all they could do was stare at her deformity?

She shook her head fiercely. No. No matter what she longed for, she couldn't have it. Not if she wanted to have a peaceful existence. The town must never know that she was such a freak.

Slowly, her fingers ran out of steam. She'd been playing each memorized piece much faster than it was supposed to be, simply to relieve her body of the pressure of the emotions inside. This piano was her heaviest chain, and her best balm. Her gift is what kept her mother pushing for more, yet Allison found peace within the ivories.

Her life in general seemed full of contradictions.

She snorted as her fingers fell silent. It seemed so unfair. Most others didn't seem to have such difficult lives.

A chirping sound came from the kitchen and Allison knew Benny had texted again. She pinched her lips together. Despite feeling calmer, she absolutely would not agree to his terms. If he thought he was going to be her friend just to get her to parade around in public like some sideshow act, then she wanted no part of his friendship.

Soon her phone rang and she clenched her hands into fists. "No," she whispered. Standing up, she walked to her bedroom. Their house wasn't large, so she wasn't able to unhear her phone ring again and again, but she also didn't have the strength to shut it off. If she held her phone in her hand, then she was not going to be able to avoid answering it.

Instead, she shut her door, grabbed her latest romance, and settled on her bed. She didn't have students for another hour and she didn't have a concert to practice for. Her time was fairly free, so she was going to enjoy herself and ignore Benny.

Her plan worked perfectly until it was time for her to teach. The doorbell rang and she hopped from her bed, grateful her phone had stopped buzzing about a half-hour ago. Smoothing back her hair, double-checking her makeup in the mirror, and putting on a smile, she opened the door. "Hello—" The words caught in her throat when she realized her student wasn't alone.

"Hey, beautiful!" Benny said cheerfully.

Allison held back the scowl she wanted to give him. Lilly didn't need her anger.

"Lilly, here, happens to be a friend of mine," Benny said. He ruffled the little girl's gorgeous red hair.

She laughed and swatted at Benny. "Leave my hair alone!" she said in her slightly garbled tone.

"Sorry, kiddo," Benny said to the child. He winked. "I can't help it when I'm around someone so pretty."

Lilly blushed and leaned into his side.

*Shoot.* Allison could tell Benny really was friends with Lilly, which made sense. Rose, Lilly's mother, was part of Benny's friend group. But that made getting rid of him harder. "Hello, Lilly," Allison said in a clear tone, making sure she was looking directly at her student so her lips were visible. "Ready to come in?"

Lilly nodded, grabbed Benny's hand, and walked in.

Allison pinched her lips, but stepped back.

Benny smirked as he walked past. "Imagine how excited I was when Rose said Lilly needed an escort today."

"Imagine," Allison grumbled under her breath. She held in a growl. That man was pushing every button she had. *Just ignore him.* Easier said than done, but advice she would take anyway.

Putting her focus on her student, Allison did her best to pretend Benny wasn't even in the room.

OOOH, SHE WAS MAD NOW. Even if he hadn't been working on getting to know her, he could tell she was mad. Steam was practically coming out her ears and he hoped Lilly would remain completely ignorant of the tension in the room.

When he'd happened to deliver Rose's mail and she'd mentioned she was in a bind this afternoon, Benny hadn't been able to believe his luck.

*Ally probably thinks I finagled this whole thing.*

He couldn't blame her if she did. This was the kind of thing he would totally do, but in this case, it had fallen into his lap. Rose was busy. Lilly had piano. He needed to speak to Ally. Perfect.

Her look when he'd shown up on her doorstep though, was priceless. He knew she'd have a hard time with his request, and he planned to retract it...for now, but today's request had been a testing of the waters. He'd wanted to see how badly she would react. He had his answer.

And now he had some groveling to do.

Pulling out his phone, he played a game while Lilly pounded the wrong keys much to Ally's delight for an entire thirty minutes. Ally had the patience of a saint if she dealt with this day after day.

*It's not like I'm much better.*

He grinned as he thought of his own pounding. Sometimes he messed up on purpose just so she'd correct him. Before he knew her, he'd spent his time trying to break through her emotionless facade. Now he did his best to bring out as much emotion as possible. Weird how things changed.

"Benny!"

He looked up from his phone and smiled wide. "Hey, Lillers. All done?"

She nodded enthusiastically, hugging her books to her chest. The girl was a perfect doll, even Benny had to admit. Her mother, Rose, was one of the most beautiful women Benny had the privilege of knowing, though he didn't find himself attracted to her the way he did to Ally.

*Good thing, or Ken would take me out.*

Benny slapped his thighs and stood up. "Your mom said she'd meet us here, so let's check outside."

"You're not leaving with her?"

Benny could tell from the surprised look on her face that Ally hadn't meant to blurt out that question.

"Oh, no," Benny said, probably a little too gleefully. "Rose just needed someone to drop Lilly off. She was able to pick her up. I'm here all afternoon, just absorbing all your knowledge as you teach." He held out his hand to Lilly, beamed at Ally, then opened the front door.

"Oh!" Rose gasped, her hand in the air. "You made it." She smiled. "Thanks, Benny. I appreciate you bringing her." She bent down and pulled Lilly up and onto her hip. "Although I didn't expect you to stick around the whole lesson." Her blue eyes turned to Ally. "How's she doing?"

Benny turned his body to the side so Ally could step up to talk, but he didn't move and give her the whole space. If she wanted to be polite to Rose, she would have to stand next to him. Inwardly, he cackled. Sometimes he was too devious for his own good.

Ally was stiff as a board as she stepped forward. Her foot landed on his toes and pressed down a little harder than Benny thought necessary. Obviously, she knew exactly what he was doing and wasn't very appreciative of his efforts.

"She's doing great," Ally assured Rose. "Her progress is just a little slower as she continues to understand the sounds she's hearing, but I don't feel like that will last."

Rose nodded, pressing Lilly's head next to her own. "Okay. Is that a problem though?"

"Oh, absolutely not!" Ally assured her. "But you might find that she doesn't want to practice if she feels like she's not making progress. But I really believe that if she'll stick it out for a bit, she'll really grow to enjoy it and will catch up with all the other kids her age."

Rose blew out a breath. "Good to know. Thank you." Her eyes darted to Benny and her lips twitched with a grin. "Thanks again, Benny. You're such a great guy."

Benny almost laughed out loud at Rose's obvious compliments. "Anytime," he said, puffing up his chest a little. If it meant he brushed up against Ally's shoulder, then all the better.

Rose laughed lightly and gave him a sly wink. "Thanks again, Allison. We'll see you next week."

Ally waved, then stepped back into the house. "Thank you for bringing Lilly," she said crisply. "But my next student should be here any minute, so if you'll..."

"Oh. Right." Benny backed into the house and walked over to plop on the sofa.

"That's not what I—" Ally was cut off when there was a knock behind her.

"Looks like your next student is here." Benny gave her an extra sweet smile, laughing inside when she ground her jaw in frustration. "Don't mind me. I'll be as quiet as a mouse."

"I'll believe that when I see it," she muttered right before opening her door. "Hello, Benjamin."

Benny nearly fell asleep a few times during the next couple of hours. The only thing that kept him awake was the hitting of sour notes during the lessons. It seemed that almost every student was under the age of twelve and still in the beginner stage.

Benny snickered quietly. *No wonder Ally was so shocked when I signed on.*

Finally, the last student had been ushered out the door. Ally stayed with her back to him and her forehead pressed against the wood. "What do you want?" she asked in a strained tone.

"For you to go to the carnival with me."

Ally turned around and she looked exhausted. If Benny wasn't doing this to help her, he might actually feel bad about the situation.

She rested her back against the door. "I was interested in the carnival," she said. "But then you had to put down a rule."

Benny shrugged and stood up from the couch, coming closer until they were toe to toe. Man, she was pretty. Outside she was nearly perfect. But it was a cold type of beauty. It wasn't until he'd started breaking down her barriers that he realized she was soft, warm, and witty as well. It was an intoxicating combination and if Benny had been looking for a romance in his life, pursuing Ally wouldn't necessarily be a bad idea. As it was though, he planned to just keep her in the friend zone. He wasn't ready to settle down and there was no way she was looking to form an attachment. Up until recently, she'd barely even wanted a friend, let alone a boyfriend.

"You told me you wouldn't force me into anything," Ally accused him.

Benny held his hands out to the side. "I wasn't forcing anything."

"You said it was a rule."

"Rule. Schmule." Benny grinned. "Since when have I been known to follow the rules?"

Her shoulders relaxed a little. "Are you saying I don't have to go without makeup?"

He shook his head. "It's always your choice." It was. But that didn't mean he wouldn't continue to push. Someone pretty wonderful was hiding behind all the hurt and the powder she wore. Benny had decided it was his duty to the world for people to meet the real her.

Ally still looked wary, though she was less angry. "Okay...if you promise not to give me grief about it."

"Done."

A small smile spread across her lips. "I've never been to a carnival."

Benny's smile wasn't small at all. "You'll love it."

# CHAPTER 14

I t had been over a week now since her mother had spoken to her, yet Allison wasn't even the least bit worried. Benny's light-heartedness had to be rubbing off on her because she was more excited about the carnival than she was worried about her failing relationship at home.

"You've really never been to a carnival?" Benny asked, glancing at her while he drove.

Allison shook her head. "Nope." She shrugged. "I mean, when I was really little, my mom took us on a few vacations, so it's not like I've never ridden a ride at an amusement park or whatever, but I've never done an actual carnival."

"You're not afraid of heights or don't get motion sickness, do you?"

She shook her head. "Not that I know of."

Benny nodded. "Perfect. Because I totally plan to take you on every ride."

"And if I do get sick?"

He shrugged. "Then I'll ride without you."

Allison punched his shoulder, but ruined the effect by laughing. "Fair enough," she said through her laughter.

"Don't damage the guns," Benny warned her, rubbing his shoulder. "You'll want to be able to hold onto these guys when you get freaked out on a ride."

Allison felt herself flush at the idea of being that close, but she rolled her eyes to hide the emotion. "Guns?"

Benny nodded seriously. "Oh, yeah. Didn't you know that you always need a ticket to be around me?"

Allison closed her eyes and shook her head. "Ticket? You totally lost me."

He took his right arm off the wheel and slowly flexed it into an impressive display. "For the gun show..."

Allison did her best to look completely unimpressed. "That's the most ridiculous thing I've ever heard."

Benny sighed dramatically. "I guess I'll just have to find another woman to impress. It shouldn't be too hard."

"You're telling me that you drug me with you and now you're going to leave me to go find a date just to build your ego?"

"Every guy needs someone to build his ego," Benny said matter-of-factly. "If you won't do it, I'll find someone who will."

Allison folded her arms over her chest. "Go for it. I dare you."

Benny's smile was way too smug. "Better watch it, or I'll take you up on that."

"I. Dare. You." Allison leaned toward him a little farther with each word. After realizing what she was doing, she backed up quickly, settling into her seat. She didn't know what it was about this guy, but he made her completely forget who she was supposed to be. The quiet, cold persona she'd perfected for the last twenty years completely disappeared whenever he was around.

Her emotions were also all over the place. One minute he drove her crazy, the next she wanted his arms around her. She nearly had whiplash just from five minutes of his company.

"Double dog?" he asked, snapping Allison out of her thoughts.

"Uh, yes?"

He gave one curt nod. "Done. I never turn down a double dog dare."

*Ah, crud.* Allison had no idea what she'd gotten into, but she couldn't back down now. She just hoped that it didn't hurt too much to watch him flirt with another woman. Her crush was ridiculous, she knew that, but that didn't mean it wasn't there.

*It's only because he's the first man to pay attention to you.*

There was probably more truth in that statement than Allison cared to admit. It's not like she didn't recognize a handsome man when she saw one, but she'd never truly gotten close to one. She'd never even had a kiss, which was far too embarrassing to admit. And if she ever actually kissed a man, then Allison prayed he wouldn't be able to tell how inexperienced she was.

"That must be it," Benny muttered under his breath.

Allison had to agree. The lineup of cars along the side of the road, including into the field of weeds, was a dead giveaway. "It's gonna be rough to find a place to park."

"Watch and learn, beautiful, watch and learn."

Allison snapped her head toward him, but Benny was concentrating on maneuvering the SUV through the crowded streets, not paying attention to her at all. That wasn't the first time he'd called her beautiful, but each time he said it, it bothered Allison a little more. It made her feel, once again, like this was all some sort of joke. Like he was teasing her or egging her on.

But when she caught him in the act, he never seemed to act as if anything was wrong. As if the term of endearment just came out naturally.

"There," Allison said softly, pointing to a spot in the dirt. Walking through the thigh-high grass would leave her itchy, but at least it was a spot.

"You going to be okay walking through the dirt?" he asked as he put the SUV in park.

Allison glanced at her sandals. "I'll live."

Benny grinned. "I like a woman who's not fussy."

*As opposed to one who wears too much makeup?*

Allison had no idea where those words had come from. It seemed the snarky side of her mind was hyper-active today. The thought, however, only depressed her, so she shoved it to the side. She was in this friendship with her eyes wide open. The longer it went on, the more she believed Benny truly wanted to be her friend, which was exciting. But she was under no illusion that he wanted anything else.

*He just took a dare to find a woman to fawn over him, for heaven's sake.*

"Ready?" Benny had opened her door, but Allison was too caught in her thoughts to notice.

"Oh, yeah. Sorry. Just daydreaming, I suppose."

"Daydreaming of the gun show?"

She blurted out laughing. "No. I can't say that was it."

Benny smiled. "Guess I'll have to just keep trying, then."

Allison frowned slightly, though she was still smiling. She didn't quite get what he meant by that, but when her eyes caught on the ferris wheel, his cryptic words no longer mattered. "Whoa." She stopped walking and craned her head back to see the very top. "That's crazy."

"Looks like fun, right?"

"I don't know..."

"Oh, no." Benny grabbed her hand and started hurrying them across the street. "No chickening out on me now. We haven't even been on a single ride."

Allison gulped as he led her to the rides. It had been way too long since she'd been on a ride at all, let alone one like these. *Please don't get sick. Please don't get sick.*

It only took them a few minutes to get some tickets and get in line for the dreaded ferris wheel. Benny beamed at her. "You're gonna love it," he assured her.

"That's what you think," Allison muttered, her eyes still trained on the top.

"That's what I know." Benny leaned in. "Aren't you glad you'll have the guns to hold onto?"

Despite herself, Allison smiled. "You won't let it go, will you?"

He shook his head. "Not until you admit how fabulous they are."

Allison laughed, her worries gone. "You'll be waiting a long time."

Benny winked. "We'll see."

"OH MY GOSH." ALLY GRIPPED the lap bar so tightly, her knuckles turned white, causing Benny to chuckle.

He leaned in close. "This is when you thank me for bringing the guns along."

She eyed him, her normally brown skin looking slightly pale. "What if I don't want to give in?"

Benny shrugged. "Your loss."

The machine jerked into motion and their car rocked back and forth as the wheel started to spin. With a squeal, she let go of the bar and grabbed his arm.

Benny flexed his arm a couple of times and Ally laughed, turning and pressing her forehead into his shoulder.

"Stop," she said through her smile.

"Not until you admit it." Benny was having a hard time holding back his own laughter as he continued to flex his arm.

"Okay!" she cried. "You win! Thank you for bringing the guns!"

Relaxing, Benny pulled out of her hold and wrapped his arm around her shoulder. "Since I won, I'm feeling generous. The guns will protect you until it's all over."

She shook a little under his hold. "You're a dork."

"Eh. I've been called worse." Benny gave a dramatic sigh and leaned his head back. Glancing in his peripheral vision, he noted her eyes were closed. "Ally," he whispered, his lips near her ear. "Open your eyes. The view is beautiful." As stupid as it sounded, his view really was beautiful. Ally has always been a stunner, but the more Benny got to know her, the more beautiful she became.

It was a new and odd phenomenon for him. He had attractive female friends, but none of them had ever felt like anything but sisters. He teased, he flirted, but ultimately he just had fun. With Ally...he found himself wanting something else. Something more. He teased and flirted with her as well, but he also wanted to talk with her. He wanted to learn about her. He wanted to find out what made her tick and use the information to make her smile and laugh. He wanted her happiness.

He shook his head and leaned back from her fruity-smelling hair. It was doing something funky to his thought processes.

"What if we fall?" she asked, her eyes still squeezed tight.

"We won't."

"How can you be sure?" A whimper escaped when the wheel stopped and their car rocked again.

"Because I brought the guns to protect you." He squeezed her a little tighter into his side. The motion felt good...and right.

She laughed and shook her head. "You never stop, do you?"

"Not until I get what I want," Benny admitted. And the lines of what he wanted were slowly blurring when it came to Ally.

"So, giving me a choice in the matter is only an illusion?" Her face had relaxed as she spoke to him, though she still kept her eyes closed.

"Absolutely not. You can resist all you want. We both have the choice whether or not to keep going after what we want." He leaned close again. "It's just a matter of who's more dedicated to the cause."

Slowly, her dark eyes fluttered open and her jaw dropped. "Oh..."

For once, Benny had nothing to say. Seeing her experience the view for the first time brought up those proud papa feelings again.

She looked all over the horizon. "It's amazing." The car jerked into action and Ally folded into herself.

"Easy..." Benny soothed, grabbing one of her hands with his free one. He rubbed her knuckles like he'd done the other night. "Just enjoy. Push everything else out."

The rest of the ride was quiet, each of them lost in their own thoughts. Benny couldn't see her head-on, so he wasn't sure what she was thinking, but he knew his own thoughts and they were dangerous enough on their own. Holding her felt a little too good and his reasons for befriending Ally began to fade into the background.

*She needs to break free,* he reminded himself as they climbed out of the car. *Your job is to help her learn to live, not keep her to yourself.*

With a firm nod and his resolve back in place, he marched them toward the house of mirrors. Maybe a little laughter would break up the pull he was struggling with again. "Ever done one of these?" he asked with a grin.

Ally smiled. "Once when I was little. And I had the bruises to prove it."

He chuckled. "Don't worry. It's easier when you're an adult."

"Oh?" Ally folded her arms over her chest and cocked a hip. "Care to make a wager on that?"

"Oh, ho!" he crowed. The spunk she hid from the world was so fun when it came out to play. "What did you have in mind?"

"First to the exit wins."

"*What* do they win?"

Ally pursed her delectable lips.

*Not delectable! She's off limits!*

"Loser buys lunch."

"Deal." Benny rubbed his hands together. "Prepare to pay up, Ally-girl. I don't like to lose."

Stepping up to the entrance, she gave him a sultry wink over her shoulder. "Neither do I."

Benny stood stunned for just a second before he came back to the present.

"Dude," the teenager taking the tickets said in a low tone. "You better hurry."

Benny grinned. "Somehow, I think I win either way," he bragged before darting inside. Immediately, he put his hands in front of him and began walking through the mirrors. His time was speedy enough and he'd only run into three mirrors by the time he slipped out the back, sure of his victory.

"It's about time."

He whipped around. "What!"

Ally was standing off to the side, all too smug in her win. She glanced at her wrist, which didn't have a watch on it, but Benny caught the message. "Have trouble?"

Benny sauntered her way, using his height to look down at her. "Never. You got a head start."

"I've been out here for at least two minutes," she said coolly, raising an eyebrow at him.

Involuntarily, Benny's eyes dropped to her lips. It took more control than he cared to admit to pull them back up to her eyes. "You're not wearing a watch."

She shrugged. "I'm a good judge of time."

He sighed. "Guess that means lunch is on me."

With a little victory giggle, Ally's calm look broke and she grinned widely. Stepping up close, she rose on tiptoe and left a kiss on his cheek. "Thanks!" she chirped before starting to walk away.

Benny snatched her hand. "Wait a second." He would never admit to how his cheek was tingling and his heart racing as he looked at her innocent face. Something was shifting here, and he was unsure of how he felt about it. But he did want to test something. Call it research.

"Hmm?" Ally raised her eyebrows in question.

"Let's try a more proper thank you." Slowly he pulled her in, brown eyes widening with every step.

"Proper thank you?" she whispered hoarsely.

He was like a man possessed. He couldn't look away and he couldn't stop himself from asking for more. "Yes." His arms moved around her waist and her hands landed on his chest, burning against his shirt.

"We shouldn't," she choked out.

"I have to know," he murmured as he slowly dropped his head. The wait was like the sweetest torture. She had plenty of time to pull away if she wanted, but Benny prayed with everything in him that she wouldn't. She had let him hold her hand and wrap his arm around her in comfort. Now he needed to know if she would let him test their connection in a deeper way.

He only hesitated once, when he could practically feel her lips, but they were just shy of touching. His heart was in his throat and his hands shook ever so slightly against her back. "Is that a yes?" he said, almost inaudibly.

Her hands crept up until they were behind his neck. "Yes..."

# CHAPTER 15

Movies and books had always made a girl's first kiss seem glamorous and romantic. Nothing Allison had ever read or seen could have prepared her for the truth.

It was heaven on Earth.

As if he knew how nervous she was, Benny was gentle in his hold and touch. His hands were splayed across her back, tucking her into his chest, and his lips played a game she could barely keep up with, but oh, how she wanted to learn.

It wasn't until a bunch of giggling broke through the haze of her mind that Allison forced herself to pull back. She was breathing heavily and could feel Benny's chest heaving just as much as hers.

A group of teenage girls walked past, whistling and laughing, but Allison didn't care. Not even a little bit. Her face felt flushed and she knew that would mean her birthmark could be seen more easily, but for the first time ever, other things came first.

"I think that might have been the best thank you I've ever gotten," Benny said in a husky tone.

The words made Allison want to close the distance between them again, but she wasn't sure how he would react to her being so bold. Plus, she needed to get a hold of herself. The tight rein she usually held on her emotions had completely snapped in the last few minutes. Instead of giving into desire, she pushed against his chest a little, gaining a few inches of distance. "I can't say I have anything to compare it to."

*Oh my gosh...anything but that!*

Nothing said *that kiss was amazing* like admitting to never having done it before. Could she be any more of a loser? Groaning, she dropped her chin and closed her eyes. "Please just forget I said that."

Benny's chest shook as he chuckled. "Actually, I don't know if I'll be able to think of anything else," he murmured before kissing the top of her head. "Thank you for trusting me to be your first."

She shook her head, words completely out of reach. What she wouldn't give for a piano right about now. Her emotions needed an outlet and expending them in another kissing session wasn't an option.

"Ready for that lunch I owe you?"

Allison wasn't sure she could eat, but she nodded anyway. Anything to get her out of the embarrassing situation she was in right now.

"Corn dogs and curly fries it is," Benny said, his smile evident in his tone.

Allison straightened and laughed softly. "I don't remember a lot from my vacations as a kid, but I do remember that was the type of food they had available at any theme park. It seems some things never change."

Benny gave her a look while they walked. "And yet some do nothing but change."

Allison frowned at his enigmatic remark. What exactly did he mean by that? Was he upset about the kiss? He was the one who had initiated it. Was she bad at it? Did it bother him to kiss someone who was so scarred? What would her mother think of all this? Would she say *I told you so*? Would she be upset or happy that Allison had finally been kissed?

Her hand began to flutter upward toward her cheek, but she stopped it midair. She didn't want to draw attention to her anxiety.

"Don't."

They stopped walking and Allison looked up at her companion. "What?"

Benny slowly shook his head. "Your wheels are spinning in the wrong direction," he said. "Don't do it. Don't ruin this."

"But what is *this*?" Allison dropped her voice to barely above a whisper. "You've told me several times that you want to be my friend, and I know I'm a little less experienced in these matters, but I don't think friends usually go around kissing each other."

Benny smirked. "Are you sure?"

She gave him a look. "Reasonably sure, yes."

"Ally..." Benny drawled. "It was a kiss. Not a marriage proposal." He shrugged. "Why does it have to mean anything?"

"You're telling me you kissed me just because I was around and available?" She started to back up, but Benny wouldn't let go of her hand.

"No." He pushed out a harsh breath. "I kissed you because I couldn't *not* kiss you."

Hope fluttered in her chest.

"You were so cute, so smug after beating me in the house of mirrors." Benny gave her a half-grin. "And you were so beautiful while we were on the ferris wheel." He shrugged. "Isn't that enough? I'm a guy who's attracted to you. So I kissed you." His grin grew. "And from the way you responded, I think you secretly have a crush on the guns you shunned earlier."

Allison rolled her eyes. "Yeah...you just totally ruined that moment." Although, he really hadn't. He had just turned it into a Benny moment. Sweet with a side of dork. That was him to a tee.

But what she really wanted to go back to was the way he said he was attracted to her. People gushed over her all the time after a concert, but no one just flat out said they found her attractive, or even better...beautiful.

He shrugged. "I can't help it. It's a gift."

She laughed under her breath. "I suppose it is." Her hand came up to her hot cheek. "But..."

Benny quickly stepped closer and put his hand over hers, pressing into her red skin. "This..." His thumb caressed her cheek. "Has nothing to do with anything."

"How can you say that?" Allison croaked. "It has to do with everything."

"Does it keep you from being an amazing pianist?"

Allison slowly shook her head.

"Does it interfere with your ability to teach?"

Again, she shook her head.

Benny leaned closer. "Did it ruin our kiss?"

Her movements were slower, but one last shake of her head answered his question.

"Then don't worry about it." He stepped back, dropping his hand. "Let's just enjoy the day, huh? A guy, a girl, a simmering attraction. Can you just let things happen the way they want to happen?"

She didn't respond right away. Truth was, she didn't know. Her whole life had been about the birthmark. Whether hiding it, or worrying about it. It might not keep her from playing piano, but it kept her from enjoying being in front of an audience. It didn't interfere with her teaching, but it meant she prepped for over an hour each morning in order to teach. And no, it didn't interfere with her kiss, but it made her self-conscious about his touch.

On the other hand, the more she tripped along in Benny's shadow, the more she wanted a chance to see the sun for herself. She wanted exactly what he was offering, but was nervous about reaching out to take it.

"Ally?"

His nickname broke through her thoughts. Here she was Ally. Not Allison. Not Ms. Mayer. Ally sounded fun and carefree. If that's what Benny thought she was, then who was Ally to argue? "I'd like that," she finally answered.

"Good," Benny said, turning around and grabbing her hand before walking forward. "Because I'm starving."

BENNY LAUGHED AT ALLY'S face. "You should try it sometime." He offered his corn dog, slathered in what he called "plastic cheese", but she waved him away.

"I don't think there's any real food in that," she responded.

"Exactly." Benny took another bite and closed his eyes as the salty cheesy goodness spread across his taste buds. "That's exactly why I call it plastic cheese."

"And yet you eat it." She shook her head and took a dainty bite of her own corn dog. Mustard only.

"Who wouldn't?"

"Me."

"Then you haven't lived." Benny waggled his eyebrows. He loved the way Allison always grinned when he acted stupid. Not that he didn't always behave that way, but he especially did it for Allison's benefit. Being a goof was only fun when he had an audience, and his had been shrinking lately.

No matter how ridiculous he had gotten, it hadn't stopped anyone from pairing up and marrying themselves into oblivion. Now he had his own captive audience, and he was planning to enjoy it to the fullest.

*Just like that kiss.*

Yeah...the kiss. He really shouldn't have broken that boundary between them, but Benny couldn't find it within himself to regret it either. The kiss had shaken him all the way down to his flip-flops, even though he'd been able to tell that Ally was a little inexperienced.

She had been slightly hesitant for the first few moments before reciprocating his affection.

Despite all that, he would never have guessed he was her first kiss at all. She had to be in her upper twenties. It seemed odd to go that long without ever kissing anyone.

*But Ally is a special case.*

It was true. Her seclusion from society had come early in life, so in a weird way, it made sense. "Have you ever been on a date?" The words slipped from his mouth before he thought better of it. When Ally's face turned bright red, enough that her birthmark was nearly visible even through her makeup, he wanted to smack himself.

Her head dropped and she picked at the breading on her corndog. "Not anything that can actually be called a date," she muttered.

*Don't do it,* he warned himself. But as often happened in his life, Benny wanted to know more. "Not even once? In high school? Or a study date in college?"

She shook her head. "No. After the…incident, Mom convinced me it was better to just stay away from others." She sighed and looked out past him. "She was right in some ways. People are cruel and even now, if I showed them my face, most would be the same. Starting over in a new place and with a new cosmetic education let me survive, but it didn't allow for much outside of that."

"I don't believe that."

She frowned, her eyes meeting his. "What? That I haven't been on a date?"

Benny shook his head. "No. That people would ostracize you because of your birthmark. I think you're not giving others enough credit."

Her lips pinched and Benny knew he was treading on dangerous ground. He wasn't actually trying to alienate her, but he wanted her to let go of her crutch. No one else was around to do it. Which meant the responsibility fell directly in his lap. He didn't want her to just survive. He wanted her to thrive. And he was beginning to hope that maybe it would be at his side, not just at his prodding.

"I don't think you have any experience in the matter," she said tightly.

He raised his eyebrows. "Oh, yeah? Well, you're wrong."

Her dark brows pulled together. "What do you mean? Everyone loves you. You were the darling of Seaside Bay High."

He snorted. "Uh. No. I was the clown of Seaside Bay High." Benny shrugged. "But I didn't mind. Making people laugh was much better than being made fun of."

"What in the world would they have made fun of?" she asked, openly skeptical.

Benny looked around in a conspiratorial manner, then leaned in. "My mother."

She huffed a laugh. "Your mother?"

He nodded sagely. "Yep."

"Why? Because she was kind of hippy-ish?"

"Something like that."

"Benny," Allison whined. "You're going to have to give me more than that."

"Ever had your mom tell someone they were never going to have kids because Big Brother had implanted chips in all of us?"

Ally's jaw fell open.

"Or how about her convincing theory that aliens were playing with us like ants in a sandbox?" He raised his eyebrows. "Hmm?"

"Uh, no. My mom has a lot of issues, but I don't think those are any of them."

"Yeah, well, when my mom got going, she did a wonderful job of making me and Mel the laughing stock of the whole high school."

"How did you turn that around?" Ally asked. "I never saw anyone make fun of you."

Benny grinned. "Were you watching?"

She rolled her eyes. "Just answer the question."

"I'll take that as a yes." He buffed his nails on his shirt, reveling in her laughter. "But to answer your question...I became the lovable comic relief you see today." He held his arms out as if to present himself.

"That's it?" She grimaced.

"That's not enough?"

Her look said *no.*

"Look, people are people. Yes, as a group they're pretty dumb, but deep down we're all the same. We want to be accepted, we want to be seen for who we are, and we want to be entertained." He shrugged. "I discovered if I became an entertainer, not only was I accepted, but people would actually seek me out."

"So you don't enjoy being ridiculous?"

"Oh, no...don't get me wrong," Benny explained. "I totally enjoy it. But I pushed it because I realized what it had the ability to accomplish."

She dropped his gaze and seemed deep in thought for a few moments. "So how does this apply to my situation?"

"I had to create a persona when I was in high school to keep from being bullied. But now I have friends who take me exactly as I am, because we're all adult enough to have something stupid in our pasts." He leaned closer. "The same could be said for you. You don't have to hide behind makeup. People aren't so insecure and cruel once they've grown up."

Her hand drifted to her cheek in an unconscious gesture. "I don't know," she whispered. "I'd like to believe that, but..."

Benny grabbed her hand and toyed with her slim, delicate fingers. It was amazing that they could make such beautiful music. "Tell you what. Let's start with one first at a time. You just had your first real kiss." He winked, then grinned at her embarrassed head duck. "How about a real first date next?"

Ally chewed her bottom lip in thought and Benny did his best to keep from kissing it instead. Now that he'd had a taste of her, he was going to have a hard time keeping himself in check. Her eyes were wary when she met his again, but inside there was also a resolve and Benny sat up straighter.

"Okay."

His smile was slow but extra wide. "Okay?"

She grinned in return. "Okay."

Benny kissed her palm. "Stick with me, baby. We'll make a socializer out of you yet."

# CHAPTER 16

"Ruining everything...after all I've done...all I've sacrificed..." Allison resisted the urge to fold into herself and curl up on the couch. Her mother had not taken the news of her date well. At all. Not that Allison had expected a hug or celebratory high-five, but her mother had been muttering curses and angry words ever since Allison had announced she was going out.

She had kept it a secret for the last week, knowing her mother would be upset, but Allison was more than ready for Benny to come pick her up and provide a reprieve from the anger.

"Ungrateful child. Never was able to see a good thing when it was right in front of you." Carla sneered as she walked past the bathroom again. "You think he likes you?" She paused to look in the bathroom and Allison kept her focus on the mirror as she finished her hair. "Keep a close eye on that makeup, darling," her mother said in a derogatory tone. "We wouldn't want to frighten him off on the first date."

*Sticks and stones may break my bones, but words will never hurt me.*

Lies. All lies. Her mother's words were sharper than a fillet knife as they cut into Allison's chest. She needed air...and space. The bathroom walls were closing in on her, and she was struggling to catch her breath. Carla's words were a little too close to home, too near the truth for comfort.

"Excuse me," Allison said as she gasped for air, pushing past her mother. Allison rushed to the front door, flinging it open, and almost ran straight into Benny.

"Hello, beautiful," he said with a grin. "Couldn't wait to see me?"

"It won't last!" Carla called from down the hall. "Just wait and see!"

Benny's smile quickly disappeared as his eyes went over her shoulder and into the house. "Goodnight, Mrs. Mayer," he said in a bright, but completely false, tone. "Don't wait up!"

Taking Allison's hand, he pulled her outside, then slammed the door behind her. Allison almost let out a completely inappropriate giggle when he grumbled something about meddling mothers. "I'm sorry," she whispered hoarsely.

Benny's eyes snapped to hers. "Nope. You don't get to be sorry for her." He straightened his button-down shirt. "You're only responsible for your choices and since you chose to go out with me tonight, I have to say you have excellent taste." He winked.

Allison let out a long breath. "You look very nice," she managed, a little stronger than before. His normally unruly hair was combed back and his shirt actually looked wrinkle free, which was a completely new look. She liked it.

His eyes traveled up and down as a slow smile crept across his face. "I figured I had better dress the part if I was going to have such beauty on my arm."

Allison wanted to enjoy his words, but they were so against everything she'd been taught and experienced. "Thanks," she said out of habit, looking out to the side. She didn't want to ruin the moment by seeing the lie in his eyes.

Benny took her chin and pulled her face around until she couldn't help but see him. "You're beautiful," he said bluntly.

She opened her mouth to argue, but his thumb came up to stop her.

"Just like you're not responsible for your mother's choices, you also don't get to take responsibility for mine."

That thumb began stroking back and forth against her bottom lip, sending delightful shivers down her spine.

"I find you beautiful. Stunning. Gorgeous." His smile was softer than usual, not so overly bright and goofy. "Your birthmark doesn't take away from that and your makeup has nothing to do with it."

He was completely sincere. Everything in his face said so. Allison felt another piece of her wall crumble and fall.

"One day, I just hope you'll trust me enough to show me the real you." His grin grew. "I see pieces of her, but I can tell there's more, and I'm excited to get to know Ally without any outside influences muddling the experience."

What in the world was she supposed to say? If he had proposed marriage, Allison wasn't sure she could have been more shocked. Bit by bit, brick by brick, this man was pulling down her protection. Did he know how much internal conflict she was experiencing at his hands? Did he know how hard it was for her to set aside years of scoldings and horrific experiences to try and believe what he was saying? Did he know how much she wanted the freedom and ease of conscience that he exuded?

"Come on." Benny released her chin and tapped her on the nose. "We're far too serious for the first five minutes of a date."

"And how are dates supposed to start?" Allison asked, walking with him out to the sidewalk.

Benny's smile turned into that mischievous one that was equal parts adorable and worrisome. He stopped and turned to her. "Like this." Without warning, he grabbed the back of her head and gave her a fierce, but short kiss.

It was just enough to leave Allison completely off balance and struggling to come back down to reality when he pulled away.

"Much better, don't you think?" he asked, his voice slightly lower than normal.

She couldn't speak. His impulsive nature and the sensations running rampant through her body had completely robbed her of the ability to put together a coherent sentence.

Chuckling, Benny took her hand once more and strutted—yes, strutted—down the sidewalk.

The sight of him looking far too proud was finally enough to pull Allison back down to earth. "You look like the cat who ate the canary."

Benny turned toward her. "It was a delicious canary."

"Oh my word," Allison breathed, her hand coming up to her hot cheek. "I don't know what to think of you sometimes."

Benny laughed and shrugged. "Men are pretty simple creatures," he said. "Think of us like puppies. We like to be fed, have our heads petted, and our bellies rubbed..." He scratched his stomach as he spoke.

Allison reached over with her free hand and swatted his shoulder. "Stop. Like seriously. Stop."

"What? Didn't you ever want a puppy?"

"A puppy, yes," Allison argued. "But not a human who acted like one. The day I have to clean up a puppy pad or litter box is the day I say goodbye."

Benny's laughter grew. "So noted," he said. He waved his arm in front of them. "We're at the Clam Pot tonight. You okay with oysters?"

Allison swallowed hard. Was he serious? She enjoyed some seafood. It was impossible to live where they did and not eat some fish. But raw oysters? They were a different story.

Benny snorted in laughter. "You should see your face."

She knew. Allison *knew* he didn't mean the words the way they sounded in her head, but habit is a hard beast to conquer and she felt her face go slack before she could stop it.

"Crap," Benny muttered, stepping quickly into her personal bubble. "I didn't mean it like that, beautiful," he said softly. His free hand came up and soft fingertips caressed her mottled skin. "It slipped out before I thought about how you would take it." He gave her a pleading grin. "You were almost green when I mentioned the oysters and it made me laugh." His palm settled fully on her skin. "We don't have to eat oysters and I hope everyone sees your face, because it makes my day better with just the slightest glimpse."

"You're too much," Allison rasped.

Benny shook his head. "Until I help you see what you really are, it'll never be enough."

OKAY...THIS MOMENT was getting a little too intimate. Benny knew he was impulsive and a little wild by nature, but when he found himself wanting to whisk Ally around the corner and kiss her until she agreed with him, things were going a little too far. He stepped back, breaking the pull between them. "We're going to be late for our reservation. Come on."

"You made a reservation?" she asked. Her voice was slightly breathless and it made Benny grin to know she was affected as much as he was.

"I did."

"Wow." Ally gave him a sly look. "I didn't think you were the type to think that far ahead."

He tugged on her hand and pulled her in close. "There are a lot of things you don't know about me."

Her eyelashes fluttered as she looked up. "Maybe someday I'll get the chance."

*Aaaaand here we go again.* He tweaked her nose. "If we're lucky." He opened the door for her and ushered her inside. How did his life get this crazy? How had he gone from bemoaning every one of his friends falling in love to him feeling like he was on the edge of the precipice himself?

He'd started trailing Ally just to assuage his curiosity and give himself something to do, but now he found himself actually eager to be in her company. When he wasn't with her, he was finding ways to change that. If he couldn't make it happen, then he texted or called, just to hear her voice and laugh at her quips.

He finally understood why Jensen, Felix, and everybody else had been so unavailable while they were dating their eventual spouses. For the first time in his life, Benny didn't want to spend time with the group. He only wanted time with Ally. And the craziest thing of all was the more he spent time with her, the more he wanted to spend time with her. It made no sense and yet it made wonderful sense.

When he'd given into his attraction and kissed her at the carnival last week, something inside of him had dropped into place. As if he'd been waiting for just the right moment and now his eyes were opened.

A relationship with the right person wasn't something to be dreaded, but something to celebrate. There was something so satisfying about being with Ally and seeing her become more than she was. He not only wanted to protect her, but he wanted to push her. He wanted her to be everything she could possibly be.

He chuckled mentally. He had probably driven his friends nuts with his antics during their dating days. *Eh...what's dating without a little fun mixed in?* Okay, he wasn't exactly regretting his actions, but he was determined to do things right with Ally. She'd been through enough.

"Thank you," he said to their hostess as she seated him and Ally in a booth. It was cozy and separated a little from the other patrons. The perfect spot for a romantic date. Benny had scooted himself toward the back of the booth, but apparently Ally had different ideas.

She sat down at the edge and started to pick up her menu.

"Oh no, you don't," he muttered. Taking her elbow, he guided her farther into the booth until she was tucked right up against his side.

Ally gave him a wry look. "I don't think I can eat like this."

Benny grinned. "Eating is overrated."

She laughed. "This coming from the bottomless pit."

He turned and nuzzled his nose into her hair. Was it weird that he was obsessed with her hair? It was dark and thick and he just wanted to play with it all the time. "Maybe I'll just eat you instead."

"Benny," she whispered. "You can't say things like that." She pushed on his chest, though not very hard. "This is our first date."

"Maybe so, but we've already spent a lot of time together." He leaned in. "And if you think I'm waiting until the third date to kiss you again, you better think twice."

Her face turned bright red, even with her darkened skin. "I thought I always had a choice in the matter."

Benny nodded. "You do. I can kiss you before dinner, or after dinner. Or maybe after dessert." He did his best rakish grin. "Or all three."

"Benny," she hissed.

Chuckling, he straightened. Time to let her breathe. If she hadn't already figured it out, Benny wasn't a halfway type person. When he wanted something or decided to do something, he chipped away until it was done. And as of last week, he'd decided he wanted Ally.

But he didn't just want her the way she was now. He wanted *all* of her. He wanted her to break free of the last of the restraints her mother was keeping on her. He wanted who she could become, not who she currently was.

A few minutes later, they had ordered and were again left alone. Ally wasn't looking at him, but was playing with the cloth napkin, as if she was nervous.

Benny stopped her twitching fingers and entwined them with his own. "What's bothering you?"

She blew out a breath. "It doesn't matter."

"It does." He squeezed her fingers a couple of times until she looked at him. "It does to me."

Ally leaned back, resting her head against the booth wall. "I don't like how I left things with my mom."

The dreaded 'M' word. Benny wasn't prone to disliking people as a rule, but Mrs. Mayer had never been on his friends list. She was a little too friendly with the men in the town, and now that he was friends with Ally, she had become downright hostile.

Ally gave him a look. "I know you don't get along, but she's my mother."

He nodded. "She is. But that doesn't automatically mean you have to cater to her every whim."

Ally's eyes dropped again.

"Hey." Benny pulled her chin back up. "I wasn't trying to knock what you've done, but the more I learn about that woman, the more I want to rescue you from her."

Ally deflated a little. "This isn't about rescuing anybody," she said. "This is about fighting with the woman who has given me everything."

*Everything? Like a complex about your looks? Like a life with no friends?*

The words were on the tip of his tongue, but even Benny knew they weren't wise to say. How could he help her fix it when she couldn't see past the older woman's manipulation?

"Let's not talk about it." Ally waved off the topic. "I have a feeling we're not going to agree."

Benny silently agreed. "Okay." He played with her fingers. "How about we discuss our next date?"

She laughed softly and shook her head. "We haven't finished our first one yet. How do you know you'll even want a second one?"

"If I was going to run, I would have done so by now," he said. "Trust me. Nothing is going to scare me off at this point."

She peeked at him from under her lashes. "You're awfully bold, Mr. Frasier."

"Life's too short to wait for stuff to come to you," Benny explained. He leaned in closer and kissed her cheek. "If my mother taught me anything that was actually worthwhile, it was if you want something, grab on with two hands and never let go."

Her eyes held that longing look again. "And have you found something you want?"

He nodded slowly, then closed the last couple of inches for a sweet and entirely too-short kiss. "And I don't plan to let go."

# CHAPTER 17

Two days later, Allison's head was still spinning. It was all going too fast. Benny was completely sweeping her off her feet and Allison couldn't catch her breath enough to know how to handle it. She'd spent twenty-six years going one direction, and then Hurricane Benny burst into her life and was forcing her to turn a one-eighty.

The worst part was, she found herself happily tripping along in his wake, enjoying his smiles and kisses and all the butterflies in her stomach, but she wasn't sure she really had a good handle on what was going on.

Her fingers danced across the keys. Here was something that made sense. Black and white. Ebony and ivory. If you pressed C, you heard a C. If you pressed E, you heard an E. When put in certain orders, the notes created beautiful melody lines and it could be replicated over and over again. Allison was always sure of the outcome when she sat down to play. She was less sure of the situation with Benny.

She liked him. A lot. She enjoyed his laughter, his teasing and flirting. She enjoyed the way he lived life to the fullest and wasn't afraid to go after what he wanted. She stood in awe of his confidence and lack of worry over other people's opinions. And most of all, she appreciated how he had stepped out of his mother's shadow and built a life for himself that had nothing to do with her craziness.

Allison was drawn to every bit of him. She wanted to be with him every moment of every day, but a small part of her hesitated. *Am I drawn to him because he conquered where I failed? Or because I actually like him?*

It was a question she couldn't quite figure out.

When she was with him, it all felt so easy. She was an adult. She could make her own decisions. She had every right to make choices without her mother.

But then he would go home and leave her by herself and it would fall apart. Allison found herself lying in her room at night, staring at the ceiling as doubts and worries swirled through her head.

*What if he lets me go as quickly as he picked me up?*

*What if this is all part of an elaborate hoax?*

*What if he changes his mind?*

*What if he saw my face again and decided I wasn't beautiful?*

*What if...*

*What if...*

*What if...*

It didn't help that her mother fed those fears until they were as fat and happy as a housecat.

Benny smothered her in compliments and support, while her mother methodically shredded each and every one.

The cover on the piano slammed down and Allison was barely aware enough to pull back her fingers before they were smashed. "Mother!" she cried, looking up to see Carla's icy gaze. "You almost hurt me."

"I had to get your attention somehow." The older woman sniffed. "You've been ignoring me for weeks."

*Actually, it's been the other way around.* Allison held her tongue. She hated confrontation, but it seemed like it was here anyway. She didn't have to feed the beast, however. Folding her hands in her lap, Allison did her best to rid her face of emotion. "What can I do for you?"

Carla snorted. "If you were interested in doing anything for me, we wouldn't need to have this conversation."

Allison closed her eyes and held back a long sigh. "What would you like to discuss, mother?"

Carla slapped a stack of papers on the piano. "We can discuss the job at Eastern."

Allison pinched her lips together. It had been a few weeks since the job offer had come in. She had assumed it was gone by now. No such luck, apparently. "What about it?"

"When are you going to accept it?"

Allison's eyebrows went up. "I didn't know I was."

Carla threw back her head and groaned. "We've been over this, Allison. It's the opportunity of a lifetime." She brought her head back down and glared. "It's a steady income ten times higher than you make now. You'll still have the chance to perform and your potential for advancement has never been higher! This is how we make all our dreams come true!"

Allison bit her tongue until she was sure it would bleed. But she knew if she answered right now, she'd say something she'd regret.

"Well?" her mother pressed.

"I don't quite know what to say," Allison said carefully.

"There's nothing to say," Carla snapped. She jabbed the stack. "Sign it and email it back."

"I'm not ready to do that," Allison said, still keeping her tone as calm as possible.

Her mother's face grew alarmingly red. "It's because of him, isn't it?"

Allison didn't answer. There was nothing she could say to that accusation that would help the situation.

Slowly, Carla shook her head. "You would throw away *years!* Of work and sacrifice for something as fleeting as a boyfriend?"

"I don't know what I've decided yet," Allison said quietly. And she hadn't...for the most part. She knew she didn't want the job, but her situation with Benny was still too new to decide anything long term around it.

"Once he sees your face, he'll be out of here so fast it will make your head swim," Carla said in a dark tone.

"He's already seen it," Allison responded before she could stop herself.

Her mother's laugh could only be described as a cackle, which felt alarmingly correct for the situation. "Then you have your answer." She smirked. "He's only hanging around because he's curious. He wants a better view." She leaned her arms on the piano and bent down to Allison's face. "Once his curiosity is gone, he'll follow. You're nothing but an oddity. Something new. Bennett Frasier isn't the kind of man who'll stay when he's had his fill. He's always been the flighty type. You're just the newest toy on the shelf."

It took every bit of Allison's self-control not to break down. How did her mother know exactly what to say in order to hurt her? Or to make Allison question the truth of her situation? This was why her nights had been so sleepless. This was why she was unsure what direction she was headed or what was right.

There could be truth in Carla's words, even if it hurt. Yet Benny seemed completely sincere in his affections.

Who was Allison to believe?

There was a knock on the door and Allison realized her first student of the day had arrived.

"Go fix your face," Carla snapped, straightening her shirt.

It was only then that Allison realized she was crying. A few stray tears dribbled down her face, more than likely ruining the foundation that covered her birthmark. She stood from the piano bench and began to walk away, but her mother grabbed her arm.

"I'm only trying to protect you," Carla said softly, as if regretting her harsh words. "I've always tried to protect you."

Allison hesitated, then nodded before walking away. There would be time to go over this later. Right now she had a job to do.

BENNY WHISTLED AS HE walked up the front step for his piano lesson. He'd only had a few, but he had to admit he was actually enjoying them. Time spent with Ally was always fun, but he found himself enjoying the lesson itself as well.

Just as he reached to knock, the door opened and the student just before him came darting out.

"Whoa." Benny stepped to the side as the boy ran past. He smiled up at Ally in the doorway. "I think Jordan was ready for a break."

Ally nodded, but didn't smile back. "He's one of my most active students. Would much prefer to be playing baseball instead of pounding keys."

"Well, it's certainly not because he doesn't have a wonderful teacher." Benny winked and stepped inside. He felt like he was starting to get whiplash from Ally's moods, but he refused to give up on her. Usually when he found her like this, it was because her mother had been around. "What little boy doesn't enjoy having a beautiful teacher he gets to admire all the time?"

Her lips quirked just a little. "You're too much, Benny."

He stepped up close before she could escape to the piano. "Nope." He nuzzled her nose with his. "I'm just right. And I'm in the same position. I'm totally crushing on my teacher." Her back relaxed against his palm and Benny threw a quick prayer of thanks heavenward.

"I'm not much of a teacher if I stand here talking instead of instructing." She smiled softly, then stepped back and led him to the bench.

Benny put his music on the piano and sat down, scooting the bench back to accommodate his height.

"Did you get your practice in this week?" she asked, her eyes on his lesson book.

"Nope," Benny said cheerfully. He waited until she looked up. "I was too busy mooning over my teacher."

Ally shook her head, that same small smile on there from before. "You realize that means you don't get to pick out of the treat jar?"

"Crud." Benny snapped his fingers. "I knew there was something I was forgetting."

"Well, you can make it up this next week," Ally said, leaning in to turn his book to the correct page.

"If I'm being honest, I predict this week will be as bad as the last one." He watched the flush creep up her neck and into her face. The port wine mark was much easier to see from under her makeup when she blushed. Reaching out, Benny trailed his knuckles across her cheekbone. "You don't need to cover this, you know," he said softly.

Ally cleared her throat and leaned back. "Hands on the piano, please," she said, all business. "Let's see if I can help you along a little before you practice at home again."

The next half-hour was torturous, and not because Benny was inept at the instrument. Every time he tried to flirt with her, she turned him down flat. Apparently, bringing up the possibility of going without makeup was still too much for her.

He told himself he could be patient about it, but it was hard. He'd fought this fight multiple times already and the stronger his feelings grew, the more Benny wanted to move on to other things with her.

*Like more time on dates or kissing on park benches.*

He had to keep reminding himself of a simple truth. *You've had weeks with her. Her mother has had a lifetime.*

Breaking through Ally's barriers wasn't easy, but keeping them down was the hardest part. Without twenty-four-seven access to her, he couldn't stop Mrs. Mayer from ruining all his efforts.

He cracked his knuckles and Ally gave him a look. Little did she know he was preparing for battle. "So...we good to go?"

She nodded, her face once again on his lesson book. "Yep. Just let me finish getting this written down." Once done, she handed him the spiral notebook. "You're making good progress." She smiled. "Don't let life stop you from pushing forward."

Benny set the notebook and other books aside, then scooted himself to the edge of the bench. Patting the spot next to him, he said, "Why don't you show me?"

Ally frowned. "Show you what?"

"How to push forward." He raised a challenging eyebrow. "Share with me the fun side of piano."

Ally splayed her hands to the sides. "Playing *is* fun."

"Ah..." Benny waved a finger through the air. "But sharing is better." Again, he patted the bench, inviting her to join him.

Slowly, hesitantly, Ally slipped off her seat and sat at the piano. She shrugged. "Now what?"

Benny raised his hands and began to play one of only two songs he'd ever learned before coming to lessons, "Chopsticks."

Ally laughed, then covered her mouth with her fingers. "You can't be serious."

"Come on!" Benny hollered over his extra loud playing. "It's a classic! You know you want to!"

Ally shook her head in amusement, but raised her fingers and held them over the keys. She bobbed her head as if counting out the line, then joined him, creating a harmony to his pounding.

Benny grinned. "We're the perfect partners!"

Her laugh was more free this time and soon her fingers began to wander, improvising a simple melody line over his rhythmic playing.

"You're amazing," he shouted, his wide smile completely genuine. How did this woman not know how awesome she was? How could she let her mother walk all over her and keep her from enjoying life to its fullest?

A door slammed, shaking the small house with its impact.

Ally's fingers immediately stopped and her eyes widened. "Mother," she breathed.

Benny stopped the song as well, but he wasn't nearly as upset as she was. "Guess we were just too good for her." It was time for song number two. "We need to switch spots." He stood and scooted around the bench, pushing her to the upper keys.

"What?" Ally moved over, but was frowning again.

He had every intention of wiping that look off her face permanently. Without saying anything else, he started the bottom part for "Heart and Soul."

Ally hung her head back. "Is that all you know?"

"Pretty much." He shrugged. "I think every teenager learned those two." He leaned into her ear, whispering. "But it worked. The whole purpose of knowing any piano was to get closer to a pretty girl." Leaning back, his eyes automatically dropped to her neck so he could watch that wonderful blush again. He wasn't disappointed.

"Bennett Frasier, you're a terrible flirt." Despite her words, she began playing the upper melody, once again changing it as she saw fit.

"Actually, I think I'm a pretty decent flirt," he argued back. "I've been practicing my whole life."

"Now that I can believe," she shot back with a laugh.

"You ready for our date tonight?"

Her fingers stopped. "We had a date tonight?"

Benny also stopped playing and twisted so he could give her a gentle kiss on the forehead. "We have a date every night."

"That's...a lot of dates." Her eyes searched his and Benny did his best to stay open for her perusal.

"It is. But I promise you won't regret it."

Her back relaxed, a sure sign he was winning again. "Well, I don't know about every night, but since today is Friday, I suppose I can work something out."

"Good." He kissed her again. "Go grab some sandals and a jacket. We're going to be on the beach tonight."

She gave him a look, but didn't ask questions, which he was grateful for. She probably wouldn't be excited to find out they were going to be spending the evening with his friends. But he had a feeling that the more people he could get on his side, the better.

# CHAPTER 18

"We're going out on the beach?" Allison ducked her head against a cool wind. "Isn't it too late in the year for this?"

Benny wrapped an arm around her, tucking her into his side. "It's pretty darn close. We won't hold too many more of these before the winter hits."

Allison stuttered in her steps. "We?" What did he mean "we"? She thought they were going on a date. A cold, windy date, but a date nonetheless. She looked up to see him scratching his chin. It was a sure sign he was nervous with what he was about to tell her.

"Every Friday during the warm months, my friends and I hold a bonfire." His arm tightened just as she started to pull away. "Ally, calm down."

"Why didn't you tell me?" she asked. A sharp pain dug at her chest. Her mother's words came back to haunt her. That he was just satisfying his curiosity. Did that curiosity extend to his friends as well?

"Because I knew this is how you would react." Benny turned and hugged her against his chest, bringing his forehead down to hers. "Now listen."

He was so serious that Allison actually stopped her struggle out of surprise.

"First of all, what do you have against my friends?"

Allison gaped at him. "Me have against them? Are you kidding?" She shook her head. "I think the more appropriate statement is that they'll have a problem with me."

"Why?"

"What do you mean why?" She shook her head, tears blurring her vision. She wasn't much of a crier, but her emotions had been so out of control lately that Allison couldn't seem to help it.

"Ally," he drawled, backing up so he could cup her birthmark. "Middle school is in the past. Anything that happened there doesn't matter. You already know Rose and get along with her, so why not be willing to try with the others?" He ran his thumb along her cheekbone.

Allison didn't like to admit how much she enjoyed his touch. Especially the fact that he was so willing to touch the part of her face that she hid from the world. Her own mother wouldn't even touch it, but Benny did it all the time. As if he were making a statement. "I don't think your friends will feel the same," she whispered.

"Give them a chance," he pleaded. "Please."

She turned her head. "There's a reason I don't hang out with others."

"You hang out with me," he argued.

"I think you hung out with me first," Allison pointed out.

Benny grinned unrepentantly. "And these are some of the best people I know. Including my own sister and brother-in-law." He put a hand to the side of his mouth. "Don't tell them I said that, it'll go straight to Jensen's head."

"What if they all stare?"

He shook his head. "They won't. I can't promise there won't be questions, but there are any time we bring someone new to the group." His smile grew. "You're the first person I've ever brought other than Jack, and he ended up marrying Caro, so my track record is pretty good." His smile fell. "Wait a second. There's still another single guy in this group." He spun on his heel and started dragging her back toward the vehicle. "Nevermind. You don't need to meet them. I was wrong."

Allison laughed and pulled him to a stop. "You really want me to get to know them?"

Benny stepped up close again. "More than that, I want them to get to know *you*."

Allison pinched her lips together, her eyes drifting to the horizon as she debated. Her hair was whipping around her head, in as much chaos as her head. Benny certainly knew how to push her buttons. He was relentless. No matter that he always said she had a choice in the matter, he pushed and pushed until he got what he wanted out of sheer exasperation. But tonight...she was scared. She was scared his friends would hate her. She was scared they'd hold her past against her. She was scared someone would see behind her makeup and call her out for the freak she was.

"You're overthinking again." Benny pulled her in for a hug, kissing the top of her head. "Life isn't all daisies and roses," he whispered. "Sometimes we have to make tough choices and sometimes we have to do tough things. But often, if we look for it, those hard decisions come with great rewards." He leaned back to look her in the eye. "I *know* my friends will open their arms to you, if only because I brought you along. They might be curious, they might be hesitant, but once they see the real you, you'll have a family." He smirked. "One that sticks with you through thick and thin, even though we sometimes get on each other's nerves."

Allison swallowed hard. "You promise?"

He crossed his heart and put two fingers in the air. "Cross my heart and Scout's honor."

"Were you a Scout?"

"Yep!"

Allison felt her eyebrows shoot up. "Really?"

He puffed out his chest. "Really. Now...are you ready?"

Allison took a deep breath, then nodded. "Okay."

His grin grew to epic proportions. "You'll love it." He winked and started walking again. "And don't even think about eating healthy tonight. My sister always brings fruit and whatnot, but Caro and Jack supply enough dessert to keep us fat and happy for a week."

Allison shook her head. "I don't want to be fat."

"Don't forget the happy part."

*I wouldn't mind being happy.* She glanced at him as they walked. *And you help me be happy.* Those were words she was far from ready to speak out loud, but they were true all the same. "I won't forget," she whispered as a fire came into view. A large number of people were gathered around and Allison's heart began to beat fiercely against her chest. This was it. The moment that would make or break their blossoming relationship.

She knew Benny worshipped his friends and if they didn't accept her, Allison was positive that she and Benny would be over. And she wouldn't blame him one bit. She was an outsider and new. There was no way he would throw away a lifetime of memories for someone like her.

"Benny!"

The man who used to work the cookie truck walked up to give Benny some kind of complicated handshake. His easy-going smile turned to Allison. "For the first time ever, Benny didn't show up empty-handed." He put out his palm. "Jack Porter. Cookie baker and husband to the blonde chatting over there." He jabbed his thumb toward the woman Allison recognized as Caroline Douglas. Or apparently, it was Caroline Porter now.

Allison shook his hand. "Allison Mayer."

Benny wrapped his arm around her. "Pianist extraordinaire and date of the amazing Benny Frasier."

Jack snorted. "Poor thing." He tsked his tongue and turned back to Allison. "Come on over, we'll help you ditch him if you want."

"Don't tempt me," Allison quipped, much to Jack's amusement.

Benny leaned down as they walked closer. "Don't even think about leaving me alone with these vultures. I'll be dead before dessert."

"I thought you said they'd welcome me with open arms?"

"You, not me." Benny shook his head. "I may or may not have ticked off every person in this group at one point or another."

Allison wanted to slap her forehead, but she refrained. The more he teased, the more Allison realized just how much he must trust this group. His humor was his way of getting to know people, not a way of hurting them. Now she just had to hope his friends knew that as well.

BENNY COULD FEEL ALLY trembling beside him. He'd really pushed hard this time. Whenever she reacted badly to his prodding, he usually backed off, but this time, he had held his ground. She needed more friends. She needed more people to speak against what her mother kept planting in her head. His hope was that between him and his friends, they would help her break the ties that were holding her back.

"Wassup!" he called to Jensen, who was catering to Mel's every need. Settling her in her chair and making sure she had a plate of food and a drink. Normally, Benny would have rolled his eyes and groaned about all the lovey dovey junk floating through the air, but tonight? Tonight he stayed silent. On a small level, he was starting to understand it himself. He wasn't ready to say he was in love, but he knew he was headed that direction. It was the only explanation for his behavior and persistence.

"Hey, man," Jensen said, sitting down in his own chair and tilting his chin. He hesitated when he noticed Ally. "Allison," Jensen said carefully. "Good to see you."

Ally tucked into Benny's side a little more. "Hello, Jensen." Her eyes moved down the line. "Mel. I hear congratulations are in order."

Mel smiled softly and rubbed her small belly. "Thank you. We're very excited."

Now Benny did roll his eyes. "Okay...let's just get this out of the way." He smiled down, trying to reassure Ally. "Most of you know Ally." He looked out at the group. "She's here as my date tonight." He smirked when that raised a few eyebrows. "Ally, do you know everyone here or should I introduce you?"

She shrugged. "I know a few."

"Okay." He pointed just to the right of Mel. "You know Charli?"

Charli nodded. "Hi...Ally?" It was more of a question than a statement.

Ally nodded. "That's what Benny calls me anyway."

Charli snorted. "Be grateful it was just a shortened version of your name. Sometimes his nicknames are horrible."

"I heard that," Benny drawled.

"You were meant to."

Bronson raised his hand. "Hi, Ally. I'm Bronson. The man attached the argumentative one." He pointed to Charli.

Benny grinned when Ally smiled at Charli's indignant screech. "Bronson moved up here from California," he said in an aside.

Ally nodded.

"And you know Ken."

"Hi, Ally." Ken smiled.

"Hello," she responded.

"You already met Jack and I'm sure you know Caro."

"Actually, we've never met in person," Caro said calmly, her head tilted to the side. "But I've heard all about you."

Benny wanted to groan. Leave it to Caro to be blunt. He felt Ally stiffen beside him.

"I'm looking forward to getting to know you for myself," Caro finished.

Benny let out a breath he'd been holding. When Caro winked at him, he gave her a chin tilt. She might be feisty, but he was grateful she had his back.

"And then we have Genni and Cooper." Benny tilted his head toward Ally. "They run the bed and breakfast."

Genni gave a small wave, then her hand went back to patting the underside of the bundle she was holding. "Hi, Ally. We're glad to have you."

Cooper half stood and offered his hand. "Welcome," he added. Sitting back down, Cooper put his arm around his wife. "And the tiny one is Esther. She's sleeping or I'd introduce you more properly."

Ally's smile was small but more relaxed than before. "That's all right. Congratulations to you both and thank you."

Cooper beamed. "Thanks. We probably shouldn't have brought her tonight, but we needed to get out of the house."

"Uh-oh," Charli said. "What did Butterscotch do now?"

Ally frowned up at Benny. "Butterscotch is their dog. She's an Australian Shepherd mix and still young enough to be a handful."

"Dug up my gladiolus," Genni said with a sniff. She shot a look at Cooper. "If he would take Grayson's advice and have her trained, we wouldn't have this problem."

Cooper put his free hand in the air. "I'll get right on that, as soon as I have the time. What would you like me to let go? Mowing the lawn? Fixing the bannister?"

"Whoa, whoa, whoa." Caro put her hands in the air. "We're at a bonfire, peeps. Lovers' quarrels have to be left at the house."

Cooper grinned and kissed Genni's temple. "See, they're all on my side."

Genni swatted her husband's knee, but she was smiling. "Rose would be on my side."

"Hungry?" Benny whispered.

Ally shook her head. "Not yet." She was still holding onto him like a leech, but at least she wasn't shaking anymore.

"Why don't we sit down, then?" Pulling her along, he grabbed a couple of camping chairs and unfolded them side by side in the circle of the fire. After seeing Ally and himself settled, he tuned back to the chatter going on.

"So you teach piano lessons?" Mel asked politely.

"I do." Ally tucked a piece of hair behind her ear, but it just blew out again.

"Hold on." Caro dug through her purse. "I think I have an extra hair tie." After a moment, she raised her hand. "Ah, ha! Here it is." She stood and brought it over to Ally.

"Thank you," Ally whispered, her head slightly ducked.

"Don't worry about it." Caro waved her hand in dismissal. "We've all eaten our hair too many times out here. You learn to come prepared." She sat down and grinned at Ally. "Next time you come, you'll know what to bring."

Benny could have kissed Caro, if she wasn't married and he didn't think of her like a sister. Those words seemed to be magic and slowly, Ally straightened in her seat and began to join the conversation.

"So let me get this straight." Jack leaned forward. "You teach, plus you perform professionally? Like in one of those fancy orchestra shows?"

Ally laughed. "Yes. And let me tell you, I'd much prefer to stick with the children."

"Then why don't you?" Mel asked.

It was a good question. Ally had mentioned once that she didn't like being the center of attention, but had never said why. Benny relaxed in his seat and waited for the answer. This was exactly what he'd been hoping for. Someone other than himself to help break down her icy walls.

"My...mother...likes to have me keep my skills up," Ally said carefully. "The money from performing is helpful as well."

"Have you ever thought about just teaching full time?" Jensen asked, rubbing his jaw.

Ally shrugged. "I've been offered..." She trailed off and Benny grew very curious as to what she had been about to say. "Not seriously," she finally finished.

"Our music teacher at the high school is retiring at the end of this year," Jensen responded. "You should apply."

Ally shrugged. "Thanks. I'll think about it."

Benny made a note to clarify what she'd left unsaid, but right now he let it go. Ally was beginning to relax, her shoulders were settling into her seat, her smile was growing, and his friends were doing what they did best. Welcoming a newcomer into their familial circle. He knew tonight wasn't going to be the cure-all, but hopefully it would go a long way into helping him with his cause. Any progress was progress.

# CHAPTER 19

This was definitely not what Allison had expected. When she'd found out Benny had brought her to a bonfire with all his friends, she had been ready to tuck tail and run. What right did he have to surprise her with something like this? Now, however, she found herself grateful that he didn't like to take no for an answer.

To her surprise, the group had been fairly welcoming and now that the initial round of chatter and introductions were done, the slight amount of tension was gone and nobody seemed to think anything of her being there.

Benny rubbed his hands together. "I need food." He looked her way. "Are you sure you don't want any?"

Allison bit her lips between her teeth and shook her head. Yes, things were feeling more comfortable, but she wasn't ready to eat in front of everyone yet. That always made her extra nervous, partly because of her strict diet, and partly because she was always afraid of wiping off her makeup when she wiped her mouth.

Everyone was being nice, but Allison wasn't completely at ease yet.

"Tell me about your playing," Mel said from her right-hand side. Benny's sister was leaning forward, her whole body telling of her interest. "What made you start playing in the first place?"

Allison blinked a few times. She hadn't been asked that question in forever. "Umm...my mother was a pianist, so she started me very young."

"How young?" Mel's eyebrows shot up.

"Three."

"Whoa...are you serious?" Mel asked breathlessly. Her hand absentmindedly went to her stomach.

Allison felt her cheeks heat. "Yes. That's not that unusual for those who are in the industry."

Mel nodded sagely. "I've heard stories of some kids doing violin or piano at three or four, but I guess I wasn't sure it was real."

Allison shrugged. "It is, but it's a pretty small circle."

Mel rubbed her stomach again. "Jensen'll probably have this little one holding a guitar before he or she is two if I don't intervene."

Allison laughed as intended. "I haven't heard your husband play, but I've heard he's really good."

Mel's smile widened. "He is. He was a favorite on a reality show a couple years ago, but he came back home to marry me instead."

"Wow," Allison added, a surge of jealousy making its way into her stomach. What would it be like to have someone feel that strongly about her? Her eyes flitted to the food table where Benny was holding a plate that looked big enough for four people, and was laughing with Ken over something. Could it be like that between them? He said he was interested in her. He said she was beautiful. He went out of his way to take care of her and spend time with her.

But could he ever love her?

Allison wasn't sure anyone could. Benny talked about seeing the real her, but deep inside, she was still terrified that "the real her" would be just as horrible as she had been told as a young twelve-year-old girl. She had tried to be herself and the person who should have been the most supportive of her stabbed her in the back. The idea of Benny doing the same was enough to send Allison's heart rate through the roof. And most of all, she knew she couldn't handle another hospital like the one she'd been in before. She'd been nothing but a number. A terrified, embarrassed, and depressed girl whom they couldn't even look in the face. The doctors and nurses always seemed to be looking at her charts, never at her, and Allison had learned a valuable lesson.

No one wanted her.

Her suicide attempt had been the result of an entire school bullying her, yet the counsellors and doctors all claimed she was simply seeking attention. Apparently, they went out of their way not to give it to her.

*Perhaps it was part of the therapy.*

"Ally? Allison?"

Fingertips rested on her arm and Allison almost jumped out of her seat. "Sorry, what?"

Mel gave her a tentative smile. "I lost you for a moment."

Allison forced herself to relax. "Yeah, sorry. My mind wandered."

Mel's bright blue eyes trailed over to her brother, then back and a small smile played on her lips. "He's something, isn't he?"

A barking laugh slipped free before Allison could stop it. "That he is."

Mel laughed too before speaking again. "You'd never know it, but Benny struggled as a little boy. I didn't recognize it at the time, of course, since I was a couple years younger, but the older I get, the more I can see it in my memories. He didn't have a lot of friends until we reached middle school and he discovered he was good at making people laugh."

"He told me a little bit about that," Allison murmured. "Said he chose laughing with them instead of letting them laugh at him."

"That's a good way to put it," Mel said with a smile. "He's always been so social, a true extrovert, but with our weird upbringing, it was hard to find kids who would accept us."

"Kids can be mean," Allison said softly.

Mel sighed and sunk into her seat. "True enough. Their circles are small and anything outside that circle frightens them." She shrugged. "Sometimes, especially the teenagers, resort to hurtful words when they're frightened, instead of being curious enough to understand."

Allison snorted. "Reminds me of that cartoon with the beast and the villagers."

Mel snapped her fingers. "Exactly! He was different and the people reacted with anger instead of compassion." She shook her head. "But you know, with the right influence, people can change. Not to mention most of us get better as we grow older." Her eyes were trained on Allison, but Allison wasn't sure how to respond.

Did Mel know something about Allison's childhood? Or was she speaking generally? Or maybe even referring to how Allison behaved in school. Her mother had certainly influenced her behavior there and if she was being honest, Allison had to admit that Benny was influencing it now.

Her guidance was coming from two completely separate ends of the spectrum and Allison was quickly coming to the point where she was going to have to decide which one to follow. The situation with her mother and the job wouldn't wait forever. Yet the thought of leaving Benny or her quiet town behind made Allison sick to her stomach.

"I'll add one more thing and then I promise not to be the 'sister' again." Mel used her fingers to make quotation marks.

"No, no, you feel free to say whatever you want," Allison responded quickly.

Mel smiled. "Thank you. And I promise I'm not here to threaten you not to break my brother's heart."

Allison relaxed the tiniest amount.

"Benny puts on a wonderful show," Mel said, her voice having dropped in volume and pitch. "But he is the most loyal, determined, intelligent, and loving dork I have the privilege of knowing." Her eyes narrowed. "Once he sets his sights on something, he doesn't give up and he doesn't let go." Long, blonde hair fell across her face as she tilted her head. "And I've never seen him set his sights on a woman before."

Allison swallowed hard.

"We don't know each other well," Mel continued. "But if Benny has his heart set on you, then I think you must be worth making the effort."

This had gotten much too serious for Allison's liking. She wasn't ready to go in that deep yet, even if Benny wanted to. It would mean being vulnerable and telling him the rest of her story. "Thank you," she finally choked out. "I don't have a lot of experience with friends, but I would love to get to know you."

There. Polite and true, but nothing that would indicate more between her and Benny. That was something she would have to figure out later.

BENNY'S FEET WERE ITCHING to move, but he couldn't seem to find a good break from Ken. The talk between Mel and Ally seemed to be growing more serious by the minute and Benny found himself concerned that Ally would want to run. She didn't like to share things about herself and though he knew Mel wouldn't purposefully scare her away, Ally was still a bit on the fragile side.

"You might as well go," Ken said dryly.

Benny's head snapped back to his friend. "What?"

"I'm not really sure why you're worried she's in distress, but go before you give yourself a heart attack."

Benny rolled his eyes. "I don't have heart attacks."

"Says the guy who has no idea what I said for the last five minutes." Ken raised a single eyebrow in challenge.

"Must not have been that interesting, then," Benny shot over his shoulder as he walked away with a grin. Ken was right. He was behaving like a mother hen or something. It was ridiculous. Ally was an adult and Mel was a sweetheart. Surely nothing bad could come from the two of them being together. "Please tell me she didn't share anything embarrassing while I was gone," Benny said as he plopped down into his seat.

Ally's smile was pure mischief. "Wouldn't you like to know?"

Jensen crowed. "Finally! Somebody who can dish it back to you!"

Benny found himself rolling his eyes yet again. He seemed to be doing that a lot lately. "One quick liner doesn't mean anything."

"You must keep him on his toes," Charli called out from across the fire. "He's like a toddler and his attention wanes quickly. If he's kept you around, there has to be a reason for it."

Ally's body language shifted. Now they were entering dangerous territory. Ally wasn't one to handle hard teasing very well.

"Just because she's more interesting than the rest of you doesn't mean you have to give her grief about it," Benny said, using his best weapon of humor to diffuse the situation. His protective side was rising quickly to the surface and he actually had to push it down to keep from snapping at anybody. That wasn't like him at all.

All this time he'd been working so hard on getting Ally out of her comfort zone and it looked like he was shifting himself as well.

Now to figure out if that was a good thing or not.

The group as a whole chuckled and the topic moved on to other things, allowing Benny to relax in his seat. He twisted toward her. "Here," he said. "I brought you something."

Ally's eyes widened. "You don't mean that whole plate for me, do you?"

Benny chuckled. "I figured we would share, but if you want it, I can always go get another one."

"No, no, no," Ally said quickly. "I can't even make a dent in that."

His chuckle turned into a laugh. "I know."

Ally huffed. "Then why did you…" She shook her head. "Never mind. I don't want to know." She moved her head around as she searched the plate. "Oh my goodness, I think you got some of everything."

"Mel always brings fruit. Here." Benny turned the plate. "The strawberries will be good, along with the grapes."

Ally's grateful smile started the warm buzzing in his chest and Benny had to hold himself back from leaning in to kiss her. This pianist had him wrapped around her little finger and she had no idea. He'd never been so infatuated with a woman before. What had started as curiosity had quickly become obsession and he didn't want it to end.

"Mmm…you're right. These are good."

Benny grinned as he stuffed a whole deviled egg in his mouth. "Told you."

Ally scrunched her nose. "Chew and swallow, Benny."

He almost choked in his laughter. "Only for you," he finally managed to say. Their eyes met and Benny couldn't look away. Why in the world did he bring her to such a public place? They needed to be tucked away in his house or on a lonely bench where he could take full advantage of the way she was looking at him right now. His mind was completely caught up in wanting to kiss her, but his ears happened to still be tuned in to the group.

"Never thought I'd see the day."

Benny blinked and turned to see the entire group watching him and Ally with various expressions on their faces. Some were grinning widely, while others were in shock. It seemed like their little "moment" had awakened some of his friends to the fact that this wasn't a casual date.

"Oh my gosh," she breathed, ducking into herself.

Benny's first reaction was frustration that she was backtracking again, but he forced himself to calm down. Nobody here was trying to hurt him or Ally. They just didn't know her the way he did. "All right, guys. Knock it off," he said, giving them a look.

Felix snorted. "Excuse me? Mr. Pokes His Nose into EVERY-ONE'S Business wants us to back off?" He looked around, then came back to Benny. "I don't see a single person here that you didn't annoy to death when they were dating someone."

Ken raised his hand, but Felix brushed him off.

"It's coming," Felix prophesied. "Trust me."

Ken nodded. "Oh, I know. It just hasn't happened yet."

Benny gave Felix his best unimpressed look. "Okay, okay, I get it. Maybe I've been a little..."

"Overbearing?"

"Annoying?"

"Pushy?"

Benny rolled his eyes for the third time that night as the list continued. He knew he pushed boundaries, but someone had to do it. These guys would be a bunch of stuck in the mud without him.

Hadlee, Felix's wife, leaned forward in order to speak. "Funny," she added softly with a smile.

Benny smiled back.

"Helpful," Caro shot out, making a gun with her fingers.

"Loyal," Jensen added as more of the group got in the spirit of the game.

Ally cleared her throat and every eye turned to her. Even in the dim light of the fire Benny could see the flush in her cheeks, and he found himself waiting with bated breath for whatever she was about to say. He had a gut feeling it would be a sign of things to come.

Her dark eyes met his and she gave him a shy, sweet smile.

"Kind."

That was all he needed. He knew how important that characteristic was to her. The betrayal and bullying had all been because people weren't kind, so having her declare him so meant more than he could express without sounding like an idiot.

Grabbing her free hand with his, he kissed her palm. "And you're beautiful," he whispered, for her ears only.

Around them the rest of the group went back to ribbing each other and left the newer lovebirds alone. It wasn't until they were packing up to leave that Benny realized the lonely feeling he'd been harboring for months, even years as his friends paired off, had been absent tonight. For the first time in a long time, he'd felt complete.

He liked it.

A lot.

# CHAPTER 20

"Oh, man," Allison moaned. "I think I've eaten more sugar since meeting you than I've eaten in my entire life combined." As if to emphasize her point, she licked a drip of ice cream off her knuckle.

Walking down the boardwalk and grabbing a treat or snack had become one of her and Benny's go-to's for spending time together and each time, Allison found herself falling harder and harder. Benny was exasperating yet charming, loud but fun, and always, *always*, pushing himself into her personal circle by calling her beautiful or stunning or any other adjective he could think of.

Benny blew air on his fingernails and buffed them on his shirt. "Thank you," he said haughtily.

"What makes you think that was a compliment?" Allison teased.

Benny winked at her, a response she was becoming quite used to. "It is if I say it was."

She laughed softly. "You might think that, but when I can't fit into my dresses or pants anymore, then I might have to say otherwise."

His large, warm hand covered hers and he pulled her cone over, taking a big bite out of it. "There. I saved the dresses," he said through a mouthful of ice cream. "Now we can just enjoy."

Allison's cheeks were on fire. Another thing she was starting to get used to. Really, any emotion was becoming par for the course. She'd spent so much time refusing to acknowledge anything she felt that at first it had been completely overwhelming to allow them to linger rather than lock them away. Now, however, she went through emotions all day long. Exasperation at her mother and embarrassment with Benny seemed to be the most dominant, however.

He chuckled and rubbed the back of his finger against her cheekbone. It was funny how he always seemed to touch her birthmark side. As if he made a point of doing it, where her mother made a point of not. "One of these days, I'd love to see that delightful blush in all its glory." He leaned in and left a soft kiss on her ear. "Not covered up by makeup."

Allison closed her eyes and deflated. He was pushing for that more and more, but...she just couldn't bring herself to do it. Yet she desperately wanted to. He made her *feel* beautiful. He complimented, kissed her, touched her, said sweet nothings in her ear. No woman could walk away from that not feeling like she was Aphrodite, but then Allison went home and looked in the mirror, and it all fizzled.

Either that or her mother would make some sarcastic remark and Benny's words would fly right out the window.

He kissed her cheekbone. "I'll stop," he said, turning away from her to look out into the ocean.

Allison didn't say anything. Her thoughts were too chaotic for her to respond. She was so torn on which direction was right. Her mind just couldn't seem to be settled in one direction or another.

Benny checked his watch. "Shoot. I gotta get you home." He stood and took her hand, guiding Allison back down the boardwalk. "We don't need to give your mom any more ammunition than she already has against me, do we?" He grinned at her, but Allison could tell some of the sparkle was missing.

Her refusal to trust him was hurting Benny.

Shame and guilt began to churn and she threw her ice cream in the nearest garbage can. Would he stick around if she continued to refuse to clean off her makeup? Would he grow tired of waiting if it took her another year? Two years? Was he only trying to get a better look at her mottled skin?

Their arrival at her doorstep happened all too quickly. "Thank you for the ice cream," she said with a tremulous smile.

Benny sighed and wrapped his arms around her. "I'm not going anywhere," he whispered into her ear, as if he could read her thoughts. "I'll just keep trying to convince you of how wonderful and beautiful you are." With a kiss to her temple, he was gone.

His words were perfect, but Allison's heart was still heavy. Slowly, she walked inside, almost groaning out loud when she found her mother waiting on the couch.

"Allison," her mother said in a low tone.

"Mother." Allison closed the door behind her, but didn't move from the front entry. She crossed her arms over her chest, as if that could protect her from whatever was to come.

"They won't wait forever."

Allison sighed. "I know, Mom, but I've already told you, I don't really want to teach at a college."

Carla tsked her tongue and stood up. The glow of the lamp wasn't enough to do much but cast shadows around the front room. "I still don't understand how you could throw away this kind of opportunity for him!" She pointed to the front of the house.

"This doesn't have anything to do with Benny," Allison said calmly. "Even if he and I weren't dating, I wouldn't want to teach there."

Carla scoffed. "You think that one man showing you a little attention is enough for everyone else to accept you? Not once have I seen you step outside that door without makeup on." She smiled as if those words were a triumph, but little did Carla know that they were slowly pushing her daughter in the other direction. "I've told you before, you're just a shiny, new object to him. His friends will never accept you, this *town* will never accept you. The minute you let down your guard, they'll betray you." Her voice was rising and Allison backed up slightly at the anger in the tone. "One minute you'll feel loved and adored and the next you'll be nothing but garbage under their feet!"

Several heartbeats pulsed in Allison's chest after her mother's rampage. "You're talking about you." The words came out before Allison could think better of them, but they rang with a truth that wasn't often heard in her house. Allison stepped forward slightly. "You're talking about yourself, aren't you?"

"What?" Carla scoffed and backed up. "No. We're talking about you and your..." She waved her hand at Allison's face. The darkness couldn't hide their trembling.

"What's wrong with your hands, Mother?" So many things were beginning to make sense. Not once did Carla ever play the piano anymore, not since Allison was a young child. Not for fun, not for teaching, not for profit...nothing. She'd handed Allison off to tutors and teachers as soon as Allison knew her right hand from her left, but she never joined her daughter on the bench, despite spending years bemoaning her fate.

Carla glared and tucked her fingers into fists. "You're nothing but a child with no true experience in this world. That man will leave you so fast it'll make your head swim. He'll never introduce you to anyone in his life."

Allison shook her head, a wave of pity enveloping her as things became even more clear. "He already has," she said softly.

Carla gasped and backed up.

"And guess what?" Allison stepped forward again, crowding her mother. "They actually treated me well."

Carla snarled and continued to put distance between them.

"And..." The last words stuck in Allison's throat, but they needed to be said, as much for herself as for her mother. "And I think I'm falling in love with him."

"Don't come crying to me when he finds out the truth," Carla said as she disappeared down the hall. "I wash my hands of the whole matter."

Allison didn't chase her. Didn't demand to know answers her mother wasn't ready to give. But she did revel in the clarity of thought she had. She felt like a veil had been lifted from her eyes and she was finally seeing everything for what it really was.

And she knew exactly what she needed to do about it.

**WANT TO GO OUT TO DINNER?**

Benny stared at his phone in shock. Ally never made the first move. Ever. And after last night, he was starting to lament that she would be willing to shift at all. During their time together, she had come out of her shell and broken free from her stoic facade, but she seemed unwilling to walk away from the biggest problem of all.

Her mother and her makeup.

Most people wouldn't know it, but Benny was fairly good at reading people. It's what made him so good at pushing buttons without having to deal with consequences. His goofy behavior, however, usually kept people from realizing that he could do so.

Makeup and her piano might be what Ally used to hide from the world, but it was her mother who created that need in the first place. Not the bullies, not the looks from strangers, but her mother. For some reason, she felt the need to hold her daughter back. She kept Ally on a tight leash that kept her from not only experiencing life, but thriving like the wonderful woman she was.

So to have Ally *asking* for a date told him something had happened. Usually he spent a good chunk of their time together trying to undo whatever Mrs. Mayer had done while the two women were home together.

**You want to take me on a date? I'm flattered.**

He held the phone, anxious to see her response.

**Hardy har har. :) I guess I figured it was my turn to pay.**

Ooh, that was tempting. Benny never turned down free food. Though he hadn't exactly been worried about how often he took Ally out either. Spending money on her had been surprisingly enjoyable, which seemed completely at odds with his normal tendency to mooch.

**Can't turn that down. I always have time for a beautiful woman.**

She sent a heart emoji back and Benny stuffed the phone in his pocket before continuing with his mail delivery. If there was a pep in his step or his whistling was a little louder than usual, he was just fine with that.

He'd been so worried after the other night, feeling discouraged and concerned for Ally, and now it looked like things were going to turn out all right. It might still be a long time until she was willing to let go of her security blanket, but slowly, Benny was starting to realize that it truly didn't matter.

He had suspected for a while, and with the way this morning's news made him feel, he was even more certain that he was falling in love with the beautiful Ms Mayer. When one tiny text was enough to brighten his day and put a smile on his face, there was no way to deny that he had fallen.

And now that he had something to look forward to after work, he might as well pick up his pace and go see her as soon as possible.

He was still floating on air when he walked up her front stoop later that evening. His collar was freshly ironed, thanks to Mel, and the bouquet he had in his hands was hand-created by Rose, who assured him that the lilacs and primroses were exactly what he needed to say "beginning of love".

Benny knocked on the door, then put the flowers behind his back. He didn't want Mrs. Mayer to give him a hard time about them.

It wasn't Mrs. Mayer who answered the door, however. Ally came out, her hair covering her face as she looked at the ground. "Hey," she said breathlessly, a slight tremble in the tone.

Benny frowned. "Hey." He tried ducking his head to look at her, but she turned away, making a show of carefully closing the door. Then she spun, keeping her back to him, and began to walk down the sidewalk.

It took Benny a split second to follow. She was trying very hard to keep her face from him and it made his mind wander into all sorts of ugly scenarios. "Ally." He lightly gripped her upper arm and pulled her to a stop. "What's going on?" He stepped up to her side, but she once again ducked her head. Geez, how much hair did this woman have?

"Nothing," she said softly. "Let's just go."

He shook his head, though she couldn't see it. "No. Not until you tell me." His breathing picked up and red crowded his vision. "Did she hit you?" he ground out. It was the only thing he could think of. Mrs. Mayer, thus far, hadn't been physically abusive, at least as much as Benny had uncovered. Her usual source of attack was words, but with Ally starting to stray outside the boundaries, it was possible it had sent the woman over the edge.

"What? No!" Ally's head jerked up, her eyes wide and her mouth open in shock. "How could you even ask me that?"

Benny should have answered, but he was too busy staring. *She did it. She broke free.* He had no excuse for why his fingers were shaking when they came up to touch her red cheek. "Ally," he breathed.

She winced ever so slightly when his hand brushed her skin and he paused, giving her time to adjust.

When her eyes came back to his, they were scared, but determined and she slowly, painstakingly tilted her head until they touched.

Benny wanted to close his eyes and soak up the pride that was soaring through him at the moment, but she more than likely wouldn't understand just how big her trust made him feel. Instead, he stayed focused on her and stepped a little closer. His hand cupped her birthmark and he let his thumb brush against her cheekbone. "You. Are. So. Beautiful," he rasped, his voice low and gravelly.

If he had had any doubt about his growing feelings before, there was none now. Even with half of her face a dark, wine-colored red, this woman was the most stunning thing he had ever seen. Gone was the icy wall that kept her safe, and in its place was warmth, kindness, and a hint of shyness. All the things that had been waiting for an opportunity to break free.

Soon his thumb was wiping away tears instead of caressing soft skin and he couldn't help but pull her in close. His arms wound around her and she folded into his chest with a sob. The flowers fluttered, forgotten, to the ground.

"Thank you," he whispered into her hair. "This is the greatest gift anyone has ever given me."

Her hands tightened on the back of his shirt, creating wrinkles his sister had worked so hard to get rid of, but Benny didn't even notice. His hand rubbed up and down her back as she cried. "Shh..." he whispered. "I've got you. It's all going to be okay."

He was determined to make sure his words came true. Ally was his. She owned him heart and soul, and now that she was finally willing to give herself in return, Benny was determined not to take that gift for granted.

If there was one thing having his friends all get married first had taught him, it was that once you had a good thing, you cherished it.

His arms tightened around her. He planned to cherish this one for the rest of his life.

# CHAPTER 21

"Benny," Allison said breathlessly. "Benny!"

"Hmm?"

She laughed at his distracted tone. Though she couldn't blame him. She was having a hard time keeping her head herself. After holding her until she was done crying, Benny, in true Benny form, had whisked her down the street, tucked her into the first alcove he'd found, and proceeded to smother her with kisses.

Every inch of her face, especially the birthmarked side, had been taken care of, and she was glorying in his attention. His response to her makeup-free face had been more than she could have hoped for.

It had taken great self-control to keep from reaching for her foundation when she was in the bathroom getting ready for her date. More than once she'd reached out, only to stop herself at the last moment.

When it had been time to open the door, however, she'd lost her nerve and let her hair cover her face. Luckily, Benny hadn't been willing to allow her to hide and had pushed until he'd figured out what was going on.

"I said I would take you to dinner," Allison whispered.

"Dinner can wait." Benny brought himself back to her lips and commandeered them for several minutes before Allison forced herself to step back.

She held up a hand to keep him from following, but the playful gleam in his eyes said he wasn't going to be deterred for long. "Now hold on," she said, catching her breath. "I thought I was the one in charge tonight."

"You can be in charge later," he said, stepping up so her hand landed on his chest. Then he leaned closer. "Right now I think it's best if I keep things moving."

"We're not moving at all," Allison said, desperately trying to hold back a grin. "We've been in the same spot for who knows how long!"

Benny nodded, one side of his mouth quirking up. "Are you telling me you haven't enjoyed our time together?"

"No," she said, shaking her head. "But I'm afraid if I stay in this alley with you too much longer, I'll completely lose all rational thought."

Lunging to the side to avoid her arm, Benny caught her around the waist and pulled her in tight. "Thank heavens for that," he said right before kissing her again.

Finally giving up, Allison flung her arms around his neck and quit trying to stop the emotional wave that was drowning them both. She definitely should have learned by now that Benny wasn't one to be controlled. And since she had spent too much of her life being controlled, Allison decided it wasn't worth the effort.

*Might as well relax and enjoy.*

When Benny finally pulled back on his own, neither of them could breathe very well. "Your lips are going to be raw if I keep this up," he said, tracing her mouth with his finger.

Allison shivered at the touch. Would it ever get old? The way he made her feel? What if she and Benny broke up? Would someone else's touch do the same? So many questions, and so few answers. Only time would answer them for her.

"They already are," she said with a huff.

He grinned. "Yeah...they're a little swollen as well." He gave her a quick peck. "You look like you've been thoroughly kissed." His grin grew. "Makes a man proud."

Allison slapped his shoulder. "Are you telling me that you've essentially marked me?"

Benny shrugged, completely unrepentant as usual. "I need every man in that restaurant to know you've been taken." He stepped back, bringing her palm to his lips. "Now they will."

Allison closed her eyes and shook her head. "You're incorrigible."

Benny tilted his head forward. "Thank you."

"It wasn't a compliment."

"It was if I take it that way." With a wink, he took her hand and started walking them back out to the main street. "Where did you want to eat tonight?" he asked as they joined the masses once more.

Allison swallowed hard when she noticed a few people do double takes. Benny's response had been the stuff of dreams, but now the general public was seeing her and already she could feel her euphoria fading.

"Ally?"

"Hm?" She snapped her head in his direction.

"Where did you want to eat?" He was frowning, and his eyes were watching the people around them.

*He has to see the gawkers.*

There was no way to hide him from what was going on. At least no one had bothered to say anything yet. Stares she could work past...she hoped...but when people began asking questions, it got a lot harder.

"Uh...the cafe is fine," Allison said, fighting the urge to duck her face into his shoulder.

Benny tugged her a little close and wrapped his arm around her shoulders. "The cafe it is," he said, his tone cheerful, but slightly forced. He leaned down just a little. "Ignore them, sweetheart. You're beautiful. And we both know my opinion is the only one that matters."

She gave him a strained smile, but didn't answer. Benny's opinion might be one of the most important, but nobody wanted to walk around being stared at like a freak. It was starting to feel like middle school all over again.

A small trickle of fear worked its way down her spine, but she did her best to shake it off. It was just new. She'd never gone without makeup before. People would get used to her.

Tilting her chin in the air, Allison tried to convey confidence with every step. She was an adult now, it was going to be okay. She could handle this.

Benny pulled open the front door of the restaurant and Allison thanked him before stepping inside.

"Hi! How many?" The hostess froze once she looked up from her planning board. "Oh, hey...Benny...Allison." Sarah's eyes dropped, but kept darting up to look at Allison as if she couldn't quite control herself. "Table for two?"

"Please." Benny's voice was sharp and Sarah winced just a little.

Biting back her own emotions, Allison rested a hand on his arm. *She's young,* she reminded herself. *She's never seen me like this. The second time will be easier.*

"Holly, can you take care of these two?" Sarah kept her head down, refusing to look at all now.

Allison once again pushed away the hurt. She could do this. She could. If Benny could see past it, surely the others could as well.

ANGER AND BENNY WERE not close friends, but they were becoming bosom buddies tonight. He could hear the murmurs running through the restaurant as they walked to their table. Didn't people have anything better to do than gossip about a woman? If the chatter had been about how beautiful she was, he would have strutted her around like a prize peacock, but with each random word he caught, he realized no one seemed concerned about her beauty...or her feelings.

His scowl grew deeper and deeper as the words seemed to swirl around him, clogging his brain and ears. It was claustrophobic.

A hand on his arm caught his attention and Benny felt some of the anger drain away. "Benny," Ally whispered, her eyes darting between the girl seating them and him. "Let's sit down, huh?"

With a curt nod, he held out Ally's chair while the hostess scurried away. This was a far cry from how Benny was usually welcomed in this place and it made him embarrassed for the people running it. Hadn't they ever seen someone with a birthmark before? Granted, Ally's was large and prominent, but still...

"Benny," she hissed, reaching across the table from where he'd sat down. "Please."

He blew out a breath and pushed a hand through his hair. "I'm sorry." His chin hung down to his chest. "I'm just frustrated for you. Is this really what happened when you were a kid?"

Ally bit her lip and shrugged. "I was a child, so I didn't notice all the whispers, but I remember the pity. That was always there."

"Are you okay staying here?" He reached out and took her hand, chafing it between his own. "We don't have to stay."

Ally took a deep breath and straightened her shoulders. "I made the choice to do this. I...I don't want to go back to the way things were." Her eyes grew misty and Benny abruptly stood up, scooting his chair over so he sat at her side rather than across from her.

He rested his hand on her leg. "I am so proud of you," he whispered. "We'll do this together, okay?"

"Okay."

Benny gave her a quick kiss on the temple and then went back to his menu, trying to pretend that there weren't whispers filtering through the restaurant. Although his eyes moved along the words, his mind was somewhere else.

How could he fix this?

He was the one who had convinced Ally to come out without makeup, and he felt responsible for what was going on. How could he help make it better? He didn't want her hurting and he didn't want her to have to be brave. She had a right to a comfortable, pleasant life the same as everybody else.

"What happened to her face?" The child's voice was louder than every other person present. So was the subsequent shushing that came from her parents. "But what was it, Mama?"

Ally stiffened at Benny's side.

"She's just a kid," Benny whispered.

"I know that," Ally snapped back.

Crud. This wasn't how this was supposed to go.

"Does it hurt?"

Benny squeezed his eyes shut. He was normally very tolerant of little children, especially considering that he liked to act like one himself, but today he just wanted that little girl to be quiet. Let her take her curiosity somewhere else.

"Can I ask her?"

"Madeline, stop!" a woman hissed. "Leave it alone."

Benny's eyes popped open. He had an idea. "Ally, sweetheart..." He stood and grabbed her hand. "Come with me."

Ally pulled away when he tried to pull her to her feet. "What are you doing? I told you we could stay and eat."

Benny shook his head, smiling broadly. "I just figured it out." He leaned in closer. "They're all just curious. If you just went and talked to that little girl, everything would be all right."

Her eyes widened and she leaned away from him. "You're kidding, right?" Her voice shook ever so slightly. "Please tell me you're kidding."

"No." He shook his head adamantly. "I mean it. They're just curious. We can go speak to the little girl and everything will be fine. I know it."

Those big, dark eyes filled with tears. "Don't do this, Benny," she warned. "It won't help."

"But it will!" He grabbed for her hand again, not paying any attention to the fact that the entire restaurant was now watching them. He knew, in his heart of hearts, that if they just assuaged the curiosity, it would all calm down. Ally just needed to speak to the girl. Little children are way more forgiving than adults, so if the girl was okay with it, he knew the adults would follow. But first they needed to confront her. "Come on, sweetheart. I'll be right with you."

"Benny," Ally warned one more time, standing up from her seat and backing up. "I said no."

"And I said it will help." He gave her his most charming smile. His enthusiasm overrode everything else to the point that he didn't see the hurt flash across her face.

"So my mother was right," Ally whispered thickly.

Benny paused in trying to grab her arm. "Excuse me?"

"She said if I showed you my face, the first thing you would do was try to show it off, so people could make fun of me." She was trembling even as she straightened her shoulders and stuck her chin in the air.

"You've got to be kidding!" Benny nearly shouted. "I am nothing like your horrible mother." A loud gasp rang through the room. "I have done nothing but try to help you see what life is really like. Your mother is doing her best to keep you under her thumb." His earlier frustration was back and it began to boil over. This was not how it was supposed to go. They'd had such a promising start to the evening. He was going to confess his love. He was going to ask her to be his girlfriend. He was going to...

"My mother has spent her life protecting me," Ally defended. Her face crumpled. "From these exact type situations!" She whipped her head around to look at the restaurant and almost to a person, every adult turned away, like she was some kind of abomination or something.

It only added to Benny's anger. He felt out of control now. He wasn't used to dealing with such intensity in his emotions and everything around him was triggering it. "Come on," he said tightly, holding out his hand. "Let's take this somewhere else and we'll work it out."

Ally shook her head. "No. I'm going home."

Benny froze. "Home?"

"Yes. I'm going home and..." She took in a shuddering breath. "I never want to see you again." Her eyes roved the restaurant again. "Any of you."

His feet were frozen to the spot as she fled the small cafe. As soon as the door closed behind her, all eyes moved to him, but Benny still couldn't move.

Sarah walked up, wringing her hands. "Benny, I'm sorry. We didn't mean to—"

Benny shook his head. He felt cold. So very cold.

A soft whimper could be heard behind him and it caused Benny to turn around.

"I didn't mean it," the little girl cried into her mother's neck.

"I'm sorry," the woman mouthed to Benny. Her own eyes were wet.

Benny had no words. For a man who usually had more to say than he should, he finally found himself voiceless. With a short nod, he stormed outside. He probably should go after Ally, but right now he was too angry. They both needed to calm down, and then they could figure this out. He still felt certain she was part of his future. But how to convince her of that?

# CHAPTER 22

Allison could barely see as she stumbled home. The walk, which had only taken fifteen minutes earlier, now felt like an eternity. How could this have happened? How could her mother's words have been so prophetic?

Benny's response to her makeupless face had felt like a dream come true. He'd held her, kissed her, made her feel as if she truly was beautiful and the red half of her face didn't matter.

Then with one little suggestion, it had all fallen apart. How could he think that talking to the very people who were staring at her like some circus act would help things? They weren't just curious. She'd experienced this before. The murmurs and gossip always preceded the hatred and bullying. And Benny had wanted her to go right into the middle of it!

What happened when the little girl cried at Allison's approach? Or spoke about how ugly her skin was? What then?

Allison shook her head, dislodging some of the tears she had been fighting. Her nose began to run and she left all propriety behind when she wiped it on her sleeve. Her mother would be appalled.

Her mother.

Allison almost stopped at the thought of facing her mother. She would have to admit to her mother that she had been right. That Benny had only been looking for a chance to throw her to the wolves.

Her heart squeezed, and Allison had to stop just walking in order to concentrate on breathing. In and out. In and out. The oxygen moved from her lungs to her nose and back, but never seemed to bring her any relief. She still felt as if she would pass out at any moment. The world was closing in and her vision was growing dark.

How could she have been so foolish yet again? Didn't she learn her lesson when she was younger? Her mother had tried to protect her, tried to warn her, tried to convince her that Benny would only break her heart, and now he'd done it.

She stumbled to her knees, still gasping for air. The concrete bit into her skin through her thin pants. It was all so unfair. It wasn't like she had any control over how she'd been born.

"Miss, are you all right? Miss?"

Allison glanced up from under her lashes, not recognizing the concerned citizen who was addressing her. "I'm fine," she rasped. "Just need to breathe for a second." She made sure to keep her hair over her face. Another riot was going to be too much.

"How can I help?"

*By leaving.* The words were on the tip of Allison's tongue, but she wanted as little attention as possible and shouting would cause the exact opposite. Instead, she shook her head and waved the person off.

It took them a moment, but finally their feet disappeared from view and Allison forced herself to climb to her feet. She knew just one more minute down the boardwalk, she would find a bench. There she could ingest all that had happened without worry about people stopping. People sat on benches all the time.

It seemed like far longer than a minute, but finally Allison was able to collapse on the bench. She leaned forward, hiding her face and trying to mask her sobs. So many emotions. Life had been so much easier when she'd been filled with ice. When she'd been numb to the normal sensations of life.

She put a fist against her heart. How could it go on beating when every dream she'd begun to form had just been shattered? Dark, horrible thoughts, ones that were terribly reminiscent of her mindframe as a young twelve-year-old, began to swirl.

*You'll always be a freak.*

*How can you face anyone in this town again after today?*

*Your students will cancel and soon you'll have no one.*

*You scare small children.*

Squeezing her eyes tight, Allison pressed her palms into them. "No," she said hoarsely. "No. Not again."

She couldn't. She wouldn't. This was hard and it felt like she was being broken in two, but if there was anything Allison had learned through years of therapy and a lifetime with her mother...it was that she could survive.

She might not be happy. She might not have anything to look forward to. She might not smile again for the rest of her life, but she could definitely *survive.*

Gripping the bench on either side of her, she forced her breathing into submission. Her chest physically hurt, but Allison pushed past the pain. Breathe in, breathe out. Repeat. At first, that was all that mattered. Once she had a handle on that, she closed her eyes and began, one by one, to stuff every outrageous, out of control emotion back into the iron trunk they had come from.

She imagined herself folding them like a freshly laundered towel, then squishing the lid closed and securing it with a padlock. The key was thrown into the abyss of her mind, hopefully never to be seen again.

She could feel them pounding against the lid, aching, straining to be released, to overwhelm her once again, but Allison locked her knees and stayed strong.

She didn't need anybody.

She didn't need her mother.

She didn't need Benny.

She didn't need friends.

She didn't need support.

Surviving meant taking everything one step at a time and not letting anything get in her way. She had already walked away and broken up with Benny. That was step number one. The second was to return home.

After that, she and her mother would talk and Allison would admit she was wrong. She knew she would have to brace herself for the conversation, but once it was over, they could move on.

And if it wasn't too late, they could move on to a brand new town and a brand new job. Up to Washington where no one knew about her face and she could go back to hiding who she was.

That's it. That would be her life. Cold, but survivable.

She stood, her knees trembling just the slightest amount. With a sniff, she wiped her face, hiding the evidence of her emotions and put her head high. Who cared if anyone saw her face while she walked home? She wasn't going to be around enough to suffer any true repercussions.

Soon this town and *all* its inhabitants would just be a distant memory.

BENNY NEARLY TOOK DOWN Ally's door when he finally arrived. He'd walked around for nearly an hour trying to expel the panicked and angry energy inside of him, but it was still thrumming through his veins. Despite that, he knew he couldn't wait any longer to see her. They needed to talk and he needed to apologize. He'd pushed too hard, not listened to her boundaries or choices.

They could try again. This time he would wait for *her* to make the first move. If she didn't want to see people. Fine. If she didn't want to talk to people. Fine. If she wanted to wear makeup. Fine. He would go along with anything, just as long as she stayed in his life.

"What do you want?"

Mrs. Mayer's sneering tone was definitely not what Benny had been hoping to hear. "I need to speak with Ally," he said.

"*Allison* isn't here." Mrs. Mayer tried to shut the door, but Benny put his hand out.

"What do you mean she's not here?"

The older woman glared hard enough to melt him, if such a thing were possible. "I mean exactly what I said. She's not here." Pausing, she pushed the door open a little. "She left to be with you." Her hand went to her hip. "Why isn't she with you?"

Shame, hot like molten lava, poured through him, souring his stomach. "We...had an argument," he said as carefully as possible. "She ran off and I came to talk to her."

Mrs. Mayer snorted. "Good. Maybe she'll finally figure out where she belongs."

"And where is that?" Benny snapped. He was feeling so out of character tonight. He hadn't been this angry in years, and now he couldn't seem to calm down. "In your house? Under your control?"

"I have spent my entire life trying to protect her," Mrs. Mayer argued back. She stepped into the doorway, her presence pushing him back a couple of steps. "That's more than I can say for you."

"You've spent your whole life profiting off her," Benny shot back. "You've kept her under lock and key, forcing her to perform when she hates it. Living off her teaching instead of getting a job of your own. You're terrified that your meal ticket is going to leave and you'll finally have to take care of yourself!"

Instead of looking offended, Mrs. Mayer looked amused. "You think you know what goes on in this house?" She cocked a hip and folded her arms over her chest. "If I didn't take care of my daughter, no one else would. She's a total head case. Not only is she scarred for life, but she struggles with mental illness." One eyebrow went up. "Didn't know that, did you?"

Benny forced himself to stay still. What exactly was the woman talking about? She spoke in lies and riddles and he wasn't sure what to believe.

"Did she tell you that she tried to commit suicide when she was twelve?" Mrs. Mayer smirked as if she had won. "She was in therapy for years. I knew then that if I didn't take care of her, the world would let her die." She poked one finger into her own chest. "Without me, that girl would be useless. I gave her everything. A career. Notoriety. A path to taking care of herself, feeling useful."

"What you gave her is a complex that she will never be enough," Benny argued back. "You never listened to what she wanted, only pushed your own agenda." He leaned in and dropped his voice. "You gave her everything but what she most needed. Love."

He would never admit that he had done the same. At least he was trying to apologize and fix it. Mrs. Mayer only wanted to continue to exploit it.

"Oh, really? And you think you can offer her that?"

"Yes."

Mrs. Mayer threw her head back and laughed. "We all know you're the town comedian," she managed when her humor died down. "Good to know you're keeping up with the talent."

"This isn't a joke," Benny said tightly, his hands clenched into fists. "I love her and I refuse to let you hurt her anymore."

Mrs. Mayer's face looked like the cat who ate the canary. Her eyes glanced around his shoulder. "Well, now...it doesn't look like I'm the one who has been doing the hurting."

Benny spun and winced when he saw Ally walking up the sidewalk. Her entire body was stiff and proper, and he had a deja vu moment of when they first got to know each other. "Ally," he said, holding out his hand in supplication. "We need to talk."

"Mr. Frasier," she said in clipped tones. Instead of taking his hand, she walked right past him and into the doorway.

"Ally, please!" Panic was starting to replace his anger. How could she walk away so easily? She felt something for him, he knew it.

Slowly, she turned around. "My name is Allison."

"No." Benny shook his head. "You're Ally. That's who you're supposed to be and my stupid behavior tonight won't change that." He took a deep breath. "I love you. I came to apologize and admit how wrong I was so we can work this all out."

He could see her body starting to shake only to have her muscles grow tighter and tighter in an effort to contain the show of emotion. A vein in her neck pulsed so hard Benny worried it would burst through the skin.

"Please come speak with me." Once again he held out his hand.

Ally didn't move. Her face grew red and he could see the battle inside her gaze. Frantically, he prayed that she would give in. That she would open up to him once more.

"She doesn't want to speak to you," Mrs. Mayer interrupted. She angled her body in between Ally and himself, creating a human wall. "I think you need to leave now."

Benny shook his head yet again. "Not until she speaks to me."

"Didn't you always say it would be my choice?"

Ally's words were barely audible, but they forced Benny to pause. "Of course."

Two heartbeats went by before she spoke again. "Then I *choose* not to speak to you." Clasping her hands in front of her, she turned and disappeared into the house.

Benny couldn't move. It was just like at the restaurant. He was cemented to the floor in shock and his words failed him once more.

Mrs. Mayer stepped back through the door, keeping her eyes on him as she reached for it. "It looks like you have your answer," she said smugly, shaking her head with a little victory movement. "Good night."

The door slammed straight in his face, but Benny still took several seconds to move. All the anger that had been boiling through him before had turned to dark despair.

The man who once made fun of his friends for falling in love had finally experienced his own bliss, only to have it ripped away, taking the most important pieces of himself with it.

He wasn't sure how he got home that night, but no matter how long he lay in bed, sleep refused to come. His entire body ached, like when he caught the flu and his heart felt as if someone had tried to carve it out with a spoon.

Rolling to his side, he stared into the darkness, one question pounding over and over again through his brain.

*What have I done?*

# CHAPTER 23

*If I don't argue, it'll be over soon.*

Allison told herself that over and over again while her mother paced and ranted in front of her. It had been going on for a half an hour, ever since Benny left, and Allison prayed it wouldn't last much longer. Surely her mother would run out of steam eventually.

"When I think of all the times I warned you..." Carla trailed off, her shoulders slumping. She rubbed her forehead. "We could have avoided all of this, if only you'd learn to listen."

*I have listened!*

No matter how hard she tried, Allison couldn't seem to quiet the little voice inside. The one that rebelled against her mother's strict rules. The one that Benny's boldness had brought to life and nurtured with every charming smile, every flirty wink, and every toe-curling kiss.

She had managed to keep the voice from being spoken out loud, but that part of her seemed to have a mind of its own. It didn't want to go in the trunk she had stuffed the rest of her life into. It refused to be quiet and it refused to be hidden. Benny's interference had led Allison to feeling like she had seen the sun for the first time ever, and now she couldn't quite get herself to turn her back on it.

"After everything I've done...all I've sacrificed..."

"And just what have you sacrificed, Mother?" Apparently, she couldn't keep the voice in her head either.

Carla spun, her jaw dropped. "What?"

Slowly, Allison stood from her seat. "Please, enlighten me, since you haven't done so a million times during my life, just what it was you gave up all because I was born with a birthmark on my face."

Carla folded her arms over her chest and huffed. "You simply wouldn't understand," she argued.

"Wouldn't understand?" Allison stepped forward. "What wouldn't I understand? What it's like to be lonely? What it's like to not have fun? What it's like to be friendless? What it's like to be an outcast? Or to be called a freak?" Her eyes were swimming again, but Allison ignored the tears. It was finally time for her to stand up for herself, against her mother and Benny.

Carla shrunk back. "I gave up everything for you," she said hoarsely.

Allison shook her head. The memory of her mother's shaking hands was vivid in her mind. "No. I don't think you did. I think your body gave up and you used me to make up for it." Allison laughed darkly. "After all, I was the perfect candidate, wasn't I? A shy, quiet girl with a talent for music and a birthmark that made it difficult to make friends." She slowly moved her head back and forth. "And when your own career fell apart, you used *me* to try and get back on top." Pushing her hand through her hair, Allison walked away, her back to her mother. "Only it didn't work, did it?" She faced her once more. "Because I wasn't as driven as you were. I didn't want the limelight." She took a couple of steps in her mother's direction. "All I wanted was a peaceful existence with a loving family, a couple of good friends, and the opportunity to share music with children."

Walking away again, Allison realized all the red flags she had been ignoring for so long. How did she not see? "But you refused me all those things." She faced her mother once more. "You were so desperate to be seen that you played on my own insecurities until I nearly killed myself as a child. A child!" she cried. Her hands were fisted and an unknown rage sought to drown her in its depths. "When you should have comforted me at the loss of my friends and the bullying at school, you instead used it to help you control me. You broke me down further, until I no longer had a desire to live. Until I thought the world would be better without me."

Her chest was heaving with emotion at this point. The trunk she had so carefully locked had busted open, spilling everything into one chaotic dump. Her pain, her loneliness, her hope, her anger...and her love for Benny.

Yes, she loved him. And if he was to be believed, he loved her as well. But just like her mother, he had tried to push her into his own agenda, and from this moment on, Allison vowed she would never let someone else do that again.

If there was going to be one good thing that could come out of this, it was that she would rise, like a phoenix from the ashes, and become her own woman. No one was going to tell her who she was or what she could do. No one. Not even the man who owned her heart.

"You made sure to ruin every good thing in my life so that you could try to gain back the career that you could no longer be a part of."

Carla whimpered and shook her head. "It wasn't like that."

"Oh?" Allison's voice was cold and her tears had dried up. "Then tell me, what was it like? When did you get the news?" She tilted her head. "What was it? Arthritis? A nerve disease?"

In that moment, while watching Carla shrink into herself, her darkest secrets finally brought to light, Allison found herself feeling sorry for the woman. She looked fragile and broken, and pitiful.

"I just wanted to be the best," Carla whispered thickly, sinking into the couch. She looked at her hands, which were more bent than Allison recalled them being. "I could have been the best. But as soon as my diagnosis came out, they dropped me faster than a hot poker." She scowled. "As if I hadn't spent years climbing the charts. Years catering to their every whims." She looked up, tears glistening in the soft lamplight. "And then your father decided he had no need for a wife who was a has-been." She sniffed and wiped at her face. "It was just after he left that I found out I was pregnant."

Allison didn't bother to address the lies her mother had told her over the years. The ones that Carla had told about it all being Allison's fault. It wasn't worth it at this point. Her father was just as shallow as her mother, and that she had already known. All she knew for sure was that she wanted out.

Marching to her room, she stopped in the hall closet to grab her suitcase.

"What are you doing?" Carla screeched.

"I'm leaving," Allison said. She opened the suitcase on her bed and began putting her clothes inside. "What I can't carry tonight, I'll come for as soon as I can."

"You can't leave! Who will pay the rent?"

Allison turned to look at her mother. "Arthritis or not, you are perfectly capable of paying your own bills from here on out. I'm done."

"But...the job! At Eastern! What will I tell them?"

"What you should have told them from the beginning," Allison said coolly. "That I'm not interested." She tossed a few toiletries on top of the clothes and zippered it shut. Holding the handle, she turned to look one more time at her mother. "Again, I'll be back to pick up the rest of my stuff. Goodbye."

Allison's heart banged painfully against her chest as she got in her car and left. She knew, deep down, that she wouldn't be able to leave her mother in a lurch. That wasn't who she wanted to be...it wasn't who she *was*.

But tonight she needed space. She needed time to examine herself and who she wanted to be and what she planned to do with herself. Her mother and Benny would only muddle up her ability to do that.

She backed out into the street and then began driving away from town. For now she would gain distance. Later she would gain perspective. One step at a time.

*I SHOULDN'T HAVE LEFT. Should never have left.*

Benny lay on his couch with his arm over his eyes. It was amazing how he could work so hard for so long to build something and in the span of a few seconds, it could completely crumble.

The last few months with Ally had been interesting and wonderful. At first she'd been something new. Next she had been fun. And finally, he had lost his heart to the shy and struggling woman. So why was he at home, feeling more broken than he ever had before?

Even when his mother had left to go "find herself" in California, he hadn't felt this much emotional turmoil. Ally had somehow burrowed under his skin and he couldn't get rid of her. He did *want* to get rid of her. He wanted her at his side so he could hold and hug and love and encourage.

His ability to read people had completely failed him tonight. Usually he knew when he needed to stop, though he didn't play it off that way. He was known among his friends for pushing boundaries, but he had been so certain that speaking to that little girl would cure everything. His eagerness had led him to pushing Ally past what she could handle, and it had cost him everything.

He groaned and turned his head to the side. Someone needed to invent a cure for a broken heart because it was far and away the worst pain Benny had ever experienced. Ally had been so cold, so controlled. Basically she had gone back to every wall he had broken down.

And it was all his fault.

"Benny?" A knock came at his door. "Benny? Are you in there?"

Benny groaned again. He didn't want to see anyone at the moment. Least of all, Ken.

"Benny! Open up or I'm going to have to do something drastic!" Ken shouted through the door.

Feeling as if he'd been hit by a Mack truck, Benny drug himself off the couch. "I'm comin'," he grumbled. He opened the door, then immediately turned around, not waiting for Ken to enter.

"What happened tonight?" Ken asked as soon as he stepped inside. "We got a call about a disturbance at the cafe and then a concerned neighbor mentioned you were screaming at someone at the Mayer house."

Benny cracked open an eyelid long enough to see Ken standing in his uniform, his hands on his hips.

"I drove by, but it was dark, so I came here instead."

Benny sighed, long and loud. "Nothing happened."

"Eye witnesses would say otherwise," Ken snapped. He pulled out his phone, thumbs hovering over the keyboard. "Better start talking or I'm going to have to take you in."

"Ally broke up with me," Benny whispered hoarsely.

"What was that?" Ken stepped closer.

Benny threw his arm off his face and sat up. "She broke up with me!" he shouted.

Ken stared at him, then his hands slowly fell to his sides. "What happened?" he asked more calmly. "I've never seen you like this."

Benny shook his head. "I'm an idiot. That's what happened." He huffed a sarcastic laugh. "Not that everybody didn't know that to begin with, but it doesn't usually come back to bite me in the backside."

Ken stepped backward until he could sit on Benny's recliner. He stuffed his phone in the pocket of his shirt and leaned forward onto his elbows. "Why don't you start from the beginning?"

"What are you? My shrink?" Benny snapped. He closed his eyes and pinched the bridge of his nose. When was he going to get a hold of himself? This wasn't who he was. He was the clown. The funny man. The one who got along with everyone and made friends with strangers. Drama he was familiar with, but not this dark kind that felt like it was eating his soul.

"No," Ken said softly. "I'm your friend."

Benny fell back against the cushions. "Good to know I have one of those."

Ken rolled his eyes. "You have plenty of those," he said wryly. "Most are just busy at the moment, but it doesn't mean they love you any less."

Benny nodded. "Yeah...I know." He stared at his hands. He'd never thought of them as capable of killing something, but tonight they had killed something beautiful. He wasn't sure he'd ever look at them the same again.

"Benny," Ken encouraged. "Come on, man. Spit it out."

Benny glanced up, feeling thoroughly fatigued. "You really want it from the beginning?"

Ken nodded. "Yep. I'm the only bachelor friend you've got. If anyone is gonna commiserate about lost love with you...it's me."

Benny acknowledged the truth with another nod. "Fine. But remember that you asked for it."

It took close to thirty minutes to spill the whole story and Ken's blue eyes were as wide as dinner plates by the time Benny was done. "You told her to go *talk* to the kid?"

Benny groaned and threw his head back against the cushions. "I know. It seems so stupid now, but I just *knew* that if she could address the child's questions, it would fade into nothing." He raised his head. "The girl wasn't scared, she was interested. I still believe that if Ally had just talked to her, told her about the birthmark, the little girl would have gone happily on her way and the adults would have calmed down." He sat up straighter. "I'm not saying no one will ever say an unkind thing again, but that wasn't what we were experiencing tonight. People stared, not out of horror, but because it was something they didn't see every day."

Ken gave him a disbelieving look. "And you don't think that makes Ally feel like the odd man out? How would you like to be stared at, even if no one is being mean about it?"

"I know," Benny agreed. "I get it. Believe me, I've spent the last hour understanding it more and more, but..." He shook his head. "It doesn't really matter now anyway, does it? She told me she never wanted to see me again."

Ken snorted. "And you intend to obey that directive? Seriously?"

Benny jerked back in offense. "What? Are you saying I don't know how to follow the rules?"

Ken raised a single eyebrow. No words were necessary.

"Okay, fine, I'm not the best person for that, but I'm also not going to push myself on Ally if she doesn't feel the same for me that I feel for her." Benny grimaced. "Even I'm not that desperate."

"You sound it tonight," Ken said.

"I know," Benny agreed. "I suppose everything changes when you fall in love."

"Well." Ken slapped his knees and stood up. "I gotta get back to work."

"What?" Benny jumped to his feet. "You're not going to help me figure it out?"

Ken shrugged. "What's there to figure out? You love her. Go after her."

"But she said to leave her alone."

Ken stepped forward to put a hand on Benny's shoulder. "I'm sure you can figure something out." He chuckled. "In fact, I'm pretty interested to hear what you come up with." Letting go, Ken sauntered to the door. "Oh, and if you need more help, the women are all meeting on Friday for their flower arranging class." He looked over his shoulder. "They've solved a lot of problems around those blooms."

"You just want an excuse to go see Rose," Benny grumbled rudely. He wasn't in the mood to care at the moment.

Ken gave him a mock salute. "Now you see how I'm working to solve my own problems." With a final grin, Ken disappeared out the door, leaving Benny to his thoughts and pain.

Plopping back on the couch, Benny thought about what his friend said. Did he love her? Yes. Did he love her enough to chase her? Yes.

*But what if—*

Thoughts of Ally's smiles, laughter, and kisses pushed against the worry and Benny straightened. Ken was right. If he loved her, he should go after her. He was sure her feelings had been similar to his and he'd be darned if he was going to let that go to waste.

Tomorrow night, with the help of a few select women, Benny was going to hatch a plan. And it was going to be good.

# CHAPTER 24

"Well..." Mr. Mangleson, the Principal of Jacques Cousteau Elementary School, flipped through the papers on his desk once again. "You're more than qualified for the position, Ms. Mayer." He looked up at her, seeming slightly bemused. "I'm not sure I quite understand why someone with your qualifications would be looking to work at an elementary school." He leaned back and took off his glasses. "And in a subbing position that has no guarantee of permanency."

Allison gave the nice older gentleman her best smile. "I've always enjoyed working with children best," she said honestly. "I know I could teach at a higher level, but giving piano lessons out of my home has been one of my favorite jobs. And I'm all right with the job only lasting a few months. At the end of it, if there's no room for me, I'm happy to look around elsewhere."

There was something so nice about small towns. Allison hadn't gone very far when she'd left home two nights ago. Instead, she'd driven until she was tired and had ended up only two towns down from Seaside Bay.

After a good night's rest in a hotel, she'd walked around, enjoying a leisurely brunch and the sound of the sea. No one stared at her or gaped at her face, which of course, had been covered in makeup. She had just been one more body in the crowd. It was lovely.

For the first time ever, she was free to create who *she* wanted to be. And she wanted more than what her mother offered, but maybe a little less than what Benny was pushing for. She wanted to be known for being kind. She wanted to have a few friends, even if she didn't share her whole life story with them. She wanted to have a job she looked forward to. And she wanted to choose each aspect of her life as it came along.

During her walk, she'd picked up a newspaper, something she hadn't done since she was a young child, and sat on the beach reading. A Help Wanted ad had caught her attention.

In a move that had seemed like divine intervention, Allison had stumbled across a long-term subbing position for the music teacher at their local elementary school. Apparently, the one they had was just about to take maternity leave for several months. It had been perfect.

Allison had called and gotten an appointment almost instantaneously. Now she was in the interview, trying to show the principal that she would still be able to teach children, even if her credentials said she was educated enough for adults.

Mr. Mangleson shrugged. "While I worry you're going to find yourself bored, I can't really turn you away either. We haven't had any other candidates for this position, and I really didn't want the children to go without music for half the school year."

Allison did her best not to gloat. She had been counting on them being desperate. She was desperate as well, but was hiding it.

Leaning across his desk, Mr. Mangleson smiled and held out his hand. "Welcome to the team."

Allison let out the breath she had been holding. "Thank you so much, Principal Mangleson. I promise not to let you down."

"See that you don't let the children down and I think we'll be on good terms," he said kindly. His grandfatherly style lent a calmness to the office and Allison guessed that the children loved him just as much as he appeared to love them. She would enjoy working under someone so dedicated to their charges.

She stood, offered her goodbyes once more, and left. Once outside in the semi-sunny day, Allison put her face to the sky and took in a deep, salty breath. This was going to be the start of something good, she could feel it.

Turning to her right, she began walking back to her hotel. Now that she had a job, she needed to find a place to live. Perhaps the newspaper could help with that as well. There had to be a few long-term rentals around the area.

She began to swing her arms as she walked, feeling more carefree and at peace than she had ever been. It wasn't until she climbed the stairs to her hotel room that Allison began to slow down. The hotel was a stark reminder of why she had come running in the middle of the night, leaving behind everything she knew and had once loved.

She locked the door once inside, not willing to take any chances, and then plopped herself on the edge of the bed. Her suitcase sat on a chair, wide open and messy since she'd rifled through everything to find a suitable outfit for her interview this morning. The sleeve of a brown T-shirt poked through the pile of clothes and Allison had to close her eyes to the memories.

She had always thought brown was too dull on her. With her brown hair and brown eyes and lightly browned skin, she felt it made her look monotone, but she still had a few pieces in her wardrobe. The day she had been wearing that T-shirt, Benny had practically accosted her on the sidewalk.

Allison couldn't help the small grin that pulled at her mouth as she thought of him jumping into her personal bubble, completely uncaring as to whether or not she wished to speak to him. He'd made the comment that the brown brought out a golden tone in her eyes. It had caught Allison completely off guard.

A few minutes later, he'd bounded away, disappearing as if he'd never been there in the first place.

Yet somehow, the shirt had become a favorite. And even in her angry state the other night, she had brought it along.

Allison stood up and slowly walked over, picking up the shirt and fingering it gently. She wasn't sad she'd left. She wasn't sad about the new job. She wasn't even sad about having a falling out with her mother. But she was sad about Benny.

If she was being true to herself, Allison knew that she never would have had the courage to leave if it hadn't been for him. He may have gone too far in the end, and she wasn't sure she believed his declaration of love as anything but desperation, but she would always be grateful that he opened her eyes to life outside of her tiny bungalow.

Her mother had a lot to answer for, but Allison wasn't sure she would ever go down that road. She loathed the idea of digging up the past and hurting them both with the lies and suffering both of them had faced.

She dropped the shirt and straightened her shoulders. No. It was better to move forward. There would probably always be a hole in her heart when it came to Bennett Frasier, but she could still live a good life.

She would start her new job next week, and today she would find someplace to live. Once she had a few weeks under her belt, Allison was sure that time would begin to heal her wounds. She would eventually forgive her mother and work to let go of Benny.

It was funny how Benny had been in her life such a short time compared to her mother, yet Allison knew that letting him go was going to be a much harder job than forgiveness.

Apparently when the heart was involved, matters always got complicated.

"YOU DID WHAT?" CARO screeched, jerking upright from where she was leaning against Jack's shoulder.

Benny sighed and deflated in his seat, his chin hanging down to his chest. "I've already called myself every name in the book," he grumbled, forcing himself to look up. "Including a few my mother would have washed my mouth out for, so please...just don't."

Jack squeezed the back of Caro's neck. "Ease up, babe. He knows he messed up."

Caro huffed and folded her arms over her chest. "Good thing, because I'm not opposed to telling you again."

Hadlee cleared her throat. "Can I just make sure I understand everything?"

Benny looked her way.

"Allison has a port wine birthmark that covers half her face." She raised her eyebrows.

Benny nodded. "Yeah."

"You happened to see it one day and decided it would be fun to figure out the story behind it?"

Benny rubbed his chin. "It sounds horrible when you put it like that."

"That was horrible," Mel grumbled.

Benny sighed and pushed his long hair out of his face. "I was bored," he argued. "Bored and lonely, okay? What else do you want me to say? I wasn't planning to hurt her, but it was clear there was a story behind it all. She'd always been so closed off and I got a glimpse of why. I wanted to dig a little."

"Did it never occur to you that there was a reason she was so closed off?" Charli inserted. She put her hand up to keep Benny from replying immediately. "I'm not saying it was completely wrong, but your motivations weren't exactly pure."

Benny fell back into his seat. "I know...but it all changed."

"And you love her?" Hadlee came back into the conversation.

Benny turned toward the scientist. "Yes."

Hadlee smiled. "I hoped you'd say that." She glanced up at Felix, who was brooding as usual. "It's not like all relationships start out on the right foot," she said, her eyes darting around the room.

More than one person shifted in their seat at her words. Many of the couples in the room had had rough patches before they got together. The road to true love was rarely straight.

"I don't know if how it started matters at this point," Hadlee continued. "What matters is what Benny does going forward." She pinned Benny with an intense stare. "What are you willing to do in order to get her back?"

"I have a question."

All eyes turned to Rose, who was sitting next to Ken since he was playing with Lilly. Benny had to admit that they made a striking couple, if only Rose would allow them to be.

"Does Ally return your feelings?" Rose asked, her voice soft. "I'm glad you fell in love, Benny. But I'm not willing to help unless Ally feels the same." She shrugged. "I promise I'm not trying to be mean, but she should have a choice in this."

Benny nodded and pushed his hair back again. "No, you're right. And it's a fair question." He pinched his lips together. "Truth is, I think so, but I don't know for certain." He made a face. "We were pretty...intense before the blow up. I mean, she never backed away or made me feel like my behavior was unwelcome."

"TMI," Caro groaned, throwing her head back.

"I'm not sure what you want from me!" Benny said in a louder than normal tone. "You asked how she felt and I'm trying to explain why I think she feels the same. But the truth is, she never actually said 'I love you'. And the night I said it was the night she broke up with me."

Caro's expression fell. "I'm sorry, Benny. I shouldn't have said that. This is serious and we're here because we love you and want to help." She sniffled. "You've always helped the rest of us, and it's not fair for me to cause trouble."

Benny's eyes widened as crocodile tears began to trickle down Caro's cheeks. "Uh..." he looked to Jack for support.

Jack gathered his wife in his arms and shushed her, then gave the crowd a *What're you going to do?* look. "She's a little...out of sorts lately," he explained.

Mel gasped, her hands going over her mouth. "Is she?"

Jack looked terrified and shook his head.

Mel's shoulders fell and she pouted. "Sorry."

Jensen rubbed his wife's shoulders. "Let's get back to the topic at hand, huh?"

Most of the heads in the room nodded and Rose raised her hand. "Before we all start tossing out ideas, why don't you tell us if you've come up with anything," she said to Benny with a small smile. "You're just about the most creative person I know, not to mention you know Ally the best. How can we help you?"

Benny sat up taller. Rose was right. He had come up with a plan, but it definitely required some work and help from his friends. "I'm not sure how open she's going to be to seeing me," he said, struggling to get the words out. They made his chest hurt just to think them, let alone say them. "So I thought I would do what I do best and recruit all of you to help."

Charli leaned forward. "And just what do you do best, Mr. Mailman?"

Benny grinned. "You just said it, Charli." He winked and leaned back, folding his arms over his chest. "I make deliveries."

"You want to send her mail?" Caro frowned and looked around before coming back to Benny. "Like, mail mail?"

Benny nodded. "Yeah. She can slam the door in my face if I just walk up to see her, or easily ignore a text. But she can't ignore a package. Not when it's addressed to her."

"But what if her mother takes it?" Bronson inserted, speaking up for the first time. "How do you know Ally won't just toss it before opening it?"

"I've got a couple of ways around that," Benny said, leaning forward in his excitement. "But what I really need to know is if you're all willing to do some delivering yourself?" He looked around the room slowly. Every person there nodded and a few even smiled.

Gratitude swelled up inside Benny's chest. This is what a family was. His biological one wasn't perfect, although his sister was pretty awesome. But sometimes, it was the people you met along the way that made all the difference. He had always enjoyed his friends, but now Benny realized they were more than friends and more than just a bunch of married couples he couldn't quite relate to.

He had always used humor and jokes to fit in, but right now, in this moment of clarity, Benny realized it wasn't necessary. Every person was here because of him. Not because of his comedic sideshow, but him. Because they'd formed a group that helped, carried, and supported each other.

It was exactly the type of situation that Ally needed, and Benny grew more determined than ever to see that she got it.

# CHAPTER 25

Allison's smile at the end of the day was tired, but happy. She had just finished her first week of substitute teaching and she knew she had finally found her calling in life. She had loved teaching piano lessons, but this was better. She enjoyed interacting with the children and seeing all their expressions of emotion.

They were so unhindered in their responses to something new and exciting. Their faces lit up. They smiled easily. They laughed even easier. And when they didn't like something, they made no pretense just for manners' sake.

It was wonderful.

*Why didn't I do this earlier?* she mused as she put away the bucket of tambourines and maracas.

*Because you let your mother rule your life.*

The answer was all too easy, but instead of being upset at her mother, Allison found she was angry at herself. She had let one difficult experience overshadow her entire life, and that had led to her mother having more power than she should have had, especially after Allison had become an adult.

Pity trickled through Allison and she sighed, shaking her head. "No more," she promised herself. She hated this line of thinking, but it was difficult to get rid of. She didn't want to be bitter about her childhood or her mother. The woman obviously needed professional help, but Allison also was recognizing more and more that she, herself, needed boundaries as well.

When she was paid, Allison already planned to send some to her mother, helping with the mortgage. And eventually she would go back and visit, doing her best to close the gap she had created when she left. But a little time needed to pass first. Allison wasn't going to go back until *she* was ready, because her wants and needs mattered.

The realization brought to mind the man who had helped teach her that. Yes, he'd messed up, but he was also the reason she had been able to see past her insecurities enough to function. Knees weak, Allison stumbled to her chair. Here was one area of her life that she still wasn't seeing quite as logically.

Funny how she was already working on forgiving her mother for a lifetime of mental abuse, but whenever Allison's mind went to Benny, her body reacted more with her hormones than with her mind.

Her fingers twitched with the desire to touch his too-long hair, or the stubble on his chin. Her cheeks flushed as she thought of his knuckles gracing her cheek, especially her birthmark. Or his hands at her back, pulling her tighter into his chest as his mouth came closer-

"Allison?"

Her eyes shot open to see the PE teacher, John Davis, leaning his shoulder on her doorway. He was a handsome man, probably a year or two older than her, with cocoa-colored hair he kept in a military style buzz cut. "Oh, hi," she choked out, the heat in her cheeks increasing rather than dissipating.

"Hey." John tugged at the collar of his T-shirt. "Uh, how has your first week been?" He sent her a crooked smile. "Obviously the kids haven't eaten you alive yet, so I'm hoping that means you're settling in all right."

Allison laughed softly, grateful no one was capable of reading minds to know what she'd been daydreaming about before John showed up. "Uh, nope. No eating here." Her smile became more genuine. "Actually, I've really enjoyed it. I hope when this is all over, I'll be able to find a permanent position somewhere."

He nodded, jerking on his collar again. "Yeah, that'd be great. I mean, especially if it was in our town."

Allison waited for her heart to speed up, or her blush to become stronger. Or maybe her eyes would want to wander to his lips or muscles...but nothing happened. She had always wondered if her reaction to Benny had been because he was the first man to break through her defenses or because of the man himself. This was her third interaction with John, and with each one, it became more and more clear that Benny had a special power all his own.

"So...I was wondering," John began.

"Ms. Mayer?" The secretary, Mrs. Fields, bustled her way past John. "This just arrived for you."

Allison frowned. "I got a package?" She hadn't even told her mother where she was yet. How in the world could she be getting any mail yet?

Mrs. Fields waved a small, flat box through the air. "Yes! Special delivery." She handed Allison the box and put her hands on her hips. "Gave me a bunch of trouble about signing it, too." She rolled her eyes. "As if we just let strangers wander down the halls here." Shaking her head, she turned and hurried out.

Allison stared at the box. There was no return address, but her name was neatly written and the school's address plain as day.

"Something good?" John interrupted.

Allison jerked her head up. She had nearly forgotten he was there. *I would never have forgotten Benny was close by.* "Uh, I don't know..." She trailed off as her eyes went back down to the box. She wasn't sure why, but Allison had a sneaking feeling in the pit of her stomach that the small, innocuous box was going to contain something she wasn't ready to handle.

"Do you want some privacy to open it?"

Allison looked up again. "You know what? That would be great. Thank you." She didn't notice when he left, but she *was* grateful that it occurred without him once again trying to ask her out. She had just begun to panic when Mrs. Fields had shown up, interrupting the possibility of a date.

John was nice. But he wasn't Benny. And Allison wasn't ready to explore anything other than the real deal yet.

Her fingers shook as she pulled back the brown wrapping paper. No matter how Allison scolded herself, she just couldn't seem to make herself calm down or get rid of the feeling that something was about to happen.

Under the brown paper came a hint of pink. Gasping, Allison ripped the paper and tossed it to the floor. *Sassy Sweets and Cookies* stared at her from the top of the box, the familiar filigree design curling around the corners and causing Allison's eyes to grow misty.

A stretchy gold ribbon was tied neatly around the box and tucked under it was a small envelope. Taking a deep breath, Allison pulled out the envelope and opened it. The tiny card had a bunch of hearts on the front and her own lurched in response. Inside, the handwriting wasn't as clean as on the front of the package, but the message was clear.

**Nothing in this box is as sweet as you are, but I hope it brightens your day.**

**Craving you always,**

**Benny.**

BENNY STUFFED YET ANOTHER card into another envelope and licked another gross glue strip. "Ugh," he grumbled after tossing it in the pile of things to be mailed. He chugged a glass of water. "Pretty soon we'll be able to use my spit to make craft projects."

Ken chuckled. "Well, if I have to tie any more bows, I'll end up giving up my man card."

Benny opened his mouth to offer a funny retort, but he stopped himself. His inability to control himself is what landed him in boiling water to begin with. If he truly wanted Ally back, he was going to have to do better.

"What? No comeback?" Ken said with a grin.

*My friends know me too well.*

"I'm turning over a new leaf," Benny said, grabbing a pen to address the next package to be delivered.

Ken's large hand nearly crushed Benny's shoulder. "That's all well and good," Ken said softly. "But remember that Ally fell in love with who you were *before* the fiasco. Be yourself, maybe just be a better version of yourself."

Benny turned and rested his hip against the kitchen counter. "Wow, that was deeper than I would have expected from a police chief."

Ken grinned, then made a point of looking around. "Don't tell anyone, but I read it in a book."

"The question is, which book?" Benny pressed.

"That *is* the question," Ken said, giving Benny a mock salute.

Benny laughed under his breath. Okay, so maybe he could still joke and have fun, but he wanted to do it in a way that others weren't steamrolled by his actions. He had worked so hard to show Ally she had a choice in her life and in the end, he'd tried to take it away. He would never make that mistake again.

Well...he would *try* to never make that mistake again.

Benny slapped his forehead. Who was he kidding? He was a dork who made stupid mistakes all the time. The best he could hope for was that Ally was willing to accept him, mistakes and all. If he could prove his feelings for her were real and true, hopefully she would do just that.

It had taken him an entire weekend to track her down. After another run-in with Mrs. Mayer at her house when Benny had tried to have the box of chocolates delivered, he had thrown himself into finding where Ally had disappeared to.

He had been driven by a mixture of panic and desperation when he realized not even her mother knew where she was. In the end, she hadn't gone far, but it had been enough to give him a couple of sleepless nights.

After contacting the mail office in her new residence, Benny had gotten to work putting his expertise to work. He had started with a box of chocolates and cookies from Sassy Sweets and Cookies and then the next day, she had started receiving a letter or small gift every hour on the hour.

Benny's eyes darted to his credit card, which was sitting on the counter instead of inside his wallet where it belonged.

*Good thing I've spent years mooching off others, or I wouldn't be able to afford all this.*

"Anything else you need me to do before I leave?" Ken asked, stretching his back with a groan.

Benny shook his head. "Nah. I think I'm good." He turned and grinned. "Besides, Mel is coming over. She's been sick from the pregnancy, so she's not working at the shop at the moment."

Ken nodded and yawned. "Great." He grinned. "Good luck."

Benny had a new appreciation for his friend. It had only been a few days of having to chase Ally, and he already was ready for her to respond. Ken had been chasing Rose for years. Benny could only imagine how hard that was on a man. "Thanks," Benny said, giving a tilt of his chin. "And good luck yourself."

Ken paused, his hand on the doorknob, before looking back. "Is this where I'm supposed to say I'm too charming to need luck?"

Benny chuckled. "Sure. We can go with that."

Ken's smile wasn't quite as warm as usual, but he gave Benny one anyway before slipping through the door.

Shaking his head, Benny went back to his work. He had no idea how long he would need to keep this up before Ally would respond.

*If she responds at all.*

"No," he said out loud. He wasn't going to think that way. He'd messed up. But he was willing to apologize and Benny was positive that if she would just hear him out, Ally would be willing to forgive him.

The only real reason he could think that she would turn him down was if she didn't love him in return. He'd been honest when he'd told his friends he thought she returned his feelings, but without any actual confirmation, it was difficult to keep all the doubts at bay.

"Hey, big bro!" Mel sang as she came through his door.

"In the kitchen," Benny hollered. He watched the entrance for his sister to come back. "Wassup?"

"Not much," she said with a smile, walking over to put her purse on the counter. Her eyes were wide as she looked around. "Wow. You've been busy."

Benny eyed the stacks of mail and packages. "I suppose so."

"Do you think it's going to work?" she asked quietly.

"I think it'll get her attention," Benny said with a laugh. "And if I can get her attention, then I think my manliness will do the rest."

"Oh my gosh," Mel groaned, slugging Benny in the shoulder. "I definitely don't need to hear things like that."

"Oh? Like I wanted to see my best friend and sister making out on the couch while you were dating?" Benny shivered. "I still have nightmares."

Mel's grin grew and she pinched his cheek playfully. "If she doesn't come running after all this, then she's not worth your time."

"Oh, she's worth it," Benny corrected. "That's why I'm doing all this...because she's worth it." He pushed his hair out of his face. "The question is...am I worth her time?"

Mel shook her head. "Nope. Don't go down that road. I know you made a mistake, but we all do." She shrugged. "Jensen actually left me before he came to his senses, so have a little hope, huh?"

Benny checked the wall clock. "She should have gotten another letter five minutes ago."

"Then keep your phone on," Mel said, settling onto a stool. "Because I'm sure you'll hear from her anytime now."

# CHAPTER 26

"Another one!" Mrs. Fields came rushing into Allison's room, waving an envelope in the air. She was grinning so widely that Allison was positive the older woman's face was going to split in two. "How many does this make?" she asked breathlessly.

Allison took the card, unable to stop an incredulous laugh. "This is card number twenty-five."

"And packages?"

Allison sighed and leaned back in her chair. "Maybe...six?"

"First the chocolates and cookies," Mrs. Fields began. "Next, the small glass piano."

"The ingredients for s'mores," Allison continued, the gift reminding her of their time at the bonfire. "A book of love poems."

"And a charm bracelet with a letter charm!" Mrs. Fields clasped her hands and sighed. "This young man of yours is so romantic."

Allison huffed. She couldn't exactly deny that Mrs. Fields was right, but she was slightly irritated too. Allison had left to start a new life so she could live under the radar, until no preconceived notions. Benny was ruining that for her. Though, his persistence in wanting her attention was more than flattering.

His letters had showered her with words of love and adoration, and if she didn't already know that he tended to be on the dramatic side, she would have thought he was making fun of her. But with Benny...it was all or nothing.

It appeared that he was giving her his all.

"Are you going to read it?" Mrs. Fields asked, leaning over Allison's desk.

Allison gave the secretary a tired smile. "I was just about to head home. I'll read it there."

Mrs. Fields huffed and straightened. "Spoilsport." She spun and headed toward the door, waving over her shoulder. "Keep us updated! We have a betting pool among the administration as to how long it'll take you to forgive him!"

Allison's face heated. Some might find that funny, but she wanted nothing to do with being the object of water cooler gossip. Stuffing her things in her bag, including the card, she stormed out of her classroom. She hadn't spoken to Benny since she had arrived in this town, though he had called and texted many times. When the deliveries started arriving, however, his attempt at communication had stopped. Apparently, he was letting the mail do his speaking for him.

It only took her ten minutes to walk to her small cottage. It had been the perfect little place for her to rent, being a second residence on a property owned by a retired couple. The studio was a little side income in their older years and a perfectly quiet and safe place for a single woman to find peace.

As Allison arrived home, however, she began to slow, her eyes widening with each step.

"They started arriving a couple of hours ago," Mrs. Taylor said from behind Allison.

She was too stunned to turn to look at her landlord.

"He must have done something pretty bad," the elderly woman said with a chuckle.

Allison nodded dumbly. She still couldn't manage to look away from the dozens, upon dozens of bouquets nestled on her doorstep. Vases overflowed with every color under the sun and Allison had no idea what to do.

"Well?" Mrs. Taylor had walked up to Allison's side. She nudged her with her elbow. "Go on."

"What am I supposed to do?" Allison asked hoarsely. All the self-righteous anger that she had left school with had drained into nothing. Benny really had gone all out. Vaguely, she wondered how long he would continue if she didn't respond, but in truth, she knew this couldn't go on. She didn't want it to go on. With every card, every gift, every delivery, a little more of her heart slipped away to the man who had stolen it before she'd ever left home.

"I'd start by reading the cards," Mrs. Taylor whispered loudly. She winked, then walked back to her own home.

Slowly, as if afraid that someone would jump out and startle her, Allison walked to the flowers and pulled up the first card. Her fingers shook so violently, she almost dropped the card. Opening it up, she read,

**Yellow roses...friendship.**

She set that one down, took a moment to smell the lovely roses, then reached for the next card.

**Camellia....desire.**

"Oh my..." Allison fanned herself with that card.

**White Cala Lilly...Beauty.**

**Yellow Cala Lilly...Gratitude.**

**Pink Carnation...I will never forget you.**

**Iris...Respect.**

**Red Roses...Love.**

Her pile of cards was growing, but Allison's eyes were too full of tears to read anymore. Sniffling, she sat down on her stoop, wiping at her eyes.

Crunching gravel caught her attention and a presence caught her breath.

"You forgot this one," a deep voice she would know anywhere said from behind a massive bouquet of bright yellow daffodils and tulips.

"Benny..."

He peeked around the flowers. "Hello, beautiful," he said softly.

Allison swallowed hard and rose on shaky legs. "How did you find me?" As soon as the words were out of her mouth, she wanted to take them back. After everything that had happened, that was the first question her brain came up with?

His smile looked tired, but just as brilliant as ever. "I'll always find you," he said in a husky tone.

Allison sat right back down.

Benny walked over, set the arrangement down, and joined her on the stoop. Plucking the card from the flowers, he held it out wordlessly.

Allison couldn't turn away from his bright blue gaze as she took the note.

**Tulips...I'm sorry.**

**Daffodils...A New Beginning...Forgiveness.**

"Oh, Benny," she breathed, laying her forehead against his shoulder.

"I"ve learned a few things in the last few days," he said, resting the side of his head against hers.

"Hmm?" Allison asked, encouraging him to speak.

"First of all, I learned that I'm an idiot."

A soggy giggle slipped free. "That's an interesting thing to learn." She could feel his head nodding.

"It is. But it's also quite enlightening," he said cheerily. "I can blame a lot of behavior on being an idiot."

"I see."

"I also learned that flowers are really expensive."

Allison jerked upright, but his grin let her know he was merely teasing her. *I should have guessed that. He always likes to get a reaction.* "Does this also fall under you being an idiot?" she said in a snippy tone.

Benny shrugged. "I suppose so. Since an idiot does a lot of things other people don't normally do. Like clean out his friend's flower shop all in the name of love."

HE FELT ALLY SIGH AGAINST his shoulder. "Is that really what it was? Or just your insatiable curiosity?"

The words were painful to hear, but Benny couldn't blame her for asking them. After the way he pushed her last week, it probably seemed like he didn't care about her feelings at all. "If I tell you the whole truth, will you promise to listen before you get mad?"

She straightened, lifting her head away, but not looking at him. "That bad, huh?"

Benny took her chin and gently pulled her around until they were practically nose to nose. "The beginning isn't pretty, but the ending can be."

She blinked rapidly, her eyes full of water before pulling loose from his hold. "Might as well share it all. The ugly and the bad."

"The only ugly part of this story is my own intentions," Benny said with a snort. He leaned onto his knees, turning his head her way. "You're just as beautiful as you've ever been."

Ally shook her head and looked off into the distance.

It was time to spill everything and Benny felt his entire body heat up with embarrassment. It was an emotion he rarely felt, and he didn't like it now. "When I first saw you without makeup on, I was kind of in an odd position in life." He hung his head, shame causing his stomach to churn. "I was bored."

There was a pause before Ally scoffed. "That's it? You were *bored*?"

He took in a big breath through his nose and nodded. "Yeah. I hate being bored." He looked at her quickly. "You promised to hear me out."

Ally folded her arms over her chest, but nodded.

"All my friends were getting married and it left me feeling like the odd man out." His gaze fell to the sidewalk. "Not that it's an excuse, but I'm trying to be honest here." He pushed a hand through his hair. "So when I saw your birthmark, I felt as if I had uncovered a mystery." He gave her a half-grin. "You were always so quiet, so stoic. You didn't have any friends and refused to hardly even speak. Learning there was something different behind the mask gave me a challenge."

She pursed her lips and turned away, nodding. "I get it. I do. Thanks for telling me." When she stood to go, Benny grabbed her arm

"I'm not done, Ally," he said softly. "You promised."

She sat down, but angled herself away and it tore at Benny's heart. He was hurting her again and it killed him, but he had to tell her everything. There couldn't be any more secrets between them or their relationship would never survive.

"What started as a challenge soon became something more," he said, his voice growing husky. "The more time I spent with you, the more time I *wanted* to spend with you." He reached out to tuck her hair behind her ear, wanting to see her face.

When she flinched slightly, he dropped his hand. "Watching you begin to step outside of your shell and let yourself truly experience life was amazing, Ally. You're amazing." He leaned closer, but didn't touch. "You're stunningly beautiful. You're strong. You're talented. You're patient and kind."

She shook her head, tears beginning to spill down her cheeks. Finally facing him, her face crumbled. "How can you say those things? I was just a project to you!"

"No." Benny bravely took her face in his hands. "No, you were much more than a project, sweetheart. You were a woman who needed to break free. I just happened to get a glimpse of it before anyone else."

She let go of a choked sob, clutching his shirt. "I let myself fall for you," she said brokenly. "I took off my makeup for you." She turned her hand up, glistening brown eyes meeting his. "I wanted you to see me."

Benny groaned and brought their foreheads together. "I see you, Ally. I was dumb and it took me too long, but I see you. And the day you gave me the gift of seeing you without your security blanket will forever be ingrained in my mind."

"But then you threw me to the wolves." She pulled back, her hands clasped over her mouth as she broke down.

Benny couldn't afford to have her run again, so he wrapped his arms all the way around her. "It wasn't like that," he said hoarsely. "I know it's hard to believe me, but it wasn't like that at all."

Ally just shook her head, wetting his T-shirt with her tears.

"I had it in my mind that I was going to fix it," he whispered, his own eyes filling with tears at the memory. "I just *knew* that if you would talk to that little girl, it would all be over. I was so convinced..." He trailed off, disgusted with his own stupidity. "I didn't understand," he said. "I didn't think about how deeply you were affected by all the stares and the whispers." He waited a beat before forcing the words out of his mouth. "Your mother told me about sixth grade."

Fresh sobs spilled across his neck, vibrating in his chest as her body shook.

Benny ran his hand down her hair, shushing her with soft words of nonsense, until the shaking began to subside. "I promise I wasn't trying to hurt you. I just wanted them to see what I see. I wanted them to see how you are so beautiful that most days I feel unworthy to be in your presence. How your heart, which is better than any other person's I've ever known, had so much capacity to love every child and their horrible piano playing that came through your studio."

A dark laugh filtered into her sobs.

He kissed her temple and spoke into her hair. "I wanted them to see the real Allison Mayer. The one who's been kept hidden all these years." Pulling back slightly, he cupped her face again, wiping at her tears with his thumbs. "The Allison that put up with my stupid jokes and my crazy antics. The Allison that made me care for more than myself. The Allison that taught me what it means to love someone so completely you would do anything just to make them laugh or smile." He gave her a sad grin. "The Allison who made me feel invincible in my own life and yet in awe of who she was and what she could accomplish."

She closed her eyes, a smile mixed with a frown on her face as she shook her head. "That's not me," she insisted.

"It is," Benny said fiercely. "It's absolutely you."

Her eyes opened. "No," she said softly. "It's not. When you came into my life, you turned it upside down and someone new ended up emerging."

Benny held his breath, waiting for her to finish.

"Allison was cold and ruled by her iron-fisted mother. She let fear keep her compliant, assuming the status quo would be fine." Her fingers shook as she pushed his hair off his forehead. "Until a whirlwind forced her to open her eyes to all that she was missing." She gave him a tremulous smile. "And then Ally was born. And she has no desire to go back to who she was before."

"I think the real question is, will Ally ever consider going back to Seaside Bay?" Benny said hesitantly.

"If she had a good reason to." She raised an eyebrow.

"What about love? Is that reason enough?"

Ally leaned forward and gave his chin a small peck. "It's a good start," she whispered.

There was still a lot to talk about and Ally had yet to declare her own feelings in concrete words, but Benny couldn't wait any longer. He brought their mouths together and did his best to convey the sincerity of everything he had just told her. If she didn't come away from his kiss knowing just how much he adored her...then he figured he would need to walk away forever. There would be nothing more he could do or say than show her just how much she was in his heart.

And with the eager way she responded to him, he had a very good feeling that words were going to be completely unnecessary.

# CHAPTER 27

"I'm sorry it's not more," Ally said as she set a plate of scrambled eggs and toast in front of Benny.

He grabbed her hand and kissed her palm, sending a tingle up her arm. "It's more than I deserve. Thank you."

She laughed softly and sat down at her own seat. "I'm not sure how I feel about this serious side of you. It's...different."

Benny nodded. "Yeah, I'll admit, I feel a bit upside down."

Ally stabbed a bite of eggs and put them in her mouth. "In what way?"

He set his fork down and looked at her. "I'm terrified of doing something as stupid as I did before. Getting so caught up in my own wants that I ignore yours."

Ally shook her head. "It can't work like that, Benny. I don't want you to change for me."

"Yet that's exactly what I did to you," he said with a sigh.

Ally shook her head yet again. "No. You didn't ask me to change for you. You encouraged me to learn about myself and become who I wanted to be." She held up a finger when he tried to respond. "If I had said I wanted to teach school, would you have stopped me?"

Benny shook his head.

"If I had said I wanted to chop my hair and dye it purple, what would you have done?"

He reached out and picked up a chunk of her hair. "Buried my face in it for two days and mourned the loss, then let you do what you wanted."

Ally snorted, covering her mouth with a napkin. "You wouldn't have."

His eyes were wide with sincerity when he nodded. "I would. I love your hair."

She smiled. "Good to know, because I have no plans to cut it."

"Thank heavens," he said breathlessly. He put a hand over his heart. "Don't scare me like that."

She laughed. "But see? That's my point. My mother would have argued. Fought. Shamed. Demanded. Generally done anything she possibly could to stop me from making that choice. You would have been sad, but let me make my own choice. There's a difference."

"I suppose, but I still feel terrible."

"Another thing that makes you different," Ally added. "My mother doesn't feel bad about any of this. She used me for her own wants, never once considering that I had a mind of my own."

"Do you think you'll ever talk to her again?"

Ally pushed her eggs around. "I hope so," she admitted in a small voice. "I mean, she's my mother. I don't want to lose her completely, but I don't want her to have any more control over me." She met his concerned gaze. "Does that make me horrible or stupid?"

"Neither." He caressed her cheek. "It makes you normal. No one wants to cut ties with their family if they can help it."

"She needs help," Ally added. "Like real medical help."

Benny stuffed a big bite in his mouth and nodded. "You're right. But how are you going to help her see that?"

"I don't know yet." She glanced down, then back up. "Will you help me?"

His smile was brilliant enough to overpower the sunset. "I'd be honored."

"Good." Ally couldn't stop the contentment that began seeping into her system. And truthfully, she didn't want to. Even in the middle of her pain, her heart had still belonged to Benny. Now that he'd apologized and confessed everything, she found herself eager to resume their relationship and see where it could go.

Never in a million years would she have guessed that she would fall for a guy who loved to laugh and play as much as Benny did. It was what made him, him. And right now, she was seriously missing that side of him. She got that he was sorry for his behavior and she appreciated it, but she wanted her mailman back. But how to go about it?

"What have I missed back in Seaside Bay?" she asked, taking a drink of orange juice.

"Besides me falling apart and fighting with your mom?" He grinned. "Not much."

"I suppose I have only been gone a little over a week," Ally mused. "Not that much could have happened."

"I don't know..." Benny made a point of looking around at all the packages in her rental. "It looks like lots of things can happen in a short amount of time."

"Yeah..." Ally put her chin in her hand, leaning on the table. "How in the world did you accomplish all this?"

"With the best friends in the world," he said quickly. "I couldn't have done it without them."

"And Rose's shop? Is that the one you cleaned out?"

Benny chuckled and rubbed the back of his neck. "Yeah...she's not really happy with me about that."

"I loved it."

His eyes shot to hers. "You did?"

Ally nodded, struggling to keep holding his gaze. His bright blue eyes were so hopeful. "I did."

He leaned in. "I have to admit I'm pretty good at making deliveries. What was your favorite?"

Ally laughed softly, glad to see his sense of humor beginning to emerge. Maybe if she kept him talking, he would eventually relax enough to be the man she fell in love with. "Well, the piano was beautiful, but I have to admit I'm partial to the flowers."

Benny stood up and held out his hand. "Come on," he urged.

Ally frowned, but took his hand and stood. "Where are we going?"

"Life's too short to eat eggs for dinner," he said with a wink. "Let's go get ice cream."

"Ice cream?" Ally couldn't help but laugh some more as he dragged her out the door. "I thought we were talking about flowers."

"We were, and we're not done with that, but we need ice cream in order to fully appreciate the flowers." He kept up a swift pace as they headed into town.

The ocean breeze blew her hair around her back and Ally tucked some behind her ear. "I'm lost. What do the two have to do with each other?"

Benny grinned over at her. "Hang tight and I'll show you."

Ally smiled and happily tripped along in his wake. This. She had missed this. She had missed his excitement and boyish eagerness. She had missed him searching out adventures and bucking the rules. She had missed his smile and the flash of his blue eyes.

She had missed him. Her mailman, her hopeful boyfriend...her future.

"YOU STILL HAVEN'T TOLD me what ice cream has to do with flowers," Ally said as she crunched the last of her cone. They'd walked leisurely back to her rental while they ate their dessert, their entwined hands swinging between them.

Benny laughed. "Nothing. I just wanted ice cream."

She shook her head. "Is it always going to be like this?"

Benny sobered. "I sure hope so." He scrunched his nose. "Is this when we need to have a 'define the relationship' conversation?" He used his fingers to create quotes. Ally seemed to have forgiven him and they had both admitted to their feelings, but what came next?

Were they just going to date? Were they more than that? Was she expecting certain things from him?

Ally's smile stole his breath. "You make it sound like I'm trying to chop your hands off."

"Can you blame me? I wouldn't be able to deliver packages if you did."

She laughed and tucked her feet underneath her. "We don't have to have any conversation, but I think being on the same page would be a good move."

Benny sighed dramatically. "I agree. But first." He pulled her over against his chest, giving her a sweet kiss. "I needed nourishment."

Ally's eyes were shining as she looked up at him. "The ice cream wasn't enough?"

"Nothing is ever enough compared to you," he murmured before going in for a few more seconds. This woman had such a hold on him. He wasn't even sure how it had happened, but he was completely wrapped around her little finger. In other words, he was just as bad as all his friends that he'd been making fun of for months.

"You're such a flatterer," Ally said with a laugh, pressing against his chest to be able to look him in the eye.

"Mailmen don't flatter. We're truth tellers."

"Oh? I didn't know the two go hand in hand," Ally said with a frown.

"Just like ice cream and roses," Benny said, relaxing back on the couch.

"Oh, good heavens," Ally said in a rush of breath. "You're ridiculous."

"Maybe so, but as long as we're defining our relationship, I'm your ridiculous, so there."

She settled her head against his chest, arms wrapped around him. "I'm just fine with that. But it doesn't mean I won't call you out once in a while."

"According to Charli, someone had better or I'll eventually be out of control."

Ally snickered, then sobered. "But seriously. What's next?"

He leaned his head back, closing his eyes and simply enjoying the feel of her in his arms. "More kissing?"

She poked his ribs. "I think we're pretty good at that already."

"There's always room for more practice."

"But what about after the kissing?" she asked.

Benny cracked open an eye. "I suppose the first thing is moving you back to Seaside Bay." He stilled when her face fell. "You don't want to come back?"

Ally drew a random pattern on his sternum. "It's not that I don't want to come back, but I was just hired as a long-term substitute at the elementary school here."

"And?"

Her dark eyes were pleading for him to understand as she looked up from under her lashes. "And I've discovered that I love teaching. I don't want to quit."

Benny nodded, but didn't speak quite yet. He needed to process that. Having her a couple hours away was definitely not the kind of relationship he had in mind. He wanted her around whenever he felt the need to touch, hold, or kiss her. He wanted to take her out for ice cream after work and stop by with her mail, teasing her with more love letters.

None of that was possible if she lived in a different city.

"I think you should finish it out." The words were like ash on his tongue and his chest hurt from saying them. They were a lie. But they were also necessary.

"You do?" Ally jerked upright, leaning away from him. "It doesn't bother you to do the long-distance thing?"

Benny sat up straighter and turned to face her better. Cupping her cheek, he let his thumb roam her skin. "Of course it does. But this needs to happen because you never got that experience," he said softly. "Because as much as I want you close by, you need space to find what works for you and who you are and what you like." He swallowed hard. "Even if in the end, it doesn't mean me."

He was ill prepared to have Ally lunge at him, knocking him off balance and flat on his back. The breath whooshed out of him as she landed on his chest, but soon his breath was gone even further when her mouth landed on his.

His arms wound around her back automatically and he made good use of her attack. What man wouldn't?

"Wow," he said hoarsely when they finally came up for air. "What was that for?"

"I love you," she said fiercely. "I love you so much more than I ever thought possible." Tears filled her eyes as she continued. "I thought I would always be alone. Always be stuck in the dark without ever tasting happiness." She kissed him again. "But you changed all that. And yet even after finding what we have, you're willing to let me go in order to let me grow." She shook her head jerkily. "I don't know if it's possible to love someone more than I love you."

"Oh, it's possible," Benny said softly. Her words touched him more than he'd expected. He hadn't realized how much he needed that confession from her in order to feel whole in their relationship. "Because I love you more."

"Nope. I love you more," she argued.

Benny shook his head. "We're becoming the type of couple that I make fun of."

Ally grinned and waggled her eyebrows. "Oh, how the mighty have fallen."

He grabbed the back of her head and brought their lips right next to each other. "But what a way to go!"

# CHAPTER 28

Ally's heart was nearly choking her. She was sure at any moment she was going to throw up and ruin Benny's shoes. Or maybe her mother's bushes would be better.

"You ready for this?" Benny asked, giving her hand a squeeze.

"Nope. But it's long overdue." Ally raised her shaking hand and knocked. It was the first time she had done so in this house. For years she had lived here, feeling trapped under the wooden shingles. The house hadn't been a happy place unless she was teaching and it made her wonder for the thousandth time what she was doing here now.

"You're amazing," Benny whispered through the side of his mouth. "And beautiful."

Ally couldn't help but smile. He called her that all the time and it was getting easier to hear. The last six months had been wonderful, if a little tiring. She had finished her contract at the elementary school only last week and with Benny's help, she had moved back to Seaside Bay.

During her time away, Ally had sent her mother checks to help with the mortgage and had tried sending a few texts, but for the most part, their relationship had been nonexistent.

Now that she was back and feeling more confident in herself and her place in the world, Ally was ready to confront the one part of her life still left unfinished.

She glanced at Benny, who shrugged. "Maybe she's not home?"

Ally shook her head. "No. She has to be home. Where else would she go?" She knocked again, more forcefully this time.

The door whipped open immediately. "What do you want?" Carla snarled.

If Benny's hand hadn't automatically gone to her lower back, Ally would have backed up at the vitriol in her mother's tone.

"Hello, Mother," Ally said softly.

Hazel eyes, so like her own, glared back. "I have nothing to say to you."

Ally took a deep breath. "Well, that's fine, but I have something I want to say to you."

Carla rolled her eyes. "Unless it's to admit you're wrong and you plan to take that position with the college, I don't see how anything you have to say is worth my time."

Ally knew more than most how much words hurt, and these dug deep. She also knew, from months of spending time with children and a new set of friends, that sometimes people said things they didn't really mean when they were upset. "I love you," she said softly.

Carla opened her mouth, then paused.

"You're my mother, and I will always love you." Ally could hear the tremble in her own voice and it had nothing to do with the chilly spring weather. "But I also am learning to love myself." She gulped. "And because of that, I need to set down some boundaries between us."

"It seems to me your absence these last months has been boundary enough," Carla argued defiantly.

"No. My absence was me taking the time to figure out who I was." She stuck her chin in the air. "Would you like to know what I discovered?"

"No."

"I discovered that I love teaching in a classroom more than I love one-on-one lessons. I love having friends, especially ones who appreciate me for me and not my piano playing skills."

Carla scoffed, but the sound was softer than before.

"I've realized I hate salad, but love ice cream."

"That explains your weight gain." The words were harsh, but lacked the bite of earlier.

Ally pressed on, determined not to let her mother ruin this for her, no matter how cruel she was. "I like wearing skirts, but not dresses. I don't like candy, but I love cookies." She glanced at Benny, who was silently letting her handle this on her own. "I like walks along the beach, but hate mosquito bites."

His lips twitched at the reminder of all the bites along the back of her legs from standing outside one evening, kissing at sunset. Romantic it might have been, until the itching hit her later.

"I discovered I have more to offer than music, and that includes my looks." Ally reached inside her purse, pulling out a bag with a wet cloth. She hadn't told Benny of this plan, but deep inside she felt like it needed to be done. Putting the washcloth to her face, she scrubbed until the makeup was gone. She knew the mascara probably was smeared a little under her eyes, but the important thing was the foundation that covered her birthmark. "I am more than a birthmark," she said softly. "I deserve love and friendship and companionship." She turned her head to Benny fully this time, meaning this message for him as much as for her mother. "And I deserve to be seen for who I am beneath the powder. I *want* to be seen for who I am beneath the makeup."

Benny's eyes were shining with tears and Ally could tell he wanted to speak, but he held himself back.

She knew he would celebrate with her later, but his selfless choice to stand as support and not demand attention filled her with love. She wanted this man in her life permanently, and she hoped that now that she was back in Seaside Bay, perhaps that particular dream had a chance of coming true.

"Well, it looks like you just got it all, didn't you?" Carla asked harshly, pulling Ally's attention back. "After everything I did to protect you, you've spent all your time and energy on proving me wrong. Proving I was a horrible mother."

Ally shook her head and interrupted before her mother could go off on a tirade. "No. That's not it at all, and you know it." She stepped slightly closer. "I'm not here to say anything about your parenting. I'm here to tell you who your daughter is and ask if you want to be a part of her life."

The words hung heavy in the air, the feeling like that of silence after a bomb.

"I've moved back to Seaside Bay," Ally said softly. "I don't want us to be at odds, but I'm also not going to fight about it. If you find that you want to get together and go to lunch or something, you have my phone number." She stepped back, her shoulder against Benny's chest. "But if you do, you'll have to leave the cutting remarks and bitterness behind. I'm sorry you didn't get the career you wanted. I'm sorry you didn't get the marriage you wanted. And I'm especially sorry you didn't get the daughter you wanted. But sometimes we have to let go of what we wanted and deal with what we have."

Benny's arm reached around her shoulders, tucking her into his side more deeply.

"I'm here. I'll always be here. But I won't let you use me anymore. When you decide you're willing to follow those boundaries, let me know."

Before any tears could fall or she could beg her mother to love her, Ally turned, pulling Benny with her. Hand in hand, they walked down the sidewalk and out onto the street.

"Ice cream?" he asked, swinging their hands between them.

"Is that your favorite form of therapy?" Ally asked, her eyes stinging.

"Yep. Haven't you learned that yet?"

She laughed softly and brushed away the errant tears. "I don't think anything has sounded quite so enticing."

"Well shoot, if that's the case, I guess I'm not kissing you enough." Benny brought their hands up and he kissed her palm. "I think today is a two scoops day."

TO ASK OR NOT TO ASK. That was the question.

A question was burning a hole in Benny's tongue, but after the disastrous meeting with Mrs. Mayer, he wasn't sure it was a good time to speak to her. She hadn't been back in Seaside Bay for very long and he was desperate for her to stay, but he also didn't want to crowd her.

That was something he was learning more and more about Ally. She needed space. She'd been manipulated and hemmed in her entire life, and no matter how excited Benny was about something, he was learning to slow down and let her have a chance to think things through before pulling her along with him.

*I guess we've both changed from this,* he mused as they ate.

He glanced in his peripheral vision at Ally and realized with a start that she was still makeupless. He'd forgotten her little demonstration, one that had made him so proud, but still broke his heart when Carla slammed the door behind them. How that woman could let go of such a treasure was beyond Benny's comprehension.

"Ally," he said softly.

She looked his way. Her eyes were rimmed in red, but otherwise she seemed to be in control of herself.

"Your face is still..." He drew circles around his own face with his finger. "Are you okay with that?" He used his head and eyes to remind her they were out in public.

Only a few people had passed by their bench, but eventually someone would notice and Benny was worried it would be too much to handle today.

She laughed softly. "I know," she said, turning her face back to the ocean. "But perhaps if I'm willing to stand up to my mother over it, I need to be willing to stand up to our town as well."

Benny stilled. "Really?"

She smiled and turned toward him. "You were right," she whispered. "Though I hate to add that kind of compliment to your ego."

Benny wasn't exactly feeling like being funny, but he buffed his nails anyway, knowing it was what she expected. "My ego thanks you for your contribution."

She laughed and the sound helped him relax.

"So we confronted your mother. Now what?" He quickly licked his cone before it could melt all over his hand.

Ally squished her lips to one side. "Good question." She tapped her fingers on her knee. "Do you know if the job Jensen mentioned is still open?"

Benny raised his eyebrows. "I have no idea. But it would be pretty easy to find out." He pulled out his phone.

"It doesn't have to be right this second," Ally started to say.

Benny shook his head while he punched in the message one-handed. "No time like the present," he assured her. "There." He set his phone down. "We should know soon enough."

"Thank you," Ally said with a tender smile. "You're always looking out for me."

This was it. How much more perfect of a lead-in could he get to telling her he wanted to look out for her permanently? Benny gathered his courage and opened his mouth, but it was interrupted by a small voice.

"Hey, lady?"

It took Benny a moment to realize what was going on. His mind left the church aisle and came back to the present with a thud as he noticed a child covered in sand walking their way.

The little boy was pointing at Ally and Benny's protective side came roaring forward. He started to stand, but Ally grabbed his arm and pulled him back down.

"It's fine," she whispered, though Benny could feel her hand shaking slightly.

"Lady?" the boy asked again, stopping just a foot or two in front of them.

"Yes?" Ally asked.

Benny could see the tenseness of her muscles and he put his hand on her neck, slowly massaging. He wanted her to know she wasn't alone, but he also wanted to help her relax. His little introvert was exposing herself to the world today and he was completely in awe of her strength.

"What's the matter with your face?" The boy scrunched his nose and tilted his head to the side. A shovel and bucket hung loosely from his hands and sand covered his legs from the knee on down. It was clear he had been having a beach day before he noticed Ally on the bench.

"LINCOLN!" A frantic voice split the air and a woman began running around frantically.

"Are you Lincoln?" Ally asked.

The boy rubbed his nose on the back of his hand and nodded.

Ally waved her hand through the air until the woman spotted them and she rushed over. The mother grabbed her son against her, her eyes going wide when she got a closer look at Ally, then dropping to Lincoln's head. "Linc, you can't run off like that," she whispered loudly. "I'm so sorry," the woman said in a rush. "I didn't see him leave."

"Mom!" Lincoln cried as she began to usher him away. "I want to know what's wrong with her face."

"Shh!" the woman hissed.

"Ma'am?" Ally stood and walked over, tapping the woman on the shoulder.

The stranger stopped, but still struggled to meet Ally's eyes. "I'm sorry," she said. "He's just a little boy."

"I know," Ally said kindly.

Benny didn't move from his spot on the bench. He'd never been so riveted.

Ally squatted down so she could look Lincoln in the eye. "Lincoln. My name is Ally. And my face is all red because I was born this way. It's called a port wine birthmark."

He studied her. "Does it hurt?"

She shook her head. "No. It doesn't hurt. My skin is just colored differently than yours."

Lincoln shrugged. "Okay." He looked at his mom. "Can we go back now?"

His mother nodded, then looked at Ally. "Thank you," she said softly. "That was very kind of you." Her eyes went to Benny and back to Ally. "You two make a lovely couple." With a tentative smile and nod, the two strangers were gone.

Ally watched them go and Benny came up behind her. He wiped his sticky fingers on his shorts, then wrapped his arms around her waist from behind. "Have I told you today how amazing you are?"

Ally sniffed and wiped at her nose. "My ego thanks you," she teased, quoting him from earlier.

Benny kissed the back of her head. "I don't know if I've ever been more proud of anything in my life. Including the time I won best comedian my senior year of high school."

Ally laughed some more. "Isn't this the point where you're supposed to say 'I told you so'?"

He gave her a little squeeze. "I'm saving it for later. When you least expect it." For the first time ever, Benny knew he would never say it. He'd created a life based on laughter and jokes and even though he still enjoyed that, Ally had opened his eyes just as much as he'd opened hers.

His love for her was worth more than being funny. She was worth more.

After watching her tackle two of her biggest fears within minutes of each other, Benny knew that asking her to marry him on a whim as they ate ice cream wasn't going to be enough. She deserved his best effort. Something that let her know he was all in and he would always support her, no matter what she chose to do.

This time he didn't just want laughter. He wanted her heart.

Ally sat up straight, making sure to look as professional as she could while Principal Nielsen asked her questions.

"You do realize how overqualified you are for this position, right?" the middle-aged man asked with a smile.

Ally returned the gesture and nodded. "I do. But I've also come to understand better what I want out of life. When I got my education, I was headed in one direction. Now I'm headed in another. As you can see on my resume, I taught for several months down in Seagull Cove. While it was only a temporary position, it was eye-opening for me and I realized how much more I'd rather be in a classroom than on a stage."

The principal nodded sagely. "I won't try to say that isn't the type of enthusiasm we hope for," he said. "Teaching can be a noble profession when done correctly and we always want to hire those who truly feel the calling." He leaned back, his office chair creaking slightly. "But are you prepared to take on teenagers? They're a vastly different crowd than elementary-aged children. They can be stubborn and even belligerent at times." His eyes went to her birthmark.

Ally had taken to staying neutral in her makeup. She still wore mascara and blush and lipstick, but her foundation had been cut down by close to ninety-percent. While she wished to smooth her skin, she also made sure she didn't cover up the red completely. It was part of who she was and with Benny's help, she was seeing that those who judged her for it weren't ones she wished to have in her life anyway.

"I can't promise that some of the teens won't be...rude about your mark."

Ally nodded. "It's understandable. I know not everyone has seen a birthmark like this, but I'm finding that most people are curious, not mean." She gave him a rueful grin. "I won't say it doesn't hurt when people make comments, but it's something I've dealt with for a long time. I'm learning how to handle it, and I believe I will be able to do so with the students at Seaside Bay High."

Principal Nielsen studied her closely for a moment. "Well, Ms. Mayer. As you're probably aware, we don't get a lot of applicants for these types of positions, being such a small town. And as for the couple we do have, you are by far the most qualified. If you would like the position, it's yours."

The smile that wanted to spread across her face was almost painful and Ally had to work to keep it under control. She stood and leaned across the desk, hand out. "Thank you, Principal Nielsen. I'll make sure you don't regret it."

He rose and shook her head. "I don't doubt it. Would you like me to show you where the music room is? Or have a tour of the school?"

Ally shook her head. "Unless it's changed since I went to school here, I think I'm okay."

Principal Nielsen chuckled. "No. Not much has changed in the last ten to fifteen years. I think you'll find it's pretty much the same." He winked. "Except you'll be at the front of the classroom instead of at a desk."

"You make it sound so ominous," she joked, feeling more at ease now that the scary part of the interview was over.

"It can be," he nodded sagely. "Believe me, it can be."

A knock came on the door and Jensen poked his head in. "Well?" he asked. "What's the verdict?"

Principal Nielsen frowned. "I don't believe this was a public interview, Mr. Tanner."

Jensen grinned. "She's dating my best friend and brother-in-law. I think I'm entitled to a little insider knowledge." He stepped in more fully. "Not to mention I have a package for her."

Ally rolled her eyes. "Are you kidding? I was only coming in for an interview. Why would he send a package now?"

Jensen handed it to Ally and then leaned his hip against Principal Nielsen's desk. "You know Benny. He likes to keep people on their toes."

Principal Nielsen groaned. "As if I could ever forget him as a student. All the other teens loved him, but I was sure his teachers would all quit before he ever graduated."

Ally laughed. That sounded just like her Benny. She thought they were a perfect couple. He was the Yin to her Yang. He pushed, she held back. He preferred new, she liked safe. Somehow, between the two of them, they had learned to find a happy medium.

Using her nail, she cut the tape on the box and opened the lid. Inside was a bunch of packing peanuts and an envelope. "What's he up to?" she murmured, setting the box aside.

**Congratulations on the new job!**

She laughed and looked up. "What would have happened if I hadn't been hired?"

Jensen shrugged. "I'm sure he would have thought of something."

She nodded in agreement, then went back to the letter.

**Time to celebrate. You know where to go.**

Ally stuffed the paper back in the envelope.

"Well, where are you going?" Jensen asked.

Principal Nielsen huffed. "I don't think you were invited, Jensen."

Jensen rolled his eyes. "I don't plan to follow her, but that doesn't mean I can't ask."

Ally grabbed the box and tucked it under her arm as she stood. "We always get ice cream when we're celebrating," she explained. "I'm sure he's waiting for me."

Jensen nodded. "Good luck."

She smiled, but wondered what exactly he meant. Good luck seemed like an odd thing to say when she was just meeting her boyfriend for ice cream. "Thank you, Principal Nielsen. I'll see you soon."

"I'll get that contract sent over and if you have any questions, don't hesitate to contact me." He stood and walked her to the door.

"Will do." Ally waved as best she could. "Bye, Jensen! Thanks for bringing the delivery!"

Jensen waved back, a wide smile on his face.

He looked a little too knowing for Ally's peace of mind, but she brushed it off. Dumping the box on her way out of the school, she walked briskly down to the beach. She could have taken her car, but the temperature was so nice today that she couldn't resist walking. Her jacket was enough to keep her warm, even with the ocean breeze blowing her hair around her face.

Soon the ice cream stand came into sight and Ally's spirits lifted. She couldn't wait to tell Benny he'd been right and she'd gotten the job. She slowed as she got closer though, realizing that he wasn't there.

"Ms. Mayer?"

She turned at the voice. "Yes?"

The man who ran the cart smiled and pulled a box out from under his stand. "I was asked to give you this."

Ally nodded her thanks and studied it. Another box just like the last one. She walked over to a bench and sat down, opening it just like before.

**Ice cream will always remind me of our first date.**

**The first time I started falling in love with you.**

**Here's hoping there are many more licks of delicious goodness in our future.**

A small box sat under the envelope and Ally opened it to find a silver ice cream charm. "Oooh..." she breathed, picking it up. It would go perfectly on the charm bracelet Benny had given her when she'd lived in Seagull Cove.

It took no time at all to attach to her wrist, since the bracelet never left her person. After finishing, she glanced in the box and found yet another envelope.

**Did you know a pet chameleon was once sent through the mail?**

**Post offices are crazy places.**

**You never know what you'll find.**

Grinning like a kid on Christmas morning, Ally threw away the garbage and struck out for the post office. Apparently she was being sent on a hunt, but just what was she hunting?

BENNY HAD TO CONGRATULATE himself on how sneaky he was becoming. Ally had no idea that she was being trailed all over town. *If I ever lose my job at the post office, I'll have to take up being a private eye or something.*

Ally was currently opening her fifth gift, yet another charm for her bracelet, this one a seashell. He had tried to send her to places all over town that reminded Benny of their dating. Benches, beaches, ice cream, mail... Each time she had gotten a trinket for her bracelet, but now the time was running out.

Ducking around a corner, he practically sprinted to his SUV in order to get to his house before Ally arrived. He already had everything set up, but this time, he was part of the package.

His nerves were strained and his heart was hammering as he waited in his sitting room next to the small electric keyboard he had bought when taking piano lessons. It rarely got used anymore, unless Ally was over, but it didn't matter. It would do for his purposes.

He heard a car door shut and promptly broke out in a heavy sweat. "Geez," Benny muttered, wiping his forehead. "Are all guys this nervous?"

A soft knock came. "Benny? Please tell me this is the end of this hunt!"

He had to chuckle at that. "Come in!"

Slowly, the front door swung inward and Ally peeked inside. "Whew!" she breathed, coming in fully and making a show of wiping her forehead. "I was half afraid you were waiting here to meet me with a silly string bomb or something."

Benny tilted his head to the side and gave her a look. "Really?"

Ally gave him a look right back. "Yes, really. Just because you've calmed down around me doesn't mean I miss how much you still egg on your friends or pull stupid pranks."

He rubbed the back of his overly hot neck. "Fair enough, I suppose."

Ally clasped her hands in front of her. "So...your hunt has been fun." She jangled her bracelet. "Thank you for the new charms."

Benny nodded, still holding back from walking to her side. "It's, uh, not quite over yet."

Her eyebrows went up. "It's not? I wasn't supposed to land here?"

He nodded a little too quickly. "You were. But there's still one more clue." Stepping to the side, he waved at the keyboard.

Ally smiled adoringly at him as she walked over to pick up the small box. "You're so sweet," she said, stepping over to leave a kiss on his cheek. "What's the big occasion?"

Benny didn't answer as he waited for her to open the package.

Ally gasped and the card began to tremble as she read it. "Benny..."

Taking the box gently before she could drop it, Benny took himself to one knee. "Allison Lynn Mayer," he said in a soft tone. "I've had a lot of fun in my life. A lot of laughter. But none of my favorite memories have been anything compared to the ones I have made with you."

She began to sniffle and her hands went over her mouth.

"The day I first heard you speak, something began to shift in me. Your laughter and smile turned my world upside down." He glanced at the keyboard. "Your music melts me into goo and your face is what I dream of when I go to sleep at night."

She squeezed her eyes shut and shook her head, tears leaking down her cheeks.

"I'm not as talented as you. Not as kind as you. Heck, I'm not even as good-looking as you, but there are some things I am. I am supportive of you and the choices you make in your life." He raised an eyebrow. "Even if I don't agree with them."

She opened her eyes and laughed through the tears.

"I am protective of you. I want nothing more than for your life to be a bed of roses, though I know that's not realistic." He took a deep breath. "I am eager to see you succeed in your new job. I am excited to make new memories with you as we eat ice cream and open mail together. I am ready to have you by my side always. And..." He swallowed hard. "I am completely and irrevocably in love with you."

"Oh, Benny," she said breathlessly.

"I am also hoping and praying that you'll show a little pity to this humble mail carrier and let me stick around for more than a few minutes, a few hours and even a few days. My beautiful, stunning, courageous Ally. Will you marry me?"

Her head slowly shook from side to side and Benny felt a moment of panic that she was going to turn him down. Then she dropped to her knees and cupped his face. "Bennett Frasier. In an effort to be fair, I have to say something."

Benny tried to give her his usual smirk, but right now, he couldn't pull it off. He was too overwhelmed with all things Ally and instead, he stared at her, listening intently.

"I love you." She leaned in for a quick peck. "I love your bright and bubbly personality. I love how you drag me along for your adventures, yet are always willing to stop if I put down a boundary. I love how you opened my eyes to what I was missing and continue to introduce me to more things." She grinned. "Some more exciting than others."

He chuckled and shrugged. So, clamming at five in the morning had been a bust. Who knew she wasn't a morning person?

"I love that you want my own happiness even above your own and I cannot, for the life of me, think of a single person I would want to spend the rest of my life with." Her kiss was slower this time and Benny almost groaned when she pulled away. "I had no idea what to think when you brought that first package to my home after you started stalking me around town."

Benny tried to butt in, but she put a finger to his lips.

"That unexpected delivery was the start of the rest of my life. Thank you for choosing me," she whispered. "I will forever be grateful, and I will forever say yes."

Benny cursed the box in his hand as she kissed him yet again. He wanted to hold her close, but right now his hands were full. "Just a moment," he said, pulling back. He fumbled with the packing peanuts, tossing them every which way as he dug out the small velvet box. Opening it, he turned it to Ally, who squeaked. "I thought your charm bracelet would be getting a little full at this point," he teased.

Ally held out her hand between them. "There's always room for more charms." She admired the solitaire. "But this." She kissed him. "Is the best." She kissed him again. "Charm of all."

"I've never been afraid to admit I'm a charming guy," Benny said between kisses.

Ally groaned. "Nope. We're not going there." She glared playfully. "Just be quiet and kiss me."

"Yes, ma'am," Benny said, pulling her fully against his chest. "I thought you'd never ask."

# EPILOGUE

Rose tried not to become emotional as she watched the handsome police captain, Kenneth Wamsley, dance with her five-year-old daughter, Lilly. She tried not to smile when Lilly laughed with abandon, much louder than all the other guests at the wedding. She tried not to blush when Ken looked her way, his eyes brimming with longing and attraction.

She tried.

But she failed.

For almost five years, Rose had been holding off the attractive police officer. She had come to Seaside Bay to escape a man, not invite another into her life. But the more time went on, the more Ken got under her skin.

He was tall, handsome, and a wonderful leader...all things that would attract any woman. But it was his gentle kindness that had Rose struggling the most. That and the fact that he treated her deaf daughter as if she were his own.

Lilly adored Ken. She clung to him at every gathering and looked for him when he wasn't around.

Unfortunately, Rose often found herself doing the same.

She shook her head and forced herself to look away. She couldn't give in. Her life was not the kind that she could welcome in another relationship, no matter how much it hurt to keep telling him no.

Nobody, not even her best friends in Seaside Bay, knew why Rose had slipped in in the middle of the night. She'd shown up in town with a brand new baby in one arm and a check to purchase an older shop on Main Street. Calling the shop The Hidden Daffodil had been Rose's way of starting a new life, since daffodils were symbolic of new beginnings.

She had always been fascinated by flowers, but had never been allowed the opportunity to pursue an education in them. Well, now she could. Now she could do anything she wanted because she was free.

Mostly.

So far, Rose had managed to stay under the radar, but the feeling that one day she would be found had never quite abandoned her.

That was the main reason she always turned down Ken's invitations. She'd had a good long run in Seaside Bay. She'd started a wonderful business and had the best group of friends, who were more like family than anything else. But someday, she knew she'd have to run again. And how could she do that if she was attached to the police captain?

"Mama!" Lilly yelled, unable to recognize quite how loud she was being.

Rose turned her attention to her daughter and automatically pasted a smile on her face. She put a finger to her lips. "A little quieter, Lilly."

Lilly nodded enthusiastically. "Sorry," she said, though her face said the exact opposite. "You should come dance with us." Her pronunciation of the words was slightly off from the normal person, but the older Lilly got, the easier she was to understand. Rose was so proud of her and all her wonderful daughter had accomplished.

"You should." Ken's deep voice came from over Rose's head and slowly, she looked up.

She was an adult. She could handle this. Her smile became one of cold politeness. "Maybe another time."

"No!" Lilly stomped her foot. "Uncle Benny and Aunt Ally got married. You have to!" she whined.

"Now, Lilly—" Rose began, but Lilly started up again.

"You *never* dance," she complained. "Uncle Ken says he'll dance with you." She looked up. "Isn't that right, Uncle Ken? Don't you think my mama is beautiful enough to dance with?"

Rose was frozen in place. She couldn't look away from his intensely blue eyes, even to reprimand her daughter for being so forceful. Tantrums and demands were something new Lilly had been trying out lately and Rose was struggling to hold her headstrong daughter back. This time, however, Lilly had gone too far.

"I'd love to," Ken said, his voice huskier than before. He finally looked at Lilly, allowing Rose to suck in a much needed breath. "Why don't you go sit with Aunt Charli," he said, giving her a little push in the direction of their friends. "She's too tired to dance because of the baby in her tummy. So you keep her company while I take your mom to the dance floor."

Lilly squealed in delight. "You're gonna have so much fun, Mama!" Without another word, she rushed over and hopped in Bronson's lap, Charli's husband.

Rose followed her daughter's progress, too dumbfounded to speak.

Bronson gave them both a thumbs up, then promptly began playing a game with Lilly.

"I think that's our cue," Ken said, taking Rose's hand and gently pulling her to her feet.

"I can't—"

"Yes, you can," Ken interrupted. His voice was firm but still soft. "One dance, Rose," he implored. "That's all I'm asking."

Her heart began to race when a slow song came on and goosebumps the size of watermelons broke out across her skin when Ken grinned and pulled her in close. He kept them in the old-fashioned dance position, with one hand to the side, but Rose's hormones screamed that it wasn't enough.

"I feel like I've been bulldozed," she muttered, trying to break the spell that was quickly causing her to melt.

Ken chuckled, the sound reverberating through her. "Lilly has that effect on people."

Rose furrowed her brows. "I don't think it was just Lilly."

Ken shrugged, slowly turning them in a circle. "Think what you will, but she's the one who brought it up."

Rose sighed.

"Is it really that bad to dance with me?" Ken had never been the type to struggle with confidence and anyone who saw him in action as an officer could see that. But right now there was a vulnerability to his tone that nearly killed Rose.

"That's not it," she rasped.

He pulled her infinitesimally closer. "Then what is?"

Rose's bottom lip trembled, but she bit it between her teeth and looked away.

Ken huffed. "Why won't you let one of us in, Rose?" he pressed. "Even if it's not me." He pulled a little more and brought her temple to his cheek. "I just want to see you happy."

"I am happy." The lie tasted like bile. Her daughter was a ray of sunshine in her life and her friends were more like family, but Rose was never truly happy. She was too scared to be.

Ken shook his head ever so slightly. "Let me help."

Three simple words said in a quiet plea.

Yet they were enough to send Rose into a panic. She could lie to herself all she wanted, but Rose knew full well she had fallen in love with Captain Kenneth Wamsley. And it was that love that kept her away.

No one could protect her, but she could definitely protect him.

As soon as the music ended, she pulled back. "Thank you for the dance," she said curtly. Spinning on her heel, Rose walked to her table and grabbed her purse. It jolted, letting her know she had a text.

Keeping an eye on Lilly, Rose pulled out her phone and clicked on the icon.

**You owe me.**

The church had been far too warm only two seconds ago, but now it felt like she'd been submerged in ice. Her head swung from side to side as she tried to see if she was being watched.

She had no idea how her ex-husband had found this number, but she knew it was the start of the end. She swayed slightly, her vision blurring as she realized she wasn't breathing.

Grabbing the table, Rose took in several large breaths.

"Rose, what is it?" Ken's voice was close to her ear.

"Lilly," she choked out. "I have to get Lilly."

Ken didn't move right away and Rose felt like she was about to scream when he finally said, "Hang on. I've got her."

The twenty seconds it took for him to come back were torturous, but Rose didn't have enough strength in her legs to go herself.

"Come on," Ken said, holding out his hand. He held Lilly in one arm, up against his chest. "I'll take you home."

Love tried to overcome the panic and fear racing through her system, but Rose ruthlessly pushed it away. Love would get her or someone else killed. "I can do it," she said, reaching out for Lilly.

Her daughter put up a fuss, but Rose was insistent.

"We'll see you another time. Thank you."

Leaving her heart and any chance at happiness behind, Rose walked away from her friend's wedding and the only people in her life who had ever truly cared for her.

Leaving would be horrible, but she had survived it once. She could survive it again.

Don't Miss Rose's Story!
You can grab it on Amazon.

Lauraannbooks.com